Her Highland Hero

D1737882

TERRY SPEAR

DEDICATION

Thanks so much to Mandy Owen for your friendship
and for all you do! May your world be filled with
romance forevermore!

ACKNOWLEDGMENTS

Thanks be to those who helped me to bring this book to you: Loretta Melvin, who brainstormed with me for days and days and days, making sure I had tied up all the loose ends. Neither of us knew who the villains were until the end. But when we did? We were ready to celebrate. Vonda Sinclair and Judy Gill, my critique partners, who continue to amaze me with catching all the stuff I can't ever seem to catch. Donna Fournier, who will ensure I really have tied up all the loose ends and sometimes come up with stuff that makes me have to change a lot more stuff---laughing, Dottie Jones, who is so good at catching my dyslexic derivations of sentences that sound perfectly fine to me, and oh, yeah, her comma genius, Maria McIntyre, who is my newest beta reader to help make this the best it can be, Bonnie Gill, who is a pleasure to work with, invaluable, and falls in love with my characters time and again, and Loretta Melvin, who, after all the work she did on helping me to tie up loose ends, reread it all over again. That's dedication!

Thanks, lassies! You are the greatest!

CHAPTER 1

"He is already here, my lady!" Jane said breathlessly as the knight's daughter burst into Lady Isobel Pembroke's chamber in Torrent Castle, her dark hair plaited against her head, her dark brown eyes alight with excitement. She quickly curtseyed. When Jane saw Isobel's maid, Mary MacArthur of Isobel's mother's Highland clan, give her a disdainful look, Jane flushed bright red and lowered her head a little.

"How do you know this?" Isobel asked, certain Jane couldn't have seen this for herself—not as far as the loch was from the castle.

"Oh, my lady, Sir Travon said a farmer had sent word that the Highlanders were near the loch."

Jane was seven and ten, two years younger than Isobel. She enjoyed Jane's company because she was just like Isobel loved to be—wild, impulsive, and adventurous. When Jane wasn't helping with the sewing, she would spend time talking to Isobel about the knights she was interested in.

"Good." Isobel smiled, gladdened that she would see Marcus again. Too much time had passed since the last. Nearly a year, in fact. And she couldn't help worrying that a Highland lass would catch his fancy. That she would appeal more because she lived near him and he would see her so much more frequently.

Isobel had worked the notion up in her mind so much, that she fretted that one of these days, he wouldn't return.

Eight knights served Lord William Pembroke, Isobel's father, some of whom had manors of their own on the land surrounding Torrent Castle. Near there, the small village of Ancroft had built up close to the Scots and English border. Skirmishes between the Scots and English erupted from time to time, which was why King Henry wanted some of his loyal Norman lords living near the border. Marcus McEwan's lands were in the Highlands and adjoined the MacArthur's. His family had known her mother's, which was how Isobel knew him. And loved him.

Her brown eyes wide with intrigue, Jane said, "I am so eager about the dance. Are you not also, my lady?"

"To see Marcus, aye." Isobel didn't want to dance with the English lords that her father hoped she'd consider favorably and choose one to wed. She only wished to dance with Marcus, whom she had known since she was one and ten. She intended to wed him and no other man, if she had her way. Which she planned to.

Constant trouble between the Scots and English dictated that Lord Pembroke have a ready force of men whenever necessary. But the border region had been blissfully quiet for a fortnight. Isobel prayed it would remain so forever. Only once was she unable to see Marcus when the fighting had broken out, and it had been too dangerous for him to cross the border without him getting embroiled in the fight.

Mary said, "Och, lass, you get your hopes up every time he comes, and I love seeing him myself, but you ken 'tis folly. Your da willna allow you to marry the Highlander."

Isobel would not hear of it. She loved him. Had always loved him. Would always love him. Just as her father had loved her Highland mother.

She let out her breath in exasperation as she attempted to sit still while Mary plaited her hair. Her own red hair properly pinned atop her head, Mary narrowed her green eyes and her mouth pursed in concentration as Isobel watched her comb her hair in front.

"You know 'tis a waste of time for you to put my hair up right before I ride to the loch," Isobel said. She gave Jane a brilliant smile, telling her in a silent way

she was delighted to hear the news that Marcus
McEwan was near there.

"You shouldna be riding to the loch to see the
Highlander before the dance." Mary was her mother's
age, just as slender, and usually just as cheerful as she
had been. Mary had been like a mother to her since her
own had died.

For now, Isobel wanted her hair left down to please
Marcus, her long dark curls tossed in the breeze, not
pinned to her head like some prim and proper lady. Not
that Marcus hadn't seen her both ways, but she was sure
he delighted in seeing her as she truly felt in her heart...
adventurous, fun-loving, wild, and free.

She couldn't help herself. Ever since she'd seen him
when she was but a young girl, he'd been trying to
garner her attention. And she...his.

Although she had to admit, the way he tried to
catch her eye when he was a lad was much more
humorous than it had been for some years. Before, he'd
do *anything* to make her smile. Now, his attention was
that of a man's.

Oh, how she loved the braw Highlander, his
boldness as he'd regard her with his discerning gaze,
and how she wished he'd touch her with his hands in the
same places and not with just his eyes.

She was supposed to behave like a Norman earl's
daughter, stuffy and highborn, her chin raised high as
she looked upon the Highlander. She was supposed to
treat him as though he was beneath her.

But she hadn't and wouldn't. He was the man she'd always wanted to wed.

She'd dreamed of what it would be like giving in to the Highlander's heated interest, to see how he turned his lustful thoughts into actions, to feel his hard body pressed against her soft curves.

Her face and throat and shoulders warmed at the notion.

She'd been far wilder than her father would have liked, if he'd known, if he'd seen her climbing trees, catching fish, or hunting with her bow.

Horrors, she'd even participated in mock sword fighting down by the loch with two of Marcus's cousins while he'd watched, a small smile playing on his kissable mouth as he'd leaned against a tree.

"Do you no' want to fight the lass?" Rob, his cousin had shouted. He was dark-haired, but not quite as dark as Marcus, a little taller, with swimming blue eyes.

She remembered it as if it was yesterday. The summer warming the glen. The smell of wet grass and fish in the loch. A soft breeze caressing her hair, tossing it about as she swung a wooden sword at Rob. They would not risk *fighting* her using real swords.

She thought Marcus would step up to the challenge. Instead, he had folded his arms across his chest, his blue eyes smiling back at her as she'd caught his hot gaze. His black hair had been windswept and he looked rugged and indomitable with his sword at his side, and his *sgian dubh* tucked in his boot.

"Nay," he said, his voice throaty and dark. "The lass is made for loving, no' fighting. I prefer to watch."

His cousins had laughed, teased him for saying so, and yet, that was when she realized the change in him. He was no longer a lad with boyish interests, but a man who knew what he wanted.

Bringing her thoughts winging back to where she was now, Isobel winced as Mary accidentally pulled her hair while she tried to pin another section up.

"Mary," Isobel said in exasperation, "if you are trying to keep me from seeing Marcus before the dance, it will not work!"

Mary stopped fixing her hair and Isobel swore a faint shimmer of tears clouded her eyes.

The Highland woman had served her mother for as long as Isobel could remember. She was sweet and gentle, but firm. Though she too had a liking for Marcus and his kin, she'd warned Isobel time and again that her father would never allow her to wed him and Mary feared it would break Isobel's heart.

Isobel quickly rose from her bench and gave Mary a warm hug, loving her from the bottom of her heart. "Do not fret, Mary. My father loves me. He would not keep me from my heart's desire. I will change his mind."

Her father adored her. Probably because she reminded him of her beloved mother. She was certain that he'd come around, given time.

Mary shook her head. "Lady Ciarda encouraged

your wildness since you are half Highland lass, and she would not deny you that part of your being which needed to be set free. Much like your own dear mother had been when she was your age and younger. Except your mother was a Highland lass through and through. But you will marry an English nobleman, and he will object most strongly to this kind of behavior."

"I know you worry about me. You have naught to concern yourself with. I wish to ride as I always do before these affairs. Do you wish to come with me?"

Jane grinned and nodded though Isobel had directed the question at Mary.

Mary tsked. "If your da learns you are riding beyond the castle walls before the guests arrive, he willna be pleased."

"He is too busy to pay any attention to what I am doing. And, as I have said, I always do this. Will you go with me?"

Giving up, Mary raised her hands in defeat. "Aye. We must return early enough so I may repair your hair."

"I will have horses saddled and meet you in the inner bailey." Isobel rushed off, cloaked in wool, racing through the keep, tearing outside to the stables, chiding the groom readying her horse and Mary's for being so slow. Although he grinned the whole time, knowing whenever her father forced another dance on her, she had to leave for a while so she could handle the long night successfully.

Mary rushed down to join her, Jane following her,

looking eager to go with her also. Isobel only wanted to be alone with Marcus, but she knew she couldn't be.

"Ready a horse for Jane as well," Isobel said.

Jane's smile couldn't have stretched any further.

"My lady," a knight said, hurrying across the bailey to help her mount. Sir Travon didn't look pleased that she was planning to ride. But he didn't say anything.

The last time someone spoke to her father against her, the man was relieved of his position.

So those who served her father kept their counsel when they considered speaking to him about her behavior. She was above reproach. Except for her wicked thoughts about Marcus. No one would ever know about them though.

Once the ladies were mounted, five of her father's knights hurried to join them. They would keep their distance, but offer protection if needed.

She and her escort rode out of the outer bailey through the gate and headed for the path she knew Marcus and his cousins would take, although his cousins would not accompany him into the keep because her father would not permit it. He only allowed Marcus to attend the parties as it was his mother's dying wish. So Marcus's cousins would stay at the tavern in a nearby village across the border until Marcus rejoined them.

A couple of miles away from the castle, she saw Marcus and two of his cousins, Rob and Finbar. Her heart soared.

Grinning too broadly when she knew it wasn't ladylike in the least, especially not for an earl's daughter, and riding like a hellion, which was also something her father would strongly disapprove of, she raced to meet Marcus.

He and his cousins were smiling, but not as broadly as she, more amused, she thought. She slowed her horse's gait, worried that she was being too forward, when Marcus did not hurry to meet her. He had grown into a tall and powerfully-built Highlander, serious at times, irresistibly appealing and intriguing at all times.

But what about her? Did he think she was still nothing more than a wild girl?

He'd never once attempted a stolen kiss. Never once held her hand or scandalously took her out of sight of his kin or Mary to be alone with her. She knew he was a man of the world, not isolated like she had been. What did he really think of her? That she was still too young for him? Or not at all suitable? Just amused at a young girl's interest in him?

She wasn't a young girl any longer. Old, in fact, at the age of nine and ten.

She'd passed up suitors by the dozen. All because she'd lost her heart to one braw Highlander. If she had any say in it, she was not giving him up. Unless, he didn't want her. That notion made her heart sink like a stone tossed into the loch.

Her skin burning with chagrin, she lost her smile, pulled her gaze from Marcus's, and kicked her horse. At a gallop, she rode right past the three men and on toward the loch.

"Isobel!" Marcus snapped, sounding annoyed, in charge, and...*surprised.*

Good. He was not in charge of her, no matter what he might think. Mayhap doing the unexpected would draw him out of his complacency toward her.

She thought she heard him curse, and then the sound of hooves beat the road behind her as the men taking chase spurred her on.

She wasn't running away from them. She was riding like she'd intended. To feel the cool wind on her face and tugging at her hair. Already tendrils were falling over her shoulders swept back like her horse's mane and tail. She wished to be free of the stuffiness of the castle and all the people she'd have to socialize with in just a couple of hours and throughout the long night. To enjoy the woodland surroundings like she'd always done.

Most of the time she had taken rides like this, she'd had her maid and a knight escort, but she'd been alone with her thoughts and pretended no one accompanied her. So she could imagine the same with him. That he wasn't here to see her any more than she was here to see him.

This was her time to soak up nature, fortify herself, and return to the keep for another social event that she didn't care to attend.

She didn't need him, she reminded herself as a

couple of cursed tears rolled down her cheeks.

***

Marcus saw the abrupt change in Isobel's expression from delighted at seeing him to upset with him, but he didn't know what the matter was. He'd come to see her, hadn't he?

He looked to his cousins for counsel. Both shook their heads and shrugged as they turned their horses and chased after the lass.

Pembroke's knights kept their distance and so did Mary and Jane, to Marcus's relief. He was certain, despite her da saying no to his marrying Isobel, he'd given the order to allow him to speak with her in private as much as it could be so.

Rob said, "She is a woman. What more can I say?"

Marcus let out a frustrated breath. With any other woman, he knew just how to handle the situation. Kiss her sweetly and make her forget her annoyance. With Isobel, he couldn't dally with her in the same way. She had been raised as a Norman earl's daughter, was a lady, inexperienced in the ways of men, and her da would have his head if Marcus laid a hand on her. Not to mention, he loved her.

He wasn't afraid of the earl, but he wouldn't ruin Isobel's reputation no matter how much he wanted to kiss her, love her, and make her his wife.

God's knees, he'd already asked for her hand in marriage. Four times this year already! But her da wouldn't permit it.

Her mother's invitations had come for years, soliciting his attendance at the social activities they had given for their daughter, and then when she'd died, Isobel's da had continued to invite him at his wife's dying request. Marcus had danced with Isobel, though it had killed him not to hold her like he'd wanted to, or dance with her more than once, or watch the Englishmen dancing with her when he had wanted to…exclusively.

He was glad when she'd slip away to be with him, even though Mary, her maid, had kept a watchful eye. He loved how Isobel had treated him like he was someone special, and greeted him first before the other guests arrived. Which was the reason he always came so early.

So he couldn't fathom what the matter was this time.

Isobel reached the loch and slipped off her horse, tethered her to a birch, then hurried to the water's edge. Marcus and his cousins joined her just as she crouched, dipped her hands into the water, and splashed her face, her back to them.

"Isobel," he said, gently, handing his reins to Rob, then joining her at the loch's shore. His cousins stood nearby watching. He wished he could be alone with her, and he could kiss her like he wanted.

She rose, her head tilted back a wee bit, which meant she'd raised her chin, and her back stiffened with his approach.

"What ails you, lass?" he asked.

"I came here to be alone," she said curtly.

He glanced back at his cousins. They both raised their brows at him, Rob motioning for him to pursue the issue.

"Isobel…"

"Go. Go," she said brightly, flicking her hand in his direction, her back still to him, refusing to look at him. "I wish to be alone," she repeated.

He knew it wasn't so. Not when he'd seen how eager she was to see him. Not when he knew she'd come out just to greet him.

He drew close, smelled the fragrance of lavender and the hint of woman, felt the heat of her skin. Craved taking her into his arms and kissing her.

"What is the matter?" he asked, quietly.

When she didn't answer, he touched her shoulder, but she quickly pulled away.

He frowned. "Isobel." He grasped her arm and pulled her around so he could speak to her face to face, to see her expression and learn what was troubling her. Tears glistened in her eyes. He felt as though a fist had struck him in the belly. He dragged her into his embrace, crushing her, holding her, not letting go, and even ignoring how her da's knights would react.

Her arms went around his waist, and he knew then he'd upset her somehow. "What is wrong?"

She didn't say, or couldn't. Rob was right. Figuring out what a woman wanted was nigh to impossible. Still holding her tight against him, Marcus lifted her chin. "Tell me."

Her eyes were so incredibly blue, her dark brown hair falling over her shoulders in a cascade of silken curls, her mouth full and moist and wanting.

He kissed her, like he'd vowed never to do.

CHAPTER 2

This was what she'd waited for all her life, Isobel thought as Marcus's mouth pressed hers in a sweet, yet sizzling, caress. Her whole body melted against his as he held her close. She felt his muscles tightening with need. She didn't wish the kiss to end, didn't want him to pull away, needing him to know that she was a woman now, full grown.

"Isobel," he groaned against her mouth, his voice ragged with desire.

She couldn't say a word in response, her own breathing shallow and raspy as she wantonly kept him close, her body pressed indecently against his, her hands locked tight around his waist.

His hand cupped the back of her head, holding her in place so he could continue kissing her as if he had been starved for affection all his life.

His tongue licked her lips, encouraging her to open

to him, the touch the most erotic sensation she'd ever experienced. She parted her lips. He plunged in, tasting her, exploring, making her feel exquisitely plundered. She quickly responded in kind. Loving the feel of his heat, his exuberance.

He groaned.

His muscles tensed, as if he was about to pull away, to end this wickedness, but she clung to him, wanting it to last forever.

"Isobel," he rasped out, "I must get you safely home."

He pulled away from her, and she let out a moan of protest.

"Will you not ask for my hand in marriage, Marcus?" She had wanted it to be his idea, the warrior that he was. But she could not wait any longer. Every dance her father had for her was meant to entice her to find another man to wed. And she couldn't do it.

"Ah, lass," Marcus said, leading her to her horse, then lifted her onto it.

She noticed only then that the knights were watching for trouble, not them, thankfully, but Mary and Jane were blushing furiously as they'd witnessed the kiss. She was grateful they had not said anything to attempt to put an end to it.

"'Tis your da that is the trouble," Marcus said.

Her eyes wide, Isobel stared down at Marcus. "Nay, you only have but to ask him."

"I have, Isobel. Four times already, this year alone.

He is determined to marry you off to an Englishman or Norman." Marcus's face was so tight with distress, his dark brows furrowed, that she knew he wanted to be with her forever with all his heart like she did him.

"He cannot," she cried, not wishing to show him or his cousins her anguish, but she truly had not believed Marcus had offered for her already and her father had denied him—how many times? "You…you have asked since when?"

"Since you were six and ten, lass. I couldna have waited any longer, but still, the answer has always been nay."

He *did* love her! Though he had not said so in so many words. "Take me away with you. Now. Take me to your home in the Highlands." She would give up everything to be with him.

"Your da would send his men for you. How long before he asked for the king's help in the matter? How long before his men and the king's would starve us out? Even King David could side with him."

She wiped away a tear, and then another. "I will change his mind." She lifted her chin and kicked her horse, calling back over her shoulder, "I will wed no other, Highlander." She galloped back to the keep, leaving Marcus and his cousins behind.

***

His heart heavy, Marcus watched Isobel galloping off, her hair flying behind her like a rich dark mane. The ladies rode after her, the knights following in hot pursuit.

Marcus knew kissing her was a mistake. He knew his touching her would kindle the fire between them that he had banked for so long.

He couldn't even mount his horse until he could get his rampant need for her under control. His cousins were grinning their fool heads off, waiting for him to ride after her.

"Mayhap you should have just bedded the lass," Finbar said. "Put both of you out of misery. Mayhap her da would come around."

As if Marcus could ever be alone with the lass to make that happen.

The kiss they had shared made him only desire her more. He wanted more than anything in the world for the lady to be his wife, his lover, and the mother of his bairns, but he couldn't bring his clan into this. If he stole her away, many of his people could suffer or die should the earl and his men fight to have her returned home.

Honor bound, he could not take the lady in such a manner. She was too precious to him. He knew how much she loved her father, and it could put a wedge between them forever.

"She loves you," Rob said, "just like I said. How you ever won her over is beyond me when Finbar and I are so much brawer."

Shaking his head, unable to find the humor in the situation as much as he usually could, Marcus stiffly mounted his horse. "Unless I can change the earl's mind, there is no hope for us."

"Dinna be daft, man," Finbar said. "She is worth moving mountains for."

"He wants someone to produce an heir who will inherit his title and lands. No' a Highlander who wouldna live with her in the earl's world."

"Mayhap 'tis time for the lass to learn the truth of her heritage," Rob said darkly.

Marcus did not want to be the one to tell her the truth. The word should come from the earl. He suspected the man would not speak with her about it ever, if he could hide the secret from her forever.

"Come," Marcus said. "'Tis nearly time for the celebration, and a bonny lass awaits my first dance." Marcus wondered though. Mayhap it was time that she learned the truth even if it meant he was the one who would have to tell her. Would she hate him for it?

That's what he feared.

When he arrived at the keep, the evening did not go as planned. He was permitted the first dance and tried to keep his distance from the lass as deemed appropriate, but the way Isobel looked so adoringly at him and moved in closer than was considered proper, he heard quite a few grumbles. She was declaring her heart to him, and her actions were not lost on the assembled lords and ladies.

He loved her for it, but feared for her, too. What if her da decided to force her to wed any Englishman of his own choice just to ensure Isobel didn't ruin her chances because of the affection she showed Marcus?

An English baron by the name of Erickson swept her across the floor after that, dancing her as far away from Marcus as he could manage. He glanced in Marcus's direction, green eyes narrowed, a small smirk on his face as if telling him the lady was now his. Wanting to growl his displeasure, Marcus then noticed Lord Fenton, arms folded, his expression aggravated as he watched Isobel dance. He was another of Isobel's suitors, though after she had broken his nose years ago, Marcus wondered why the baron still wished to wed the lass—well, for the earldom, he supposed. Marcus feared for Isobel's safety should she wed him. The man was nondescript—ordinary wheat-colored hair, pale brown eyes—the only thing remarkable about him—the slightly crooked nose. Marcus smiled evilly.

As if he knew Marcus was observing him, Fenton turned to look at him, his mouth turning down even more than before. Marcus suspected Isobel had never told her da what she'd done to the man or Lord Pembroke would not have agreed to allow the baron to court her.

Standing next to Fenton, a baron named Hammersfield glanced in Marcus's direction. Hammersfield began to speak to Fenton, both eyeing Marcus with contempt. Amused at the way Hammersfield had his hair rolled to imitate King Henry's curls, Marcus eyed him back with just as much scorn. He wondered if the baron dispensed with the curls when he was engaged in combat in the field. Both men were dressed in their finery, their garments heavily embroidered to show off their wealth. Marcus, on the other hand, wore much simpler clothes, not about to have a clanswoman work so many hours on embellishing his clothes to catch Isobel's eye as if he were a bird showing off his plumage. Lord Erickson's bright red hair was already showy enough, but he wore clothes to match. If he dressed like that on the battlefield, he would be his enemies' easiest target.

Movement to his right caught Marcus's eye and he saw both Hammersfield and Fenton grinning like a couple of fools before Marcus turned to see two armed men stalking toward him. The burly men were armed and not dressed in finery like the others attending the function, both broad of chest, and looked fit enough to wield the swords they wore. He knew this was not a social call.

"Come with us," the taller of the two men said.

Marcus looked back at the dancers, but could not see Isobel. He did not wish her to make a scene should she see he was leaving so abruptly without saying goodbye when he was certain where this was headed, but he did not want her to believe he had left of his own accord, either, without saying goodbye.

He caught her maid's eye as she waited nearby, her gaze taking in all. Her expression concerned—though for him or for Isobel when she learned he was sent away—he wasn't certain. Mary nodded just once to him as if to say she would relay his regrets to her mistress.

"Do not tarry. Move." This time the black-haired man touched the hilt of his sword, the implied threat that he would use whatever force necessary.

Marcus was unarmed, his sword left with his horse. He'd never expected to have to fight any man at the earl's keep. Not that he would have been allowed to carry a weapon into the keep.

As the two men led him to the stables, the one who seemed to be in charge said, "The earl did not wish you to have to make your long journey home so late at night. 'Tis not safe, you know. Best you leave now." He smiled broadly, malice in his black eyes as he folded his arms, his thick body positioned so if Marcus took a step toward the keep, he would not be successful.

Marcus had not seen the earl this eve, but he must have been angered at Isobel's flaunting of her dancing with him.

"Aye, 'tis fortunate you were able to dance with the lady once. Run along now like a good lad, will you?" the other said condescendingly, looking just as determined to send Marcus on his way and just as sinister, though he was smaller in size, but wiry looking.

Marcus looked back at the sizeable keep, the four stone towers stretching into the diffused light of gloaming, sconces holding torches, the golden flames wavering in the breeze. He wished with all his heart that he could take Isobel away, hating that he could not. He turned on his heel and entered the stable where a lad was quickly saddling his horse.

Once Marcus had mounted his horse, he steered him through the inner bailey and beyond the gates to the road in the direction of the village across the border where his cousins waited for him at The Wildeswin. His cousins would never expect him to arrive this early, and he hoped he wouldn't upset their plans overmuch. He couldn't quit thinking about the way Isobel had kissed him back, the way she'd wanted him to marry her, the way she'd promised to change her da's mind about them. He knew the earl would not.

Marcus didn't believe threatening her da with the truth would sway him to give her up either, though he had considered it. He was thinking of other options he might try, even sending a missive to the English king, to let him know the true story. Would the king take his word over a Norman earl's? Would he even care to learn the truth and would it matter one whit? As many illegitimate children as King Henry had, most likely not.

Marcus hadn't traveled more than a half a mile beyond Lord Pembroke's castle before three men on horseback came out of the woods, all with swords drawn. They were dressed in tunics of fine wool cloth and trewes, not like the average ruffians looking to steal from a person traveling alone.

"Kill the savage who believes he is good enough to

be one of us," a brown-bearded man said, his long hair in tangles, his brown eyes narrowed.

Marcus knew then that this was not a random encounter. He didn't recognize any of the men. He was certain whoever had sent them had done so because of Isobel, probably a lord interested in her hand in marriage who was still at the party either dancing with her or watching her dance.

Marcus unsheathed his sword with a whoosh and looked from one to another, measuring them for the task.

The boldest of the men charged him. Blood hot with fury, Marcus swung his broadsword at the bearded man, cutting him down from his horse in a mighty blow. Mayhap the savage was better trained to deal with whoever these men were than they thought. Or mayhap that was why three of them were tasked to murder him.

The man lay still on the ground, blood spilling from his chest. The two men who were left hesitated, and then a younger man with his hair cut close gave a war cry and kneed his horse to take Marcus on next. Swords clashed, clanging in the cool night air, the sound ringing through the woods.

The angry clashing of swords, metal striking metal, the horses' heavy footfalls as they pranced while the two men fought, the horses' snorts, and the men's grunts filled the air.

Marcus struck a decisive blow, ripping the sword

from the man's grasp. The man quickly went for a dagger, and Marcus shoved his sword into the man's belly. He yanked his blade free.

Before the man even fell from his horse, Marcus felt a sword slicing across his back. He cursed revenge and turned his horse so quickly, he unsettled his attacker's mount. The horse reared upward, unseating the brigand. He fell to the rocky earth, landing hard on his back with an "oof," and didn't move.

Marcus waited for him to clamber to his feet and renew the attack, but the man's gray eyes grew shadowed, then stared up at him lifelessly. Blood spread over the ground from the back of the man's head.

Warily, Marcus dismounted, his own back burning with pain. The whoreson couldn't even fight him in an honest battle man to man. Though what had Marcus expected when three of them had been set upon him?

He kicked the man aside, saw the rock he'd struck his head on, and shook his head. "Next time, you will have to send a bigger force to deter me, whosoever you are that sent these men to murder me."

Before he grew too weak to manage, Marcus climbed into his saddle and rode like the devil to the tavern. When he arrived, he fell from his horse to the ground in a bloodied heap, cursing at everything he could curse. With a willpower that overtook the pain carving a swath through his back, he managed to get to his feet and stumbled to the tavern, pushing the door open, and took two steps inside.

Praying his cousins were here, his vision blurring and the peat smoke from the fire making the tavern even hazier, he couldn't see them among the men seated at the half dozen tables scattered about. With as much strength as he could muster, he shouted, "Finbar! Rob!"

The place was noisy and smelled of ale, but when he yelled, conversation ceased and all gazes swung to him.

He thought he saw his cousins rushing to aid him, but he couldn't be sure. He just hoped no one else meant to kill him as his sword fell from his weakened grasp and struck the floor right before he joined his weapon, smacking hard against the wooden planks, sending up a cloud of dust in his wake.

CHAPTER 3

Isobel wondered why Lord Erickson had swept her toward the other side of the great hall, until she realized he was trying to keep her from seeing Marcus further. After her father would not grant her hand in marriage to Marcus, she intended to prove to the assembled lords and ladies that she had chosen the Highlander as her own. No one else need ask for her hand in marriage.

She had seen the hostile looks directed at him, and some of those same men had cast the same kind of disparaging looks her way. Did they think she'd ever agree to marry any one of them? She knew her father could make that decision, if he so chose. But he'd always assured her and before that—her mother—that Isobel would have a choice.

"Some wine, my lady?" Lord Erickson asked her.

She shook her head and again looked for Marcus. Erickson had a quick temper that matched his fiery red hair. She could imagine having several redheaded bairns who each had tempers to match their father's.

Lords Fenton, Neville, and Hammersfield headed her way as if they believed it was now their turn to spend time with her. She wished to take a respite and drink some wine with Marcus. She had every intention of showing how much she loved the Highlander and no other man would have her affection.

Glancing around the hall at the collected visitors, she realized her father was nowhere in sight, and she felt a chill race down her spine. He always stayed close at hand while she danced with the gentlemen. Was another suitor offering for her, and this time her father was considering any proposal just to ensure she did not wed the Highlander?

"Lady Isobel, would you care to dance with—" Fenton didn't finish speaking when Cantrell, one of her father's servants, hurried into the great hall to talk to her father's advisor on the other side of the room.

Cantrell was a spry middle-aged man who oft ran errands for her when she needed something done—for a fee. Yet, he'd proved invaluable to her time and again. He was always crossing the border, knew everyone and one and all liked him, so he had been invaluable to her father as well since Cantrell always heard the news first about trouble brewing at the border and quickly apprised her father. She wondered if he charged her father for the information, or gave it freely.

Lord Wynfield's pudgy face reddened, his jaw

dropping. Whatever the news, it was not good. He glanced around the great hall—looking for her father? Then spied her and he quickly spoke to Cantrell and headed out with Cantrell following behind.

"Hope that it is not trouble at the border again," Hammersfield said, crossing his arms. "Whoever has the pleasure of marrying Lady Isobel will have to deal with all of this on a regular basis, I daresay."

After her father was dead! Marrying her would not mean the lord would suddenly have her father's title and his properties.

Lords Fenton and Erickson agreed. The men began to talk to one another about the unruly Scots, while Lord Neville quickly took the opportunity to offer his arm to Isobel. "A dance, my lady?"

The men quickly ceased their talk of border issues, realizing the baron had made a play for her when they had forgotten all about her. She could see that, should she have to marry any of them, she would be good for providing bairns, and an heir, but naught more.

"Excuse me, gentlemen." She rushed out of the great hall to see her father about the business with marrying Marcus, still wondering where her Highlander was, and hoping Lord Wynfield was not now telling her father that he needed to prepare for the skirmishes at the border.

"Lady Isobel!" her maid called out, hurrying to catch up to her before Isobel reached the stairs.

She turned to look at her and saw the concern

etched in Mary's face.

"Laird Marcus has left, my lady," Mary said, her words low as if she shouldn't be speaking them.

Isobel's jaw dropped. "What…" She had never considered he would leave this early, and certainly without saying his farewell. He had never done so in the past. At first confused, then furious, suspecting he had been forced to leave because of the way she had showed the assembled visitors and staff that she favored Marcus above all others, she narrowed her eyes. "Why?"

"'Tis the way of things," her maid said vaguely.

Isobel steeled her back. "Why did he leave? Tell me, Mary."

Mary wrung her hands and glanced at the stairs behind Isobel, and quickly turned her gaze back to her. "Come, my lady. Enjoy the dance."

Isobel looked over her shoulder to see if someone was standing near the stairs, but there was no one. Yet someone could be listening in the corridor above. Or even hidden from view on the narrow, tightly-curved stairs that ascended to the upper floors.

She strode past the maid and headed for the door to the inner bailey.

"My lady, where are you going?" Frantic, Mary rushed after her.

"Why did he leave?" Isobel asked Mary again, not to be thwarted in learning the truth.

Mary's expression tightened, her lips thinning, but

she didn't speak.

"'Tis fine with me. I will learn what I can on my own." Isobel hurried outside.

"My lady, you canna leave."

Having no intention of arguing with her maid, Isobel stalked toward the stables. Just as quickly, two of her father's knights headed for her, the one, the captain of the guard, Sir Halloran, his blond hair as short as any Norman's, his eyes a sharp blue. He was frowning at her like he would when he had a disagreeable task to perform. Redheaded Sir Travon, who always had smiles for her—except for tonight—stalked beside him. His green eyes were narrowed as he considered her. She knew the two men wouldn't allow her to go anywhere. Even *with* an escort.

"The dance is inside, my lady," Sir Halloran said. "You should be enjoying the celebration."

"Thank you kindly, Sir Halloran. I am getting a breath of fresh air, if it pleases you." She didn't care whether it pleased him or not.

The captain of the guard took hold of her arm, and she looked up at him, shocked and angered. No one in her father's employ had ever manhandled her. "Unhand me at once!"

"'Tis for your own good, my lady." The ogre hauled her back to the keep as Mary hurried to keep up with them.

Isobel would have the men fired. The both of them! She tried to jerk her arm free, but she couldn't get loose no matter how hard she tried.

Once inside, Sir Halloran released her and blocked the door. It seemed as though everyone had noticed her departure, and every eye was on her.

She smiled sweetly and headed for the stairs. Mary followed her up them as if she were her shadow.

When she reached her father's solar, Isobel noted the door was open and he was inside. And alone, which she was grateful for. Mary continued on down the corridor, not needed when Isobel was seeing her father. He was dark-haired like her, but his eyes were nearly black, and not blue like her own. She had her mother's beautiful cat-like eyes, she was oft told. Now his eyes narrowed at the sight of her.

"Father, I wish to wed Marcus. I love him and he loves me. That should be all that matters."

"You belong here where you will provide an heir for the earldom. You do not belong in some drafty, ill-furnished castle in the Highlands, my daughter." The diplomat that he was, he was firm, but at least he still attempted to placate her.

She would not be appeased! She glared at her father. "Did you send him away? He was invited here. A guest, like any other." Though she knew he was not a guest like any other. Only she welcomed him with open arms. Everyone else reviled him. Except for Mary, who loved to hear stories from him of home as well, and Jane, who thought Isobel and Marcus's love for each other was the most romantic notion ever.

"You were too bold with him. I would have done the same had any other man touched you the way in which he did. 'Tis not done when you are not promised to him."

"We love each other!"

"'Tis only a young girl's imaginings. You will care for the man, any man, who takes you for his wife."

"That is not so! Marcus has asked for my hand many times, and you have turned him down every one of those times? I do not imagine the love that is between us. What of my feelings for him? What of his feelings for me? Do they not matter? Did my mother mean naught more than a dowry to *you*?"

She knew he had loved her mother with all his heart. She hoped he'd see her point.

"Enough, Isobel. My title was not at stake when I took your mother to wife."

"My happiness means naught to you," Isobel blurted out. She saw the look of hurt on her father's face, but she had to break through his denial. She had to make him remember why he married her mother. Didn't Isobel deserve the same kind of love and happiness?

"Seven men have offered for you, whom I approve of, and you will spend time with them and decide which you prefer to marry."

"Marcus is the only one I will agree to wed."

Ignoring her comment, he continued to speak as if she were blithely agreeing to everyone he dictated! "You will wed in a fortnight. In that time, each of the seven men will be given the time to court you properly. If you select one before you have spent time with the others, so be it. If you cannot find it in your heart to decide on one of them, I will do the honor. I leave it to you to choose well."

She bit her lip to keep from saying no to her father. She only had one choice. If she ran away to join Marcus at Lochaven in the Highlands, her father would punish the laird and his people. She could see that now. If she went somewhere else, disappeared for several months, if she could find someone safe to stay with, mayhap her father would be so relieved to learn she was alive, he would allow her to wed Marcus. She would not give in so easily to her father's unreasonable demands. She understood about his title and the importance, but she wanted to be loved for who she was, allowed to be the way she was and not what some nobleman, who didn't love her, wished of her.

Her parents had cared deeply for one another just the way she wanted to love Marcus.

"As you wish, my lord father."

He frowned and seemed not to be taken in by her acquiescence. She'd accepted his demands too readily.

"You do not wish to know who will have the honor to court you?"

She shook her head, her chin stubbornly lifted, fighting the tears that suddenly filled her eyes.

"I only do what is best for you." He reached to take her hands, appearing somewhat unsettled that she was on the verge of tears.

She took a quick step back to avoid his touch, tears rolling down her cheeks. "May I retire to my chambers now, my lord?"

"Aye," he said coldly, not taking well to her dismissal. "You will spend time with Lord Fenton at nooning on the morrow."

"As you wish." Her voice was a choked whisper. She did not kiss her father's cheek as she always did when retiring for the night, although it was way too early for her to be abed when guests were below in the great hall waiting for her return. She could not suffer to see their smug looks when her heart was near bursting with sorrow at the way Marcus had been sent away so unkindly. She turned to leave.

"You will have an escort at all times, my daughter."

Her back to her father, she spoke to the floor covered in rushes. "Mary. Of course."

"And one of my men."

In disbelief, she turned and stared at her father. "What?"

"For your protection, daughter."

He knew her too well. She would leave now before he gave word to his advisor to have one of his men watch her.

"My safety," she said, feigning ignorance.

"Aye. You are all I have, daughter. Had you been a son, I would not be having this discussion. Now you must marry and provide an heir, before I am no longer here. I will secure a future for your son before I would leave this world."

She took a deep, steadying breath, realizing not only did he care about his title and estates, but about her welfare. Yet, marrying one of the English lords would not make her happy. Still, did he know something she didn't? That he was unwell? "You…you are not ill, are you, father?"

"Nay."

She ground her teeth. Fine. Then the truth mayhap would sway him. "Know this, since Lord Fenton is one of the men who wishes to court me, I will tell you then that I broke his nose when I was three and ten." She watched for any change in her father's expression. When his eyes widened, she thought he didn't believe her. Or he did and he couldn't believe she'd do something so violent to a prospective suitor when they were younger. "He said my mother was naught but a Highland heathen and whore."

His face reddening, he clenched his teeth so hard, he looked like he would break his jaw, but he still did not say a word.

"Do you think if he weds me, he would not seek retribution? That he would not think me beneath him because I am my mother's daughter with Highland blood coursing through me?"

"I will make it known to him that he is no longer able to court you. I will add Lord Wynfield to the list instead, who has confided in me many times over that he wishes your hand as well."

"Your seneschal?" As if there was another. "Lord Wynfield? He is more than twice my age. Surely you jest."

Her father shook his head. "The baron is a good man and mayhap you need an older man to take you in hand."

"Are we done, Father?" She didn't wait for him to reply, but tore out of his solar and into the corridor where Sir Travon waited. Her heart tripped at the sight of the knight. Except for earlier when he accompanied Sir Halloran, who forced her to return to the castle, he was usually very cordial toward her, and always had a smile for her. She suspected he would have loved to wed her, not just for the title, but because he cared for her. But her father would never consider him because of his low rank.

Her father couldn't have already told his men she was to be guarded at all times.

She hurried to her chambers, hoping the knight had some business with her father, but his footfalls a few steps behind her told her otherwise.

She turned and stopped, her action so unexpected, Sir Travon nearly ran into her. "Did you wish something of me?" she asked, her voice sharp and on edge.

Appearing not in the least bit bothered by her harshness, he shook his head. "Only following orders."

He gave her a crooked smile.

She shut herself up in her chamber, vowing to find a way out of this nightmare. She would not wed one of the Englishmen or Normans seeking her hand.

The door opened and Mary hurried into her chamber, frowning at her. "You are not returning to the great hall? Your suitors await you. They wish to dance with you."

"Mary, you of all people know how I feel about Marcus."

"Aye, and also how we canna always have our own way. I left my people behind to stay with your mother, to protect her, to be her companion when she was so far from home. We were childhood friends, you ken? She loved your da as much as you do. I had to sacrifice my Highland ways and my Highland family, but now I am here for you."

"Oh, Mary." She took her maid's hands in her own. "If you wish to return—"

"Nay, my place is here. Someday I would love to cradle your bairns."

"If they are Marcus's," Isobel said bitterly. She turned and strode to the window, then peered out at the hills, the trees, and loch in the distance.

"Do you want me to take down your hair?" Mary asked.

Isobel wanted to leave and steal away with Marcus. That's all she wanted to do.

***

Marcus hadn't felt this bad in a long time as a healer stitched his wound shut and used some kind of herbs in a poultice on the injury. Finbar and Rob were standing nearby, arms folded, brows furrowed, their eyes narrowed with worry. The sun shown into the small room furnished with a bed, chest, table, and a chair. He must be in the tavern, though he wished he was home, and Isobel was with him.

"I will live." Though the way Marcus was feeling, sore, aching, his back burning, he wasn't certain. His voice was dry and raspy. He was lying on his stomach and thought if he had to move from this position, he'd never make it.

"Can we resituate him so that he can sit and drink some mead?" Finbar asked the healer.

"Aye, but carefully. His belly may not be able to take any food or drink so soon. Take a care that you dinna pull his stitches loose."

Marcus wanted something to drink, but he wasn't sure he wanted it that bad.

"Aye, we will take the best of care of him. Come on, old man," Finbar said as he and Rob helped Marcus to sit up.

His head swam as soon as he did, his stomach roiling, his back raging with pain.

"He is going down," Rob warned and caught Marcus before he fell off the bed and onto the floor.

When the darkness faded, Marcus realized he was sitting up in bed against the pillows and sunlight no longer shown through the window but was replaced by nightfall.

He groaned. "How long have I been out?"

"Three days." Rob poured him a tankard of mead.

"My horse…"

"He is being cared for at the stable in the village." Rob handed him the tankard.

Marcus noticed then that Finbar was no longer in the room. "Where is your brother?"

"The word has spread that you were attacked by the Sassenach. Because of the incident, skirmishes at the border have begun. Finbar is watching the situation and trying to negotiate with Isobel's da."

Marcus swallowed several gulps of mead to soothe his parched throat. "Isobel?"

"From what we have learned, she is safe, locked up in the castle, but fine."

"Does she know about…" Marcus let out his breath in exasperation. "About me?"

"I am certain that her da and his staff will attempt to keep the news from her. How are you feeling?"

"Better."

Rob looked skeptical.

"Like I have been run over by a hundred galloping horses ridden by the MacLauchlan clansmen, if you must really know, but I am not as dizzy as earlier. And my appetite has returned."

"Good. We will return home as soon as you are able to travel. We have sent word to our kin and they will help to escort you home in case we have any more trouble along the way."

Marcus grunted. But he knew Rob was right. He wanted to fight every last one of the brigands with his own sword. The way he was feeling, he didn't think he could ride anywhere very far and still stay upon his horse, or even stand still and swing his sword.

He wished more than anything to get word to Isobel, and yet he knew there could never be anything more between them as much as he wished it were so. It was best if he never returned to see her. The notion made him ill. He wanted her more than he wanted anything else in his life.

"She must be yours, Marcus. Somehow we must make it happen."

How? That was the question he had pondered ever since he was a lad and never had he found a solution to make it happen.

Footfalls tromped up the stairs and then headed toward his room and Rob drew his sword.

"'Tis me," Finbar called out. "With more of our clansmen."

Rob unbolted the door.

Finbar walked in and Marcus could see at least six of his men hovering about the door, peering in, seeing how he fared. He was heartened by the sight of them.

Then redheaded Alroy, his green eyes sparkling with good cheer, slapped a fellow clansman on the shoulder. "I told you he would be ready to fight."

Marcus managed a small smile and his men cheered him.

CHAPTER 4

Unable to sleep, Isobel had tossed and turned in bed, or paced across her bedchamber floor, wanting to tell Marcus how sorry she was that her father had forced him to leave the dance.

Isobel refused to break her fast the morning after the dance, nor would she attend the nooning or evening meals. Her father would not permit her maid to have a tray brought to her chamber, although Mary sneaked a bit of cheese and bread to her.

It did not matter. Isobel couldn't have choked down a meal if she'd tried. She couldn't sit in her room for another whole day in silent protest either. She had to oversee the household staff. For two more days, she had no appetite, and she would not break her fast, but when she went to the kitchen with Mary to check on the meal, she noted Cook and her assistants seemed troubled, worried looks cast her way, though no one said a word.

Maybe they thought she would try to eat in the kitchen and not with the rest of their people in the great hall. But she had no intention of eating either place. Once she was done with the kitchen staff, she said to Mary, "I wish to take a ride." Isobel headed for the corridor that led out to the inner bailey. "You do not have to ride with me. I will have a knight escort and you need to break your fast."

"Nay, I will eat later." Mary looked ill at ease, but only followed her and said not another word.

Isobel intended to take a ride to the loch—with her unwelcome escort. She wanted to remember the kiss she had shared with Marcus there and pray that he would return to see her soon and not wait another long year. But what if her father forced her to wed by then? A fortnight, he had warned. She was certain he would, too. She had to leave before that happened, and…and find someplace she could live for a time until her father gave in and let her wed the Highlander who held her heart hostage.

Sir Travon silently trailed them as she made her way down the corridor past one of the rooms. Men's voices inside caught her attention, and she abruptly stopped when she recognized them. All of them were her suitors. What were they still doing here?

"No doubt he has already forced himself upon her," Lord Neville said, sounding annoyed.

Were they talking about her? Isobel suspected so. Furious beyond reason, she knew the men probably thought as much, but she had not expected them to discuss it among themselves in her father's own castle.

"Forced himself. Nay. She offered herself willingly, of that I have no doubt," Lord Erickson said. "All anyone needs to see is the way she behaved at the dance. The way she pulled him closer. The way she looked up at him so…wantonly."

She was ready to march right in and break Lord Neville's and Lord Erickson's noses this time.

Sir Travon cleared his throat, and she looked back at him, having forgotten all about him. He motioned for her to continue on her way as if saying this was a man's matter, and she should not be listening in. She glared at her father's knight and stood her ground. And listened to hear more of what her suitors thought of her. Because she had no doubt they were discussing *her* behavior toward Marcus.

"Mayhap she needs a firmer hand," Lord Hammersfield said, his voice disdainful. "We have been polite, mayhap overmuch, trying to win the lady over who wishes not what polite society dictates. 'Twas obvious to anyone who watched her and the Highlander that more has been going on betwixt the two. We must remember what her mother was."

Sensing her fury, Sir Travon stepped forward and reached for her arm, but not quickly enough. She threw the door open to the room and stormed in.

Startled, the men all glanced in her direction, their eyes widening. All three men had been lounging on benches, but they all bolted from them and stood, looking like they'd been caught stealing from the kirk and were at once rendered speechless.

"*What* exactly *was* my mother?" she demanded of Lord Hammersfield, the English baron's blond hair, long and twisted into ringlets like King Henry's as it hung over his shoulders, though he did not wear the beard. His cold gray eyes were fixed on her, his mouth surly. As usual, he was dressed impeccably, the finest wool tunic reaching to the floor, the over tunic, resting at his knees, and both heavily embroidered.

The men could discuss her all they wanted, but when it came to her mother, she would defend her honor to the death.

"A clan chief's daughter. That was what she was. He was an earl, too, if you did not know this. So what did this make her, Lord Hammersfield? You tell me," Isobel growled.

Though she glared at the baron, she noted the other men had taken a step away from him as if distancing themselves from the lord and her anger.

"I beg pardon," he said coldly.

He was not cowed by her sharp tongue, nor would he think any better of her or her mother if he wed Isobel. Most likely he would make her pay for her insolence if he took her to wife. She could see in his narrowed eyes he would love to do just that.

"And you, Lord Neville," she said, turning her wrath on the next of her suitors, his blue eyes just as narrowed, his black-bearded chin raised a notch as if he wouldn't be submissive in front of her, his thin lips pursed in annoyance. His garments were just as richly embroidered, but instead of wearing colors of the forest like Hammersfield did, Neville's clothes were brighter like one of King Henry's peacocks. "When I take a husband to my bed, he will be the first to lay with me. You can believe all you wish, but Laird McEwan has always been most honorable. Whoever my husband is, he will find me a virgin wife."

The men cast each other glances. She couldn't read their veiled expressions. Were they glad the one who got the prize would not be taking a wife who might be breeding a savage bastard, or that the chosen husband would be the first to plant his seed in her? Or mayhap they'd prefer that the initial bedding had been done, that she might even be a more experienced wife rather than a green girl. Maybe they thought she lied.

She turned her wrath on Lord Erickson next, his red hair wild in massive curls, making his head seem twice its size, his green eyes rounded as if he couldn't believe she'd speak her mind thus. Like the others, he wore clothes fashioned similarly to their king, his garments in varying shades of green that matched his sage green eyes. "If I were to wed you, sir, you would have to force yourself upon me as I would never comply willingly."

They stared back at her red-faced, jaws taut, but none said a word. Though she suspected Lord

Hammersmith was fighting the urge to speak his mind from the way he was keeping his jaws clamped together and his hands curled into fists. She could just imagine what he'd say. Whether she came willingly to his bed or no', she would have his heir. Then he would find pleasure in a whore, an English whore, not a Scottish one, when the duty was done.

"Oh, and my father has dismissed one of my suitors, already," she added sweetly as she turned to leave, "if you did not know—per my recommendation. My father's advisor, Lord Wynfield has offered suit. Never has he said an ill word about my mother or me. You might remember that in the future."

Her cheeks hot with anger, she stalked out of the room, not bothering to shut the door.

Waiting for her, Sir Travon raised his brows at her, but he didn't dare say a word. He'd tell his fellow knights all about her outburst, she was certain. And she didn't care. Mary's cheeks were red, her eyes round, but other than being mortified and probably shocked, she didn't speak a word to her either.

Lord Erickson said to the other suitors, "Now where were we?"

The door shut and Lord Neville said, "Changing tactics."

If she could not wed Marcus, she knew her future here would be bleak. As much as she admired her father's advisor, at thirty-nine, he was twenty years her senior. He was more her father's age than a husband's.

If she could find no way out of this nightmare, she would concede…

She shook her head. She could not wed the baron. *Ever*. She loved Marcus and would never marry any other man than him.

Mary and the knight followed Isobel outside the keep. The day was awash in gray—the sky, the clouds, and every space in between. She felt swallowed up by the dreary bleakness, unable to shake off an impending doom.

"Lady Isobel?" Mary said as Isobel continued toward the stables.

His expression stormy, Lord Wynfield, her father's senchanal, and two knights crossed the baily to stop her. He wore his blond hair cropped short like many Normans did, when she loved Marcus's longer hair and wished someday to run her fingers through the strands.

"You must remain inside today, my lady," Lord Wynfield said, his voice firm but gentle.

She knew then something was the matter and wondered again about Cantrell's bringing him some disagreeable news at the dance. "What is wrong?"

"Skirmishes again at the border. Your father has left to try and talk some sense into those who are fighting."

Scots. Like her father, around her, the baron was careful not to call them barbarians or savages.

"Father," she said her heart wizening. She had not seen him since the night of the dance. What if she never saw him again? He had always been successful with negotiations in the past, but as dangerous as the fighting could be…

"He will be all right, my lady. He left word that he did not wish you to venture outside the keep until he returned."

"Who is instigating the border fight?" she quickly asked, praying Marcus was not involved because her father had sent him away.

"McEwan had nothing to do with this. At least we do not believe so," Lord Wynfield said, understanding her fear, and attempting to set it aside.

Which she more than appreciated.

"He would not," she said adamantly. He was an honorable man.

Lord Wynfield guided her back into the keep, dismissing the two knights who had accompanied him. Though Sir Travon still trailed close behind them and her maid continued to stay nearby.

Her father's advisor cleared his throat. "Laird McEwan was wounded, Lady Isobel. If some of the Scots thought this had anything to do with us, some may have retaliated. As far as we know, his clan members are not involved."

She barely heard anything beyond the words, *He was wounded.*

She seized Lord Wynfield's arm, her heart pounding furiously. "How…when…he was not fighting. I do not understand."

"He was set upon by…a thief, and the brigand wounded him. But we have word Laird McEwan lives."

She clung to Lord Wynfield's arm, more to keep her knees from buckling than to keep him from going anywhere now, as she felt lightheaded, her stomach queasy. He reached out to take hold of her arms to steady her, but she shook her head and took a step away from him. She didn't want to be comforted by him or anyone else on her father's staff. Any of them who could have been involved in sending Marcus away from the castle during the dance.

She had to see Marcus.

"When did this happen?" she asked, her eyes narrowed. It had to have been when he left her castle, but somewhere close to the border if the Scots there were fighting.

Lord Wynfield looked ill at ease to have to mention it.

"After the celebration? When he was forced to leave here?"

He glanced at Sir Travon and appeared to be trying to decide whether to tell her the truth or not.

"I will learn the truth, or some wildly exaggerated version of it. Which would you rather me hear?" she asked, her tone cold.

"After the dance, only a short distance from the castle."

"That was the news Cantrell brought to you?"

"Aye. We do not know the exact circumstances.

Your father wishes to speak to Laird McEwan to determine what had happened, but no one of his clan will permit it."

"Take me to see Marcus."

"Your father would not permit it. 'Tis too dangerous for you to cross the border to the village, not with the fighting going on, my lady."

She narrowed her eyes at him. "This is all your fault." She didn't mean him personally, but she knew he would not want her wedding the Highlander any more than her father would.

When Lord Wynfield did not deny it, she knew then—her father had given him the order, and he had given word to the men who had escorted Marcus out of the keep.

"How bad is he?" She fought valiantly to keep the tears at bay, to believe he was not wounded badly, and that the man who did this to him would pay with his life.

"He is recovering, so I am told, from the little word that we could get concerning his condition."

"Has father's physician seen to him?" Considering that Marcus was injured on her father's land while being forced to leave the castle through no fault of his own, and now the Scots had retaliated, wouldn't peace come easier if in good faith her father sent his own physician to care for Marcus?

"I have had word that a healer has seen to his injury."

"I want to see him for myself." And she would, no matter the obstacle that stood in her way.

"'Tis not possible, my lady."

She would make it possible, one way or another.

***

In the small tavern room, Finbar offered Marcus another bowl of fish broth. "Fortunately, you will live," Finbar said cheerfully, but then his happy countenance darkened. "Which will not be the same for whosoever paid to have you murdered. I am certain he will be surprised to learn that it will take more than three burly men to kill you, however."

"Then he will try again." Rob leaned against the wall, his arms folded across his chest, appearing ill at ease.

"The dead men were paid well, I hope," Marcus said wryly, still confined to the bed at the tavern, feeling out of sorts and in too much pain. Every muscle in his back ached, and he had not the strength to leave the bed since he had been struck down two days ago.

"Aye," Rob said. "We collected the gold from each of the three men for your safekeeping."

"Did you learn anything about the lord who ordered my death?" Marcus tried to take another sip of broth, wanting to mend as quickly as he could so he'd be able to fight again when necessary.

"Nay," Finbar said. "A few Scots took offense to the notion that Englishmen attempted to murder a clan chief when he was only traveling through the area, at the invitation of Lord Pembroke. They have started several skirmishes along the border."

"The Scots will pay with their lives. For what?" Marcus asked.

"Honor. Pride," Rob said. "One of their own. Even if they are not Highlanders. Well worth the dying for. You know how it is with some men. Any excuse and they will take it."

"Aye, which is the same for the other side as well. What of Isobel?" Marcus wanted word about her most of all, but not wanting to hear what he suspected would be the way of things now. Her father would push the wedding forward, forcing her to make the choice between any of the suitors who had come forward.

"Mary sent word that Lord Pembroke said she would wed in a fortnight. He has offered her a choice of seven men," Rob said.

"Fenton?"

Rob shook his head. "The lass told her da finally how she had broken his nose and feared retribution. Her da substituted his advisor as the seventh man."

"Wynfield? He is nearly as old as her da!" Marcus cursed and shoved the broth aside.

"Mary said because of the border uprisings and that Lord Pembroke fears Lady Isobel will try to run away, she is being kept under guard in the keep," Finbar said.

"Good, I am glad he is aware of what she might attempt to do." As much as Marcus would love to see her again, he didn't under the current circumstances.

"Lord Wynfield wishes to speak with you. He believes if you talk to the men who are battling the English, they will listen to you and the continued bloodshed will be averted." Finbar arched a brow. "We would ride on your behalf if you wish it."

Rob snorted. "The Scots would only listen to Marcus. He is the clan chief and the one so grievously wounded. Except he canna ride for now."

Marcus considered his options, then smiled. "Tell Lord Pembroke I will speak on his behalf, if he will grant me the marriage to his daughter."

His cousins both smiled at him.

"If he doesna?" Rob asked.

"The devil take him. I didna instigate this fight, and I willna stop it."

Rob bowed to him. "I will get word to him at once."

Rob left the room and Finbar barred the door behind him.

Marcus frowned. "I worry about him taking the message alone to Lord Wynfield."

"Naught to worry about," Finbar said. "Several of our allies have gathered to watch our backs. And the six that came from home are here. 'Tis as safe as it ever is."

Marcus just hoped that Pembroke would keep his daughter at home and safe from harm. If she learned Marcus had been injured, she would attempt to see him at great personal risk to herself, and he prayed she would not, but he knew her better.

CHAPTER 5

For days, Isobel had plotted and planned a way to escape the confines of the castle to find a way to see Marcus. She had given Mary coins to pay a servant to slip across the border and visit the tavern where it was reported that Marcus was staying. But they could not learn how badly injured he was, only that his cousins were staying close at hand, and several more of his clansmen had arrived to protect him. That meant he had to be injured enough that he could not fight, and she worried even more that he could be dying. She was furious with her father and everyone else who might have had a hand in this.

She wanted desperately to be with Marcus, to see for herself that he was all right and that Cantrell had not said so only to protect her feelings.

Mary slipped into Isobel's chamber and whispered, "I know what you are thinking of doing, my lady."

Mary would. She always knew what Isobel planned to do, sometimes even before she thought of it.

"You will help me?"

"You will leave whether I help you or no'."

Isobel frowned at her. "Then what do you wish to tell me."

"You are tired after your fright concerning Marcus. You will eat—"

Isobel had no appetite and hadn't since her father had sent Marcus away.

"You will, my lady, or I willna help you." Mary looked sternly at her, her mind made up.

"All right."

"That way you will make an appearance in the great hall to show you are there. You will do the duties you normally perform and when your knight escort is distracted, slip back to the postern gate. You will leave by the postern gates that are being left open later than usual because of the men returning who have been wounded in the skirmishes." Mary paused. "Cantrell, who has been going across the border to learn about Laird McEwan, asked for more coin."

"But I have given him so much already."

"He said he has to bribe several to keep this secret."

Isobel's heart beat faster. "He was not to mention this to anyone."

"A servant canna do anything he or she wishes. He has to have permission, so he has to use the money to bribe others to look the other way."

"All right. But I will run out of shillings before long." Isobel gave Mary the coins.

"He has hidden clothes behind the washing barrels. Dress in the alcove and with the borrowed brat covering your head and hair, everyone will believe you are a male servant, no' a woman," Mary said, frowning, "though God forbid anything should happen to you. 'Tis no' safe for a lass or a man to venture toward the border. Cantrell has gotten word to a couple of Laird McEwan's men that you wish to see Marcus and they have agreed to escort you from the woods near the keep. You just need to slip past the chaos at the postern gate, and I will help to see that you leave without incident. But you *must* return within a few hours. I willna agree to aid you if you dinna."

"I cannot stay with Marcus," Isobel said, "or my father would have him thrown in the dungeon, wounded or not, and I can see a full-fledged battle ensuing. I just wish to see him."

"Aye, lass. A thick fog cloaks the area, which can be good, but also can be bad. Mind the time. I have warned McEwan's men thus as well. The laird doesna know you are coming to see him. He would say no."

Overwhelmed with hopeful joy, Isobel threw her arms around Mary and hugged her.

"There, there, lass. 'Tis what I would have wanted done for me if I were in your shoes. And I know you will go anyway to see him, so I would rather we did this in the safest manner possible."

"Thank you, Mary."

"Aye, well, once you have departed the grounds, I will return to your chamber, bolt the door, and talk away to you in a scolding way, pretending to be speaking with you while you are ignoring me. The knight will hear me and believe you are here as I dinna talk to myself, usually. Then I will say something about you going to sleep and will lapse into silence."

Isobel prayed it would work.

"It is time."

With her stomach jumping with fluttery worry, she and Mary departed the chamber with the knight in tow. At the meal, Isobel ate as much as she could force herself to, too upset over Marcus's injury and too unsettled about traveling across the border with the men fighting to eat very much. Mary was watching her and so she ate as much of the fish soup, venison, and bread that she could manage, before she slipped away to the kitchen to speak to Cook about the meal for the next day. Afterward, she stopped at the billets where men injured in the skirmishes were being cared for. Once she began to aid the healer, she noticed her knight escort left, probably figuring she would be there for a while, and he could take care of personal business.

She finished bandaging a soldier's arm, then left the billets and found the change of clothes where Cantrell had hidden them behind a barrel of soapy water. The washer women were busy hanging the clothes to dry and thankfully didn't notice her. Unless he had bribed them to—look the other way.

Fearing she would be caught at any moment, Isobel changed into the servant's clothes—trewes, a brown wool tunic, and then fastened the gray brat at her throat. She tucked her own clothes behind the washer barrels and hoped no one would find them. After pulling the wool brat over her head to cloak her hair and face, she hurried out of the keep and saw Mary watching for her, her brows furrowed with concern.

Isobel kept her head low so no one would see her face as she headed for the back gate. The thing of it was, with so many coming and going through the postern gate, no one paid her any mind. Not when she was wearing men's clothes and leaving, not coming in. When she returned, they might inspect her some, but by then the deed would be done.

Thanking God that no one detained her, she stalked through the gate and headed for the woods, gladdened to see the gray fog cloaking the area. Several more hours of light remained, so she had to hurry to meet up with her escort in the cover of the woods and then go from there, and return well before it grew dark.

Her skin chilled with trepidation and heart pounding, she quickly made her way to the edge of the forest, praying that she would run into the right men or she could be in serious trouble.

When she saw Rob on foot, his sword drawn, two horses nearby, she nearly cried out with relief. "'Tis me," she said, hoping no one else would hear her but Rob and his kinsmen serving as her escort and not her own men.

"My lady." Rob quickly helped her to mount the spare horse.

She then saw six men, all wearing trewes and tunics, all nodding their greetings, several fighting smiles, though she knew this was a deadly business and if her men found her with the Highlanders, they would attempt to kill every one of them for taking off with her. But she suspected the men were glad to see her when she wished to visit Marcus and maybe even lift his spirits.

"They are all of the clan," Rob said. "Come, we must ride quickly and return as soon as we can. We want no one to learn that you have slipped away."

"Aye. Is he…is he well?"

"Aye, lass. He will want me skinned alive when he learns we have done this, but I know you, and I believed 'twas safer this way, than worrying if you'd try to do this on your own."

"Thank you, Rob."

"Marcus will not be pleased," Rob again warned her.

"I had to see him."

"Aye, lass. I know."

They traveled for some time in silence, avoiding the fighting, swords clashing and men shouting in two different areas, though they could not see the men battling for the woods and distance they were from Isobel and her escort. Trying to avoid any encounters with the men made for a longer journey, and her stomach tightened with concern all the more. When they left the cover of the woods, a shout from somewhere in the distance startled her and her heart did a little skip. Instantly, her skin chilled as she realized someone had spied their small party and warned his own people. Men on horseback suddenly appeared out of the fog as they left the woods and rode toward them. Ten of them. She held tightly onto her reins as her borrowed horse made a step back, and she feared he would bolt.

Her party halted, and Marcus's men unsheathed swords while they circled around her to protect her. She loved Marcus's kin. With all her heart, she wanted so to be part of his family.

Her skin prickling with fear though, she slipped her *sgian dubh* out of its sheath hidden beneath the brat, the one Marcus had given her when she was a young girl. She treasured it, but she didn't believe she could fight men who wielded swords. If one of them lost his, she could get it and use the training she'd learned when she was but a wee lass fighting Rob and Finbar in mock battle and maybe gain the advantage. They wouldn't expect that she could fight.

Then again, they probably thought her a lad and not a woman the way she was dressed. A lad would have trained how to fight in the Highlands from a young age.

"Hold!" Rob shouted. "We are kin to Marcus McEwan."

They had to be Scots. His hair black as his eyes, the man in charge eyed Isobel with suspicion, most likely because Rob's men surrounded her in a protective way.

"Who be the lad?" the man asked, his voice a command.

Good, they did not know she was a woman.

"Marcus's nephew. He wants to see him at once, to give him the order personally that he should not be here attempting to fight the Sassenach on Marcus's behalf," Rob said.

She had never heard Rob use that term in referring to the English before, but she supposed he had to, to show which side he was on. She hoped the man was unaware that Marcus did not have a nephew.

The Scot smiled a little. Was it because he thought her a wild lad to attempt to fight in the battle on behalf of his uncle, or that he didn't believe Rob?

"You have too small a party. We will ride with you to the tavern."

"My thanks be to you," Rob said and he and his men sheathed their swords.

"Dwyer's the name." He looked at the *sgian dubh* clutched in Isobel's fist and she finally slipped it under her cloak. Why would a lad not be carrying a sword, she feared Dwyer would wonder.

She was glad that Rob and his men had not had to fight the English, and that the Scots would help them gain safe passage.

No one spoke any further as they headed again for the village, and when she saw the scattered cottages, the two shops and the one tavern, she felt both relief and apprehension.

When they reached the two-story stone tavern, one of the men took hold of her reins while Rob helped her down.

What surprised her next was that the man who was in charge of her Scots' escort joined her and Rob. She was afraid he knew just who she was and what her business here entailed.

"My lady," Dwyer said with admiration. "Do ye plan to leave with the laird and his kin when he is well enough to travel?"

Assuming he knew very well who she was, she shook her head. "I fear what would happen to the laird and his kin if my father were to learn of it."

"Then you only wished to see his lairdship and return this day?"

"Aye. I shall not be long. I do not want anyone to learn I have gone."

"Then with your permission and Rob's, we would feel honored to return you home again once you are done."

"But the risk—"

"Nay. The clan of the McEwan and their kin, the

MacNeill clansmen, have fought alongside us numerous times. We know his lairdship was wounded because he had been with you and was turned out of the castle. We only wish the two of you the best. We pledge ourselves to returning you safely."

"Thank you," she said, feeling choked up.

"Aye, my lady. We will be waiting." Dwyer and the other men moved off then to water their horses.

Rob walked with her to the door of the tavern.

"He was cut on the back and is weak," Rob said, preparing her for what she would see. "He was sitting up earlier and eating some. He may be sleeping now."

"He is not with fever?"

"Nay."

She felt some relief at his words, but until she saw him or knew he was fully recovered, she would worry.

They entered the tavern where men were eating and drinking, though the noise from their conversation visibly died down when the new arrivals appeared, everyone checking to see if they were friend or foe. Many nodded a greeting to Rob, and she suspected they were some of the men sent to watch over Marcus.

A few regarded her with a discerning eye. She hoped she looked like a young man and not like a woman dressed in men's garments. She wondered if that's what had given her away with the Scots across the border was Rob and his men circling her to protect her and that she had no sword, only a *sgian dubh* to protect herself in a fight.

They moved to the stairs and she felt strange when she didn't have skirts to lift while she ascended the stairs. She kept her cloak closed so that no one there would see her trewes. She felt too exposed in them, having never worn a tunic that would show off the shape of her legs. Her father would have had a fit.

When they reached the landing, she saw two men standing on either side of a door. Both straightened when they saw her and bowed their heads in greeting. She returned their greeting with her own.

Rob knocked on the door. "I have returned with the bundle."

"Good." Finbar sounded vastly relieved. The bolt slid back and then the door opened. Finbar gave her a small smile. "He is asleep, but do come in, my lady."

Isobel entered the room, then saw Marcus, his face peaceful in sleep, his blanket resting at his hips, his chest bare. She had seen many men like this when she tended to the wounded, so she was not shocked. And she had seen Marcus's chest before when he fought his cousins in playful combat. She swore it had been just to show off his muscles. She had loved them and him for showing them off.

She hurried across the floor and placed her hand over his forehead, but his skin was cool to the touch. No fever. Thank God.

Finbar pulled the chair over to the bed so that she could sit beside Marcus.

"We will be outside the room. If you need

anything, just let us know," Finbar said.

"Aye, thank you."

He bowed his head and he and Rob left, then shut the door.

Isobel leaned over and kissed Marcus's cheek. He didn't stir and she knew she should let him rest. That sleep would help to heal him. But she also believed that if he knew she was here, sitting beside him, encouraging him to get well, he would mend all the faster. If only the situation could be different between them and she was sitting at his bedside in his chambers back home. She would not leave his side until he was well again.

Then again, if things were different, he wouldn't be suffering from any kind of wound inflicted by the English.

She worried that she didn't have much time to stay.

She ran her hand over his arm, loving the feel of his muscles, his skin. She looked back at his face and was startled to see him staring at her as if he were seeing a ghost.

"'Tis me," she quickly said.

"What are you doing here?" Marcus attempted to sit up.

She jumped up and helped him sit. "I came to see you. I had to know that you were well. I had to tell you that I love you with all my heart."

"You crossed the border? With the skirmishes going on? What were you thinking?"

She scowled at him. "I was thinking that I loved you, and I had to be with you. That was what I was thinking!"

He smiled a little, though he grimaced also and appeared to still be very much in pain.

"You shouldna be here. It will be as difficult for you to return as it was to get here."

"'Twas not difficult coming here." She wouldn't admit how scared she had been when they had come across the group of Scots looking to fight them, until Rob had told them who they were. Or how hearing the fighting going on in the distance had made her heart race with fear. "I would not have stayed away. I had to see you for myself."

"You have seen me." He sounded furious. "Tell Rob you wish to return now. Before you are missed. Before you are in further danger."

She narrowed her eyes at him. "I will not leave just yet." She rose and found a flask of mead and brought it to him, then sat back down as she watched him drink it. "I am so sorry that my father sent you away. And that you were injured. If your cousins had met back at the keep at the appointed hour so that there were three of you riding together, the attack would never have happened."

"One of your suitors had to have hired the men," Marcus said angrily.

"What? One of my suitors?" Her heart began to pound furiously. "The man who attacked you was not a thief? Lord Wynfield said he was but that they did not know more than that. How...how do you know he was not a thief?"

"The timing, the close proximity to the castle. They lay in wait like a pack of wolves, like they knew just when I was leaving because they knew I would be forcibly sent away. Then they attacked. The last one who struck me in the back had been too cowardly to face me man to man in a fair fight. They were paid in gold. But the three brigands have paid for their crimes. The man who hired them hasna."

"Three men?" She scarce could breathe, imagining Marcus fighting for his life against three armed men.

She couldn't believe the English could be so bloodthirsty, and yet here they called the Highlanders savages. What concerned her most was that her father was the one who had given the order to have Marcus sent away. He could not have had anything to do with the men attacking Marcus. She wouldn't believe it of him.

"You do not know who hired them?" Overwhelmed with the truth of the matter, she had assumed the man only a thief, who would attack anyone he believed would make it worth his while.

"Nay. There were too many attacking to hold polite conversation."

"I...I am so sorry, Marcus." She bit her lip and took his hand and squeezed it.

"Dear lass, you had naught to do with it."

"If I had not held you so close, flaunting the way I feel about you in front of the others, showing them that I love you—" Her eyes filled with tears and she hated that she could not hold them back, but it was all her fault that he had been sent away and then attacked.

"Ahh, Isobel, come here." He reached out his arms to hold her, though he grimaced as if the movement caused him much pain.

She willingly went to him, wanting to hold him close, and pressed herself gently against his chest, trying to be so careful not to hurt him further. She needed his touch as much as she suspected he needed hers.

"You had naught to do with this," he repeated. "'Twas my fault for holding you close at the dance and stirring your da's ire."

"He was angry with me over it. Not with you," she said vehemently.

He stroked her back and sighed deeply. "Though I shouldna wish you were here, you canna know how much it means to me to hold you like this. But you shouldna have come."

"'Tis the same for me. I wished to see you, to feel you, to know you were…were going to live."

He kissed the top of her head. "Three brigands couldna get the best of me."

She frowned at him because one had.

"And live," he amended with a small smile.

"Can I see your wound?" She couldn't help

worrying about him, though he furrowed his brow at her and she could see he didn't like being fussed over.

"I havena seen it, but I imagine it doesna look pretty," he warned.

"I just want to see if it is healing well."

He let his breath out. "You shouldna be here."

She thought he said so because he was afraid of how she'd view his fresh wound and be sickened by it.

"I must leave soon," she admitted, "as much as I would love to stay with you until you are fully recovered." Then she smiled a little. "Mayhap if I did stay with you, my father would change his mind about us."

Marcus snorted. "He would know I couldna have you, no' as wounded as I am."

Disappointed that they could not make her staying with him work in their favor, she made him lean forward a bit and ran her finger over his uninjured skin—the wound not bright red as if it were infected, but a lighter pink. "The healer did well with her stitches. It appears to be healing."

"Good."

"Are you really angry that I have come to see you?" She sat back down on the chair. If she had it to do all over again, she would do naught differently.

"Aye, lass. 'Tis no' safe for you with the fighting going on. If anyone was to learn who you were, he could ransom you for concessions from your da. Besides, thieving brigands are out there who could harm you." He glanced down at her trewes and shook his head. "You shouldna be dressed like that."

She pulled her brat over her legs.

"I had your men escort me here and there were others who joined us and will help me to return home."

"And they are just as much at risk. Beyond that, I dinna want *them* seeing you dressed thus, either."

"The brat covered my clothes." Though not all the way as she rode there. She sighed and took his hand and lifted it to her lips and kissed him. "I would not have stayed away."

His beautiful eyes gazed at her, and she knew he was only worried about her, trying to pretend he did not wish to see her. "Isobel." He looked away. "It can never be."

Her heart took a dive and she bit her lip. "Do not say that. My father *will* change his mind. I will make sure of it."

Marcus considered her again, his expression weary. "His title and lands are too important. Dinna you see? He will never agree that we should wed."

Isobel fought the tears welling up in her eyes. She would never give Marcus up. Never.

He reached out to her again, and this time she sat next to him on the bed. He folded his arms around her and held on tight, despite his injury, for one last time. She treasured feeling his arms around her, and she would cherish this moment forever.

Then he kissed her forehead. "You must go."

She felt safe here in his arms. She didn't want to go. She wanted to be with him like this always.

Someone knocked on the door. Rob said through the closed door, "I must return our guest."

"Aye." But Marcus sounded like he truly didn't wish it.

Rob opened the door. "Come, we must go."

She kissed Marcus then, with the passion she felt for him, and he returned the kiss just as passionately. Then she reluctantly left the bed, their hands clasped. "I will wed no other," she vowed again to have Marcus for her husband.

She pressed her lips against his warm and willing mouth one last time, her heart weighing heavily. With the fear of returning safely to her keep, that they would be in the midst of a fight where men on either side would be killed or badly injured, and trying to slip back inside the keep without anyone noticing, she felt anxious all over again. At least she knew that for now, Marcus was alive and on the mend.

She assumed that he would give his cousins hell after she was returned safely to the keep. She loved them for helping her to see him, and she vowed to repay them someday.

"I have to go. I...I love you, Marcus. Get well so that I may see you again soon."

He didn't repeat her sentiment. She swallowed hard, afraid he had decided they had no chance to be together and after this last incident, he no longer would fight the inevitable. But *she* would.

Rob closed the door after her and hurried her down the stairs and out of the tavern. Before long, they were riding once again across the border with the Scots at their side and were headed back to her keep.

When they were only a mile or so from her castle, a force of a dozen men—her father's men—led by Sir Halloran, captain of the guard, charged her and her escort. Her heart couldn't have beat any faster with fear.

Rob and his escort and that of the Scot's quickly drew swords and encircled her as before, only with a larger force this time.

"Nay!" she shouted as loud as she could manage and rode through her escort to reach her men. "Hold! 'Tis me! Lady Isobel! They are not here to fight, but to escort me home safely! Let them return to the border without a fight!"

Rob and some of the others had rejoined her, not allowing her to face the Englishmen alone, should they not believe who she was. She pushed back the cloak, some of her hair loose and falling about her shoulders.

Her men looked furious with her, maybe a little worried. "I will not return to the keep and will fight you myself if you battle with these men," she warned.

"Aye, be off with you then," Sir Halloran said to her escort. "We will not fight you here. Come, Lady Isobel, we will escort you back to the keep."

"After the Scots and the Highlanders are gone," she said. She didn't want them to be pursued after she was returned to the keep.

"Aye." Sir Halloran scowled at her, looking highly displeased.

She hurried to dismount and handed the reins to one of Rob's men. Then she said good bye to Rob, telling him in private that she would wed Marcus and that he better not marry a Highland lass in the meantime or he would wish he hadn't.

Rob smiled and bowed to her. The party turned and headed back toward the border.

Sir Halloran rode forth then and she knew he meant to lift her into his saddle, but she feared that once he had hold of her, he'd return her to the keep and the other men would go after her escort.

She quickly pulled out her *sgian dubh* and took a stance that said she was serious about this. She would not be thwarted in her task.

"My lady," Sir Halloran said, trying to persuade her to listen to reason and sounding perfectly disgruntled. "If your father knew what you have done, he would have all our heads."

She wouldn't budge and he finally waited for her to agree to let him take her home. When the horses' hooves had faded off in the distance, and she turned to see that her escort was long gone, she sheathed her *sgian dubh*. The knight dismounted and lifted her onto his saddle.

"I could have taken you," he said, "easily. But I wished to show goodwill toward the men who returned you safely."

"Thank you."

"But your father will be most displeased."

She knew she could only further displease him if she continued to want to be with Marcus and her father denied her the chance to do so.

Now that she knew Marcus would live, the next time she left the castle, it would be to find a safe haven far from her father's reach, and she prayed he would change his mind about wedding her to someone other than Marcus.

CHAPTER 6

Marcus couldn't believe that Isobel had managed to see him alone and while the fighting was going on. Though he had been glad to share a moment with her, he wouldn't stop worrying about her safety until Rob returned safely himself. Marcus scowled at Finbar.

"Mary said her charge would find a way to slip out somehow to see you as determined as she was. She thought it safer for her if she had an escort," Finbar explained, his arms folded, his demeanor as stubborn as any of his kinsmen.

Still feeling tired, Marcus couldn't agree or disagree with Finbar's comment. But if Isobel didn't make it safely back, or his own kinsmen died en route...

He took a deep breath and closed his eyes. As soon as he heard voices speaking low in the room, he woke to find candlelight reflecting off the walls and Rob had returned safely.

"Isobel?" he asked immediately.

"She protected us." Rob smiled. "With her *sgian dubh*, she threatened her da's people if they should ride into battle against us. They left us in peace. The good news is that Pembroke arranged a tentative peace between the Scots and the English. I spoke with him myself, and he sends his regrets about your injury. He asked if there were any more men who attacked you, or just the one. When I told him there were three, he fully intended to find the others and hunt them down."

"Three was enough. Why would he know of only the one?"

Rob shrugged. "I wonder if whoever paid them tried to get rid of the bodies to hide the evidence. Since the men who attacked you are dead, he felt the matter closed."

"You told him what the one man said, aye? These men were doing a task for another, most likely a lord vying for Isobel's hand in marriage."

"Aye. I told him just that. Pembroke did not feel that was the case. No evidence exists to back up the claim."

"'Tis as plain as the tusks on a wild boar." Marcus grunted. "If a peace agreement of sorts has been reached, the bad news is Pembroke doesna need me to convince the Scots to stand down in exchange for my wedding Isobel."

"Aye. The other good news is that before we parted

ways, he said he willna have Isobel wed anyone for a couple of months. He wouldna say for certain why, but I got the impression he was rethinking the situation as far as your injury was concerned and wouldna want his daughter to marry a man who would have had you killed. But know this, the lass will wed you—her words—and if you wed another in the interim, it will go badly for you."

Marcus smiled. He loved her and if it was in his power to do so, they would be wed.

***

After returning to Lochaven, and for two months, Marcus had continued to beseech Pembroke to allow him to marry his daughter. He wasn't about to give up his clan, nor did his people want him to, but if it was the only way to have Isobel, he had to consider it might be his only choice. Still, he didn't believe Pembroke would want a Highlander to take his place should he die, or that Marcus's child would someday hold the title and lands. For all that time, Marcus had corresponded with Isobel as well. Though it was rare for Highlanders—and many of the English and Normans did not know how to read or write—Isobel's mother had learned, and she had been adamant that both Isobel and Marcus acquire the craft so they could send missives to each other to keep in touch.

Thankfully, Pembroke had allowed the correspondence between them to continue. Marcus often thought he did so because it was easier to keep them apart that way. Pembroke had to know that if he had not allowed them to write to one another, Marcus would have showed up in person. If someone had tried to kill him again?

More skirmishes would have ensued. Better to keep the peace this way. Marcus didn't mind, well, overmuch, that her da was breaking the seals on her missives to Marcus, nor that he did the same with Marcus's letters to Isobel, as evidenced by Lord Pembroke's seal affixed to both—as long as they were allowed to correspond.

Following the hunt that morn and while his people who had grievances gathered to speak with him about them, Marcus once more read Isobel's words.

My beloved,

Even though my father has said I must soon see the men who wish to court me, he has made no mention of a pending date. I think he is softening his views to allow us to wed. Though you know the way he is. He will not say so in so many words, but he has mentioned about his nephew, John, a number of times. I believe if he allows the two of us to wed and me to leave here, my cousin will fill my place should my father no longer wish to manage the estate. 'Tis good news, aye? With all my heart and forever yours, Isobel

Finbar stalked into the great hall, his dark blond hair disheveled, his blue eyes shifting to the missive in Marcus's hands. His cousin knew the only missives he ever received were sent by messenger from Isobel.

"The first of our clansman wishes to lodge a complaint about one of the sheep herders allowing his sheep to graze near his cottage. And the others are all waiting to see you."

"Aye, call them in."

Finbar did so, and his people lined up one by one to hear how he would resolve their difficulties with their neighbors or family members.

He had only listened to two complaints when he heard footfalls in a rush headed for the great hall. Thinking it was another clansman with a gripe, who worried he'd missed the time that Marcus had set aside for dealing with the issues, he listened to the next one.

When Marcus saw a red-faced Rob hurrying to see him, and a quick comment to those waiting in line that they must vacate the great hall at once, Marcus raised his brows at him.

It was not Rob's place to send his people away. At once, Marcus knew the matter had to be of grave importance for him to do so. Still, his people did not vacate the room, moving somewhat toward the doorway, but still waiting to hear if Marcus wished them gone.

Marcus motioned to them to leave. "Go. I will see to your complaints as soon as I can."

"Not today, but several days from now," Rob said.

Marcus lifted his head a bit. This did not sound good. "We will let you know when I can meet with you again."

"Aye, laird," several said and made their way slowly out of the great hall.

He was certain they wished to learn what the trouble was as much as Marcus did.

"What is the difficulty, Rob?"

"Lord Pembroke's daughter could be in grave danger, Marcus," Rob warned, his blue eyes flashing with indignation as he paced about the great hall, his hair unkempt as if he'd been outside in the cold wind recently. He hadn't been on the hunt earlier, but instead in the village. "'Tis your duty to secure the lass and bring her here before anything untoward can happen to her. You promised her mother you would."

Marcus stared at his cousin in astonishment.

Rob continued as if he couldn't speak fast enough. "Lord Pembroke always had a kind word to say about our clan and his Lady Pembroke had been a good friend of your mother's. God rest their souls. We owe it to his daughter to keep her safe. She loves you and we know how you feel about her."

Her father would not allow Marcus to protect the lass. Rob knew that. Her da would protect her.

"Has someone taken her from her castle?"

"Nay, 'tis worse."

When he was riled, Rob often got his facts out of order and Marcus was attempting, without success, to understand what the truth of the matter really was without interrupting him and asking. Had Lady Isobel been betrothed to someone when she had vowed to wed

Marcus instead? 'Twas what Marcus suspected Rob was saying. If Marcus rushed him in his attempt to get at the truth, he knew Rob would make even more of a muddle of it.

Instead, he offered the facts in the situation his cousin knew very well. "Her da would no' agree to my taking her to wife. I have beseeched him incessantly. He will no' change his mind. He is the one who will keep her safe, no' me." Marcus gave a disgruntled exhale of breath and frowned even more at his cousin as he sat at the head table. "Wait, she hasna run away, has she?"

"Marcus," Rob said, barely getting the words out. "Word comes that his lordship is already dead."

Marcus stared at his cousin in disbelief, and then abruptly rose from his chair, the legs scraping the stone floor.

Before he could speak, Rob said, "Whoever has murdered him will blame the Highlanders for his death and whoever has done this dastardly deed will spirit Pembroke's daughter away before—"

"Where has Lord Pembroke died? When? Have you evidence that any of this is true?" His thoughts were swirling, stumbling over one another...Isobel, the earl, who had done such a thing?

If someone pretended to be her friend now in her time of grief...

Marcus cursed under his breath. "The lady could be in grave danger."

TERRY SPEAR

"Aye, that is what I have been trying to say. 'Tis rumor of the most reliable source. One of James MacNeill's brothers, Angus, was passing through our lands on some business and had news that his cousin, Niall, has wed a French countess and learned of Lord Pembroke's death. He knew you would be concerned for her safety. He had to return to Rondover Castle, but said if you need his and our cousins, the Chattan brothers' help, they would be at your disposal."

Marcus couldn't believe the news about Isobel's da. "Where did the killing take place?"

"Near the hillside village of Chirnside in one of the scattered hamlets. 'Tis what Angus related. For fear of King Henry's hearing of the news that someone from the area has murdered one of his devoted lords, the body has been taken further south. Hopefully, to hide the fact he died up there and not nearer his own castle or on English soil."

"And Lady Isobel?" Marcus clenched and unclenched his fists, fearing for her safety. If he did secure her and bring her to the Highlands to stay safely under his roof, would King Henry believe Marcus had her da murdered and then secreted her away?

God's wounds, Marcus had wanted the lass since she had bloodied Lord Fenton's nose when the baron had made some degrading comment about her Highland heritage.

"You still want her, I know it," Rob said, despite the fact Marcus was already stalking toward the keep's

84

entryway. "We are leaving right away then?"

Marcus cast a reproachful look over his shoulder, indicating that his cousin had to be daft not to realize it. When he saw the grin on Rob's face, Marcus shook his head and reached for the door to the inner bailey.

Before he could grasp the handle, the door swung wide and one of his clansmen, who had recently joined their ranks, stood before him dressed for the journey, his blond hair looking as wild as Rob's, his blue eyes narrowed, mouth pinched, grim as if he was going into battle. And ready for it.

Leith gave Marcus a nod in greeting. "We are going, aye?"

"With or without me, it appears," Marcus said, seeing several of his men throwing packs onto their horses' backs, already saddled as dark clouds gathered overhead.

The fury of the storm would soon break loose.

Lasses were scurrying out of the keep, bringing food for the expedition, prepared in a rush, their faces flushed and anxious. Brief kisses and hugs were exchanged with their men. No telling when the men would return to the keep. If ever.

Even Marcus's own horse was ready and his bags packed, and he gave a dark laugh. Sometimes, he thought his men knew him too well.

***

Isobel had been on edge for the last two months, worried her father would change his mind and decide she had to see the men who wished to court her again. But he hadn't discovered who was behind Marcus's attack and for now, her father was still having his men look into it. She had learned through a servant that Marcus had been regularly corresponding with her father, trying to convince him to allow her marriage to him. She prayed he'd be successful one of these times.

She'd also learned her father had read every one of the missives and kept them, which was good news. He was not tossing them in the fire, unopened. Even so, he was keeping her well-guarded after she had left the keep, escorted by Marcus's kin, to see him. She knew the captain of the guard had to have told her father, though he had not spoken to her of the incident. She wondered if the fact his kin had taken her to see Marcus, then returned her safe and sound had made a positive impression on her father.

A few of the servants had even hoped her father would relent after the unprovoked attack on Marcus and the way he had tried so valiantly to earn her hand in marriage in a civil way. But her father still hadn't budged on the issue. Her cousin, John, was visiting soon and she hoped then her father would declare that he wanted him to take his place upon his death while Isobel could marry Marcus.

As far as she knew, her father had not told John this, so she didn't know if it was something that was viable or just something she hoped with all her heart would happen. She suspected her father wanted to see how John managed the staff and the Scots at the border before deciding.

Before she retired to her bedchambers early that evening, Isobel sensed that something was dreadfully wrong as she slipped closer to the doorway of her father's solar. She slowed her pace as a maid hurried past her, eyes lowered, and then Isobel stopped before she reached the open doorway.

To her knowledge her father had once more journeyed to Scotland at the request of King Henry to help quell the Scottish rebellions along the border. Which, while King Henry ruled, were still uncertain with the Anglo-Norman influence pushing northward to Cumberland. Though William of Normandy invaded in 1093 and incorporated it into England, the region had been dominated by many wars and border skirmishes between England and Scotland since then. Because Henry had married King David of Scotland's daughter, relations were generally good, though the skirmishes did continue. Which was why King Henry had given Isobel's father permission to build his castle near the border to quell such rebellions.

While her father was away, his advisor, Lord Wynfield, was left in charge of the castle. Her father was the greatest diplomat and often was able to settle the trouble brewing at the border with naught but a word. Rarely, if ever, did he have to resort to the use of a weapon, he was that good at negotiations.

She had learned that the last time, when Marcus

had been injured by one of her own people, her father had finally convinced the Scots to quit fighting. But also that he had asked Marcus's help in stopping the skirmishes. Marcus had offered only to help at the price of taking Isobel as his bride. She loved him for it. And she wished her father had agreed.

But her father had won the peace without giving her over to the Highlander. She was not disappointed that the hostilities had ended. Only disappointed that her father still would not allow her to wed Marcus.

The staff normally greeted her cheerily when they passed her by, but now they examined the rushes on the floor as they avoided looking directly at her while they hurried about their business. That concerned her. Several knights guarding from the wall walk that evening were dressed in chain mail, while double the guards were posted. Isobel had noticed the high state of alert, but she was unable to ascertain the reason for such concern.

Isobel peeked into the room where several of her father's vassal lords and some of his knights were having a conference with Lord Wynfield, who was standing squarely in the center of the group. The short, stocky man's puffy cheeks, usually punctuated by dimples, were plain ruddy this stormy night as he snapped at one of the servants and scowled at the knights. She had only seen Wynfield in such an aggravated state on one other occasion when her mother had died unexpectedly from a raging fever while her father had been away on business in Scotland two years earlier.

Again, she was reminded why she did not wish to wed him.

Isobel attempted to discover what had upset the baron so as she leaned against the stone wall outside her father's solar.

Lord Wynfield cleared his throat. "King Henry will have to be made aware of this as soon as possible." From the dark tone of the baron's voice, whatever the news was, it was not good.

More rampant fighting, she feared and maybe her father needed reinforcements.

For an instant, all remained silent. Afterward, the men spoke all at once in such a confusing deluge that she could not understand their words. "One at a time, gentlemen," Lord Wynfield said.

Standing closest to the doorway, Sir Halloran said, "What of Lady Isobel?"

The mention of her name sent shivers cascading down her spine as she stood obscured by the wall leading to the doorway. One of the knights walked over to close the door and frowned to see her standing there. "Excuse me, my lady." Sir Edward closed the door.

She leaned against it to listen, but unable to discern any more of the men's conversation muffled by the massive oak, she headed down the corridor to her bedchamber, hating that she did not know any more about what was going on than before.

When she entered her room, Mary rushed to greet her. Her green eyes were narrowed and her red brows pinched in a frown. She appeared just as shook up about something as everyone else was. "Are you retiring to your bedchambers for the evening already, my lady?"

"Aye, Mary. Lord Wynfield's mood is too stormy for me. He has everyone upset to no end. Whatever is the matter, do you know?"

"I would not know, my lady."

Yet the way her maid refused to look her in the eye, Isobel knew differently. She also knew if the baron didn't want anyone to enlighten Isobel as to the matter, the staff would hold their tongues.

Already, rain was pelting the stone walls, the winds howling through the arrow-sized windows, and lightning streaked across the black sky, highlighting mountains of clouds. Thunder boomed in its wake, warning the storm had only just begun.

She didn't think the night and all its secrets would ever end.

She was mistaken.

CHAPTER 7

The stormy journey had taken Marcus and his five men five days to reach Torrent Castle near the village of Ancroft and learn Lady Isobel was no longer there.

Lord Wynfield stonily greeted him. "I warn you not to interfere with my decision to send Lady Isobel south to stay with someone safe."

"When did she leave?"

"Two weeks ago."

Marcus didn't believe it. Only ten days had passed between the time the word had reached him of her da's death and he and his men had traveled there. "Before her da was murdered?"

Lord Wynfield led him into the great hall to sup with him and Pembroke's staff. The baron didn't say anything in response. Afraid he'd be caught up in the lie?

Marcus had overheard servants talking and they

had said Isobel would be staying with King Henry and his wife, Matilda. Isobel would serve as a companion to Matilda in Westminster where the queen preferred to remain.

Marcus was not happy about that at all. Isobel would have too far to travel and anything could happen before she reached Westminster. Beyond that, King Henry had enjoyed a number of sexual partners resulting in numerous illegitimate children. Though he supported many of them, Marcus didn't want Isobel to be subjected to Henry's prowess if he found her as lovely as Marcus did.

At least, Lord Wynfield had Cook prepare a meal for Marcus and his men while stable hands took care of their mounts. In the meantime, Marcus tried to determine which route Lady Isobel had taken with her escort. He wondered though, why Lord Wynfield had even told him that much.

Although Pembroke's staff often looked at the Scots as savages with their noses stuck high in the air, and many kept their eyes averted as if they couldn't be bothered to even look disdainfully their way, this time the atmosphere was different. Darker. Gloomier. As if the raging storm outside had managed to slip inside the keep's walls. And yet, several nodded to Marcus with the slightest of greetings as if they were glad to see him, but didn't want to get caught showing their respect.

Marcus hurried to eat before they took their leave to determine if they could even catch up to Lady

Isobel's escort. If she had left a few days ago, they might not be able to. Especially if Marcus and his clansmen ran into trouble with the English.

"I will say again, Laird McEwan, I am doing what the earl would have wished." Lord Wynfield's face was flushed with annoyance. He was a well-fed man, from all appearances, and had probably not raised a sword in many a year. He was usually fairly agreeable, from what Marcus had observed of the man during his infrequent visits, except when it came to Marcus's interest in Isobel.

Marcus was certain Wynfield was a good man as far as Norman lords went, but he was not at all happy with the idea that a Highlander entertained notions of marrying the lass. Especially when the seneschal contemplated wedding the lady himself.

"Do you ken who murdered Lord Pembroke?" Marcus queried, lifting a chunk of bread, white, unlike the way his brethren prepared the much heartier brown bread, before he took a bite.

"*You* had motive. *You* wanted to claim the earl's daughter as your wife."

Marcus glowered at the baron, surprised to hear the man say such. "I had naught but respect for Lord Pembroke. I deeply admire his daughter…"

Revealing his own belief that Marcus much more than admired the lass, Rob snorted.

Marcus cast him an annoyed look, then focused his wrath again on the baron. "You ken I didna have anything to do with it, aye?" He didn't want *anyone* to believe he had murdered the earl.

Wynfield took a deep breath and shook his head. "You had motive. But unless you paid the murderers, I do not believe you were behind the killing. A Norman lord of some consequence, from the description of his dress, his saddle, and his weaponry, murdered him. But the witness did not recognize the men."

"Men?"

"Aye. Four. All of them wore garments fashioned from the finest wool. The shepherd believed the men knew Lord Pembroke, and he recognized them, or he would have shouted a warning. Had they looked like common thugs and thieves, he would have avoided them. As it was, they called to him, and he went willingly to greet them. "

"Lord Pembroke was alone at the time?" Marcus asked in disbelief.

"The two knights with him were also murdered."

Marcus absorbed that, then said, "They were dressed in their lordly Norman clothes so Lord Pembroke would believe he had nothing to fear from them. Did he know them?"

"That we do not know for certain."

"The shepherd did not hear an exchange of names?"

"Nay," Lord Wynfield said.

"Why did you not send for me so I could protect Lady Isobel?"

"You are a Highlander!" the baron said, slamming his fist on the table, his face red with fury.

Marcus glanced up to see two of the earl's knights watching them at the entrance to the great hall. He said to the baron in a low voice, "Aye, and 'twas no' a Highlander who murdered Lord Pembroke, but a Norman."

"You cannot go after her."

Marcus would not listen to the baron, who could very well have sent the lady into danger. "Where is her escort headed?" He knew the destination, but not the route they would take.

Lord Wynfield stiffened his back and narrowed his eyes. "Listen to me. She will marry an English lord. Not a Highlander. I have done what I felt was my duty to the earl and to the lady herself."

"Have you considered that the same lord who murdered her da might very well attempt to marry her? Mayhap Lord Pembroke wouldna allow him to marry her already. Mayhap the *gentleman* will force himself on the lady so she has no other choice. What if after he has her title, he has no other use for her? Have you considered this?"

Wynfield's face drained of color.

"Where. Is. The. Lady?" Marcus asked, gritting out the words.

"She is gone and will soon be safe in another's care. If you wish to rest here the eve and continue on your journey home, I will make the arrangements."

If she had left so long ago, she would have already reached her destination. Marcus knew the baron had been lying.

With barely controlled animosity, Marcus said, "For your generosity, my lord, I must thank you for the food, but we must be on our way."

He glimpsed Isobel's maid, Mary, who was stretching her neck, trying to see around the two knights standing in the entryway. The maid had served Isobel's mother as her companion from her Highland clan, and when Isobel had been born, she'd devoted herself to the lass. He was surprised she had not gone with Lady Isobel since she'd often accompanied her when he had visited the castle in the past. That doubly concerned him.

Marcus frowned at Lord Wynfield. "Mayhap we should stay here the night."

Rob interjected, "He doesna like that we are Highland—"

Marcus motioned for his silence, his gaze still locked onto the baron's as if they were fighting in a battle. The man sat like stone, his expression giving naught away now. What was going on? Was the lady still here within the castle walls? Marcus would learn the truth if he stayed here. Trying to get back into the castle without permission if he learned afterwards that the lass was here, he would find nigh to impossible.

On the other hand, if Isobel had already left, he didn't want to lose any more precious time in tracking her down.

Mary motioned around the knights for Marcus to come with her. Sir Travon glanced back at her, and she quickly dropped her hand to her side. She smiled brightly at the knight.

Marcus said to the baron, "Should we stay?" He glanced at Mary to see if she would warn him one way or another as to what he should do.

Sir Travon was again watching Marcus, and Mary quickly shook her head, saying no.

"We will go." Marcus immediately rose from his bench, his men following suit. "Again, I thank you for your hospitality."

Lord Wynfield gave him a stiff nod, and then allowed them to leave on their own.

"What was that all about?" Rob said in a hushed voice to Marcus as they headed for the entrance to the great hall, but Mary was no longer standing there. The two knights moved out of their way, their expressions full of distrust.

"I will speak to you of the matter when we are on our way," Marcus said to his cousin in a low voice meant only for his ears.

When Marcus and his men reached the noisy bailey and the stables, he saw Mary rushing to meet with them, a couple of sacks in her arms. "I have brought some provisions for you, my laird."

"Thank you, Mary. Why did you no' go with Lady Isobel?" Marcus asked, unable to keep from frowning as he waited to hear her response.

"They are taking her to see King Henry," she said in a whisper, her eyes filled with tears. "He will find her a husband. If he doesna take her as a mistress first. Her mother wished her to wed you. Her da would hear naught of it, but I dinna believe he would have sent his daughter to live with the king. He wished to know who she wed even if he couldna agree to allow the two of you to marry. I beg of you, find the wee lass and hide her somewhere safe. I fear the same man who killed her da wishes the earldom and the lady as his bride. He cares naught for her, mostly, I believe because of her fondness for you and her Highland heritage, but for the position and the monies her lands receive. If he doesna meet up with her on the road, I fear he will seek an audience with King Henry and attempt to convince him he desires the lass for his wife. The king is always looking for money to aid him in battling his brother. If the lord has enough money, he could easily buy her, thereby gaining her da's title, the castle, and the revenues from the lands."

Feeling as Mary did, Marcus nodded. "Do you ken which lord he is?"

"Nay," Mary said, as Rob took the sacks of food from her and added them to his own bags. "As soon as word reached me that you were here, I had Cook prepare food for you, and then I tried to get your attention. Most feel as you do. That she is in grave danger and they wish you well. The men who escorted her left this verra morning only shortly before you arrived. Lord Wynfield couldn't decide until today if he should send her away or no'. It shouldna take you very long to catch them. Hide her, my laird. If you can see a place in your household for me when she is settled, fetch me. Please."

"Aye," Marcus said, thanking her loudly for the food as if that was the reason for their brief visit.

"She belongs with you," Mary said again.

"Aye, she does. I will fetch *you* when the time is right." He would take the Highland woman to his keep no matter what happened in Lady Isobel's case, though he didn't wish to think anything other than that he would find her safe and then he'd hie her away to his home and hers.

With great relief, Mary nodded. He wished he could take her with them now. But it would only make the situation more suspect, and he was certain she'd slow them down.

"God speed," she said softly. "Take the road through the forest to the west, and then where it branches off south."

"Aye." Then they were on their way, but not before he noticed Lord Wynfield had been monitoring their actions the whole time Mary had been speaking to them. Would he send men to ensure the Highlanders went home? If Marcus and his men took the road that Isobel and her escort traveled, would the baron's men try to stop them?

CHAPTER 8

Isobel knew something was terribly wrong as she and her escort headed south, the wind whipping at her cloak, the frigid air chilling her, though her escort would not tell her what the matter was. Only that she must serve as a companion to the queen, and she feared King Henry might decide a husband for her. Or worse, he might take a liking to her and attempt to seduce her like he had so many other women. If Isobel could, she hoped to slip away and seek Marcus out. If no one ever learned she had joined him...yet, the way would be so dangerous for a lady traveling alone.

Lord Wynfield would not even allow her to take Mary with her, citing that the woman would not fare well on the journey. If it had not been for that, Isobel would have forced Lord Wynfield to relent and allow her maid to accompany her after seeing Mary's eyes filled with tears as she tried so bravely to see Isobel off without shedding them. Just as Isobel had fought her own at having to leave Mary behind.

Isobel suspected her father had decided she should wed an English lord and was sending her somewhere else far away so she would never see Marcus again. And that ensuring Mary stayed behind would be in the Highland woman's best interest. No one would treat her ill in her father's household, but they might in someone else's. Mary could very well be ridiculed for her Highland roots. So with a heavy heart, Isobel had left Mary behind, a woman who had been like a mother to her.

Why this morn, of all times with a storm threatening overhead and the weather so bitterly cold would Lord Wynfield have insisted Isobel leave at once.? Why had he not waited until her father had arrived to see her off, if this was what her father had wished?

He had been gone for ten days, which was not all that unusual, but she kept expecting him to return home at any time. And he had not.

Lord Wynfield's mood had not improved by morn, and he was not one to question when in such a state. Although she did anyway. Which had only earned her more harsh words from him. She suspected it was because he wished to wed her and if she was in the king's court, Wynfield would lose the chance.

Which made her think about Laird Marcus McEwan again and finding a way to safely slip away.

She knew her father had only allowed her mother to invite Marcus to their holdings because of how close her mother had been to his, and seeing him had helped her mother overcome some of her longing for her Highland home. Her father had respected and admired Marcus's father and his clan as he had never had any trouble with them, so there was no difficulty there. And it was her mother's dying wish—so Isobel had been thankful her father had honored it. But her father was a Norman, through and through, and if he hadn't fallen in love with her mother on one of his journeys to quell the differences between the Scots and the English and met her mother then when she was traveling close to the border, he would have married an English lady.

Isobel and her escort rode at a trot, the wind whipping around them, chilling her through to the bone. It would take them an interminable amount of time to reach Westminster. If she'd had a choice, she would have enough sense to stay out of weather like this. The rain again threatened to spill from the darkening clouds. Creeks that had once trickled through the forest now overflowed their banks.

She shivered incessantly, trying to gather what warmth she could from her horse, drawing her cloak tighter as the three knights, three guards, and one maid rode single-file along the narrow trail.

Although it was dawn, the darkling day made it appear as though the sun had sunk below the horizon again. The men escorting her did not speak a word and their silence unnerved her even more.

The maid, a waspish young woman that hated all things Scottish and who had not held her tongue about such whenever Isobel had been within hearing, was the only one who made a sound. She grumbled and grouched and made the journey even more disagreeable.

"Halt your caterwauling," Sir Edward, riding behind the maid, said.

Then, except for the howling of the wind through the trees and the clopping of horses' hooves on the leaf-littered trail, no other sound intruded.

Until Isobel heard an arrow slicing through the air and a knight's grunt before he fell from his horse. Then the sound of chaos reigned.

Her heart in her throat, she glanced around to see if she could aid the knight and was about to dismount when Sir Edward shouted, "*Go*, my lady!"

She feared he would not have said so if he didn't believe they were doomed to fail at protecting her.

Heart racing, Isobel felt a surge of panic. Where was she to run to? She did not know which direction...wait, no, she did. The arrows were coming from the east. Her first instinct was to head off the trail to the west through the woods. But she thought to race back toward the safety of her castle in a northerly direction also. Riding along the trail, she would be an easier target though. And she suspected her attackers would assume she'd go that way first.

She fled west away from the only home she'd ever known, her blood chilled, as the rain decided at that moment to add to the chaos and fell in drenching sheets.

She couldn't allow herself to think of the fate of the men or of the sour-tongued maid as Isobel hurried to make her escape. All she could think of was to hide herself and return to help anyone she could later when the danger was past. If the danger passed.

The sound of swords clashing caught her attention as she continued to ride through the tangled forest. She prayed her men would kill every last one of the brigands and that her own men suffered no losses. When she came to a river rushing south, blocking her path, she headed north, knowing she could never ford the rising waters. She assumed no one in their right mind would be out in this weather, except for those in her escort and the men who had ambushed them, and she would be safe enough on her own, if she did not freeze to death first.

She didn't stop pushing her horse, fearing her own men hadn't survived the skirmish when no one followed after her. If she reached a village soon, she could send word to Lord Wynfield about the plight of her escort and herself.

The rain was still coming down so hard, she didn't see a man's approach from the east until it was too late.

"Looky what we have here," he said in a deep, gruff voice. He rode up beside her and jerked the reins from her frozen, mitten-covered hands.

Her heart gave a start, and she realized then how ill-equipped she was to handle anyone out here. Although she did have her *sgian dubh*, and she would use it if she had to. She didn't recognize the man, though she was certain he was a common enough thief, his brown hair and beard shaggy, his blue eyes glacial, and his clothes patched and filthy.

"What are ye doing out here all alone?" His eyes roamed over her as if he was sizing her up for the price she might bring.

Still, she nearly sighed with relief. He wasn't one of the men who had attacked her escort or he would have known who she was and what she was doing out here all alone. That didn't make him any less dangerous though.

Water streamed down his face because he had no brat to form a hood like she had. Bulky and haggard, he looked like a ruffian, not a trained knight or mercenary or whatever the men were who had attacked hers.

"My escort is back there," she said, her voice hushed in case any of the men who had set upon her escort were following her as she motioned in the general direction. "They were attacked and our assailants are searching for me now."

At least she assumed they would be, unless her escort had killed them and were now searching for her.

The man looked back over his shoulder. "Would they pay a ransom for ye?"

"They are armed knights and would no doubt prefer killing you," she said quite seriously, with no hint of amusement in her tone of voice.

He seemed to think about that for a moment

She again considered her dagger. "I must go. They could catch up to me at any moment."

He frowned at her. "Would *your* people pay a ransom for ye?"

Her mouth parted as she stared at him in disbelief, then finally found her voice. "Not to a dead man. Were you not listening to me? These men killed my escort." Though she prayed it wasn't so. "They are knights! Think you they would let you live if you knew about their traitorous deeds?"

For a moment, he seemed to consider her sincerity. Then he nodded. "For now, go free." He let go of her reins and then as suddenly as he had appeared, he melted back into the pouring rain and disappeared into the woods. That's when she heard horses coming, and she cursed silently to herself for allowing the man to hold her up for so long.

Her blood pounding with fear that those following her would catch up, she rode as fast as she could through the tangled woods, praying her horse would not stumble and injure himself, until she found a clearing and saw a farmer's cottage. At once, she realized she could not stop there or the men following her would most likely kill the farmer and his family, too.

That's when she thought she heard a Highlander's

brogue as a man shouted, "Isobel, stop!"

Marcus? It couldn't be.

She jerked her horse to a stop and turned, not believing it could be who she thought it was.

But it was. Laird Marcus McEwan, his cousins Rob, Finbar, and two more of his kin headed straight for her.

"Marcus," she whispered, not believing her eyes. "Oh, Marcus." She wept with joy as she galloped toward him as he rushed to join her.

His grim expression told her they were still in grave danger.

***

Marcus wanted nothing more than to pull the bedraggled Isobel from her horse and hold her close, to assure himself she truly was all right and to assure her he was here for her now. But he had to be prepared to fight. He just had to get her somewhere out of this weather before she caught her death. And he couldn't believe his fortune that not only had they met up with her doomed escort, only able to save one of her knights and kill their attackers, but that they had managed to find her before anyone else did.

"The men," she said, her words a whisper and over the pounding rain, he could barely hear her sweet voice.

She was as he last remembered her, except wetter and exhaustion was evident in the dark circles beneath her eyes.

"The brigands who attacked your escort are dead."

He didn't want to tell her what had become of her own men. "One of my men carried one of your wounded knights back to Pembroke Castle."

"The others?" she asked, so fretful, he hated telling her the truth.

He shook his head.

"The maid?" she whispered as if it hurt to ask.

"Drowned in the river when she tried to cross it."

Isobel let out a pitiful gasp, her face so pale he thought she might faint. He drew closer and grabbed her hand. Despite wearing mittens, her hand was cold and wet "We must get you out of this frigid wind and rain." He feared she would be ill before long. "I would have you ride with me, but it would slow us down. I am afraid others may learn you were no' taken hostage as planned and come for you. I will have to be free to fight. Can you ride alone, my lady?"

If she couldn't, he would take her in his arms and gladly. But he still felt they would be better off if she could ride her own horse for longer.

"Aye." Her voice was determined, but she looked as though she would not make it.

"It willna be long." But he knew it would. Even traversing a short distance would make it seem as though they rode forever in this kind of weather.

"The cottage," she said.

"Nay."

She nodded and they traveled side by side in the open meadow, two of his men following behind, Rob ahead of them, Finbar and Alroy flanking them. They stayed close as it was so difficult to see in the pounding rain, they could easily lose sight of each other.

Marcus was grateful they had found Isobel unharmed, but they were far from being safe from danger. He wanted Isobel to talk to him, to ensure she didn't drift away into a silent, cold death. But he didn't want to talk to her about her da's demise, or anything else that might upset her.

"We will return for Mary and take her to my home the first chance we get," he finally said.

"Mary."

"Aye. She wishes it. She said Lord Wynfield would not allow you to take her with you."

"Aye." Isobel's voice shook with cold. "Why...why would she want to leave?"

"Because you had left." He glanced again at her. She was staring at her horse, her head bent in the driving rain, trying to keep it out of her face, her hood hiding her expression.

"You will be my wife." He'd decided the moment he'd learned Lord Pembroke was dead. Nothing would stop him now. Though King Henry could be a problem if some of her suitors brought the issue to him.

She jerked her head around and stared at Marcus, her blue eyes wide and lips parted.

"If 'tis what you desire." He tried to smile, but he was so cold himself, he felt his frozen face would crack with the effort. He wished to give her a choice, but if she was not certain about him, he would ensure she changed her way of thinking.

"But…but my father…he will not permit it."

With incredulity, he stared at her. Lord Wynfield had not told her about her da's death? God's wounds, man. Now Marcus was left with the task?

Marcus had been certain the baron would have warned her about it, and the danger she might face on her journey to see the king.

Och, Marcus could not be the bearer of bad news when she could be near death herself. He would wait until they were safe and dry and warm again. He wanted to wait until they were home in the Highlands, but he felt she should know of her da's death before that.

Would it ease her suffering if he told her the whole truth? That her da was not who she thought he was? He wasn't sure that was something he should speak of now. Mayhap never. She believed she was the daughter of a Norman earl when she was truly the bastard daughter of a Highland laird. He wanted her to know she was all Highlander, no part of her heritage being of Norman descent. On the other hand, the knowledge she was a bastard and not an earl's daughter, raised by a man not her da, and shunned by the one who was—might not be the most welcome of tidings for the lass at this point.

She didn't say anything more, and he lapsed back into silence.

After they had traveled for some miles, Isobel

warily asked, "Why are we not headed for Pembroke Castle?"

He thought she realized he was not taking her home. Not when Lord Wynfield had the notion of sending her away. What if he did so again? Marcus knew she'd be in danger all over again. He would not permit it.

"Nay, too risky."

"I do not understand. Traveling beyond the castle walls is dangerous. Surely we would have been to my castle by now. And it would be safer there." She paused and stared at Marcus. "Who attacked us? And why? If your man takes my knight home, my father will be concerned as to why I have not been taken there as well."

"You were no longer at the site of the battle, my lady. My clansman left with no knowledge of what had become of you. While he took your knight to your castle to seek aid for him as quickly as he could, we had to chase you down. We will go to my hunting lodge, which is closer by a day's ride, and then to Lochaven after that."

"You did not answer my question. Why are you not taking me home? Marcus?" she asked, staring at him now. "What…why were you there? My father did not send word for you, did he?" Then her face paled. "My father has not returned home. What is wrong?"

"My lady…Isobel—"

"Riders," Rob warned.

They could barely see the men in the gray rain drenching the glen, but they could hear the horses' hooves, and Marcus feared the riders might have been with the men who had attacked Isobel's escort.

But then he could make out their clothes and realized they were Highlanders, some wearing furs, their tunics belted at the waist, some with beards, all with longer hair.

Seven men swarmed around them as Marcus and his men readied their swords.

"Who would be out in foul weather like this other than men thinking to steal our cattle…," the red bearded man, who appeared to be in charge said, shifting his stern gaze from Marcus to Isobel, "…*or* our women?"

"We are just passing through," Marcus returned in Gaelic. "The lady is my bride."

Isobel glanced at Marcus, her eyes wide, and he realized her mother must have taught her some Gaelic. Though he had not known it was so. Unless she really didn't understand what was being said and was only surprised to hear him speaking Gaelic.

"And who are you?" the man asked Marcus.

"The McEwan."

"Ah." He leered at Isobel. "Then where have you stolen the lady from? No one except for a clansman who wished a stolen bride would be out in this weather, bringing his woman home when so far from there."

If Marcus said she was Lord Pembroke's daughter he feared the word would reach English ears too quickly that he had her with him and where he was headed.

"I have not taken her against her da's will," Marcus said.

The man shook his head. "She appears to be with you of her own accord, but I still dinna believe you."

Which was not an ideal situation for Marcus and his men and Isobel to be in. "From which clan do you hail?" Marcus asked.

"Kerr."

God's knees. The Kerr clansmen were known to be cattle thieves. No wonder they thought the same of Marcus and his party. Though men did not haul a woman with them when stealing cattle. So he suspected something else was untoward.

"We have a hunting lodge this way. Come and we will get out of this weather." He smiled at Isobel. "She is quiet. Subservient? I like that in a woman."

"I am neither," Isobel said in Gaelic, her voice terse.

Marcus smiled a little at her, unable to curb the urge, and glad she did indeed know Gaelic.

The Kerr clansman laughed. "And spirited."

Marcus had no fight with the Kerr clan as they lived too far from where Marcus's lands were and so they did not bother *his* cattle, but he still didn't wish any of them knowing Isobel's background. They might not wish any trouble with the English if they should take offense that the Kerr took them in.

"Which clan are you from?" the Kerr asked Isobel.

She opened her mouth to speak, but Marcus said for her, "MacArthur."

Isobel closed her gaping mouth.

Her mother was of the Clan MacArthur. But her da was Laird Laren MacLauchlan, unbeknownst to her.

Laren had denied his daughter's existence when her mother was with child and Marcus didn't want the Kerr clansmen to learn MacLauchlan had a daughter now. What if now that the man who had raised her was dead, the MacLauchlan would want to claim his daughter and give her in marriage to one of *his* loyal men or to encourage clan ties with another clan? Bad blood would always exist between them after some of the MacLauchlan clan killed Marcus's da and his men as they were attempting to cross their lands to reach home. Marcus swore his mother died from a broken heart shortly thereafter—her will to live gone. If he hadn't been voted in to take over the clan when he was six and ten and needed to keep his anger at bay, he would have led his men into MacLauchlan territory and killed every last one of the brigands. But he didn't know who had actually murdered his da or the three men with him.

Marcus was sure Isobel's surprised expression had all to do with his mentioning her mother's Highland clan and ignoring that she was the daughter of the earl of Pembroke.

The Kerr had been watching the exchange, and Marcus was afraid he'd gather more from what was not said and draw his own conclusions. The man finally smiled. "Come."

They rode off in the pouring rain that never let up, not even when Marcus was helping Isobel down from her horse at the wooden two-story hunting lodge, nor when they hurried as fast as humanly possible inside.

A maid led her away, but Marcus couldn't help feeling unsettled when Isobel was out of his sight. But she had to get out of her wet garments and warm herself before a fire. Still, he feared she'd suddenly just be taken away and he'd lose her again.

She glanced back in his direction, her face anxious and she looked as though she had the very same concern. He would not lose her again, ever, he vowed.

CHAPTER 9

Chilled to the bone, Isobel followed a female servant to a room where the woman started a fire, and she gave her a plaid to cover herself while she dried her clothes by the hearth.

A small staff was preparing a meal for her escort while Isobel waited in the room, her wet clothes dripping on the stone hearth. She shivered while she pondered what was going on that Marcus had been reluctant to talk with her about.

The maid said, "I will bring up a meal when 'tis done."

"Thank you," Isobel said, and the lady quickly left the room, shutting the door behind her.

Isobel drew closer to the fire, tired, feeling anxious. She knew Marcus was also.

Only a short time had passed when someone knocked on the chamber door. Expecting a servant had brought up a meal, though she hadn't thought it would be ready this quickly, she called out, "Come."

Marcus quickly opened the door, and she let out a small gasp. He entered the room and shut the door, further shocking her.

"What…what are you doing here?"

He took in her appearance from her wet hair to her body wrapped only in the plaid, and her bare feet. "Isobel…" He moved across the floor, his gaze focused on hers.

This was so unlike him and she was afraid of what she'd learn now. "What has happened?" she whispered, knowing that something terrible had to have happened or Marcus wouldn't have come for her and rescued her, nor would Lord Wynfield have sent her away before her father had arrived home. Nor would Marcus approach her alone in a chamber when she was nearly naked.

Marcus drew close, rested his hands on her shoulders, and looked down at her. "I didna wish to be the one who gives you these ill-tidings. I thought Lord Wynfield had apprised you of the truth. Apparently he hadna."

"What truth? Tell me." She barely spoke the words, fearing what she would hear, that like her mother had died…

"Lord Pembroke is dead."

"Dead?" She stifled a cry, her eyes instantly filling with tears. She felt her knees buckle and Marcus instantly swept her off her feet and sat down on the edge of a bed, holding her in his lap.

Her heart breaking, she had sensed that more had been wrong the night Lord Wynfield had been so distraught, and believed he had known something awful had come to pass. Yet she couldn't believe it was really true. And that Lord Wynfield hadn't told her. She loved her father and she didn't want to believe it.

"Nay. He could not be."

"'Twas the word we received, lass."

"How...how did he die?" Her words were filled with anguish, forced out against her will. If he had died because his heart had given out, or some other such malady, though little comfort that would be...but if not...

"He was murdered. A witness said the men who killed him were dressed as Normans and wore clothes befitting nobility. Lord Pembroke..." Marcus rubbed her arm and held her tighter. "Isobel..."

Her body chilled to the core, she bit her lip to hold back the tears, trying to make sense of it, hating to hear the truth. The men who had attacked her own escort— Normans also? The same men who had killed her father? Then killed her escort? Was the same man in charge of the ones who had tried to murder Marcus?

She looked up at him, her eyes blurry with tears. "Where...where is he?"

"I dinna know for certain. Once I learned of this treachery, I had to ensure you would be safe."

"Lord Wynfield..."

"He thought it best to send you to stay with King Henry's court. That he would keep you safe. I feared you and your escort might be attacked by the same men who killed Lord Pembroke on your journey there. Had you found your way there without incident, I suspect whosoever this was would seek to have your hand, offering payment to King Henry for the honor."

Every thought tumbled over the next. She was so distraught, she couldn't grasp some of what Marcus was saying. "When...when you spoke of who my people were to the Kerr, why did you not mention my father is Lord Pembroke? Were you afraid he would warn Lord Wynfield I was not returning to Pembroke Castle?"

"He may have wondered how I had made you my wife, or if I had truly done so."

She brushed away tears trailing down her cheeks and frowned at him. "You should not have said I was your wife."

"Ah, lass." Marcus pulled her tight against his body.

"I cannot believe it. My father..." She choked back a sob.

"'Tis true. If I could have done anything to have prevented it, you know I would have. But now that we are here, how would I have explained your presence? Besides, I had already asked for your hand in marriage. Lord Pembroke wouldna accept. Now you are free to marry me."

"I have no say in it either?"

His dark brows deeply furrowing, Marcus said, "Dinna tell me you dinna want me now."

She couldn't answer him. He knew how much she loved him. She always had and always would. She wanted no other man for her husband. Even now, she knew it wasn't her choice. She frowned up at him. "I am an earl's daughter. What if King Henry willna allow me to wed you? What if 'tis the same as the trouble we had with my father?"

Marcus growled out his next words. "You are no more an earl's daughter than I am the king's son. Your da was Laird Laren MacLauchlan, but he wouldna recognized the bairn your mother was carrying as his own because he was married to another woman at the time."

Isobel's mouth gaped, and she slowly closed it. Feeling lightheaded, she couldn't believe any of it. "You are wrong! 'Tis not true!"

"I am sorry, lass," Marcus said, gentling his words, stroking her arm, holding her close. He kissed the top of her head. "I didna wish to be the one to have to tell you all of this. But if it means you are free to wed me, I wished for you to know."

Despite the upset to hear all the shocking news— her father was dead and he wasn't even her father—she knew in her heart Marcus would never lie to her. She realized then he hadn't cared one whit about her birthright. He had known all along and he had still wanted her. Though she feared King Henry would not allow her to do as she pleased, not with the earl's title and lands at stake. Would he even believe she wasn't Lord Pembroke's daughter?

"Have you proof?" she asked, her voice barely above a whisper, more tears trailing down her cheeks as she recalled the last time she had seen her father, looking worried at her at the table when they broke their fast that morn before he left on business.

Marcus narrowed his blue eyes as he stared at her. "You need proof?"

She shook her head. "Not for me. But without it, I am afraid King Henry will not believe us."

Marcus's gaze softened and he tightened his hold on her again, as if saying she was his no matter what. And she wished it with all her heart.

"Your mother confided in mine. Your true da also kens the truth. That is another situation I am concerned about. What if he learns of your da's death and Laren wants to use you as a way to tie his clan to another. He has no bairns of his own. But know this, lass," Marcus said, "you *are* mine."

CHAPTER 10

So shocked at all the news, Isobel couldn't believe Marcus's words. She knew in her heart he wouldn't lie to her about her father, and she suspected he wouldn't have even told her the truth if he hadn't believed she needed to hear it, but she was still having a hard time grasping any of it.

She bit her lip and turned her gaze from his worried one and stared into the fire. Her father, the only one she had ever known, was dead. And he hadn't even been her *real* father.

"Did he know?" she asked so quietly, she wondered if Marcus had even heard her. Had her mother pretended that Isobel was Lord Pembroke's own child?

"Aye, lass. He kenned your mother was with bairn, that she had no husband, and that she was hiding her…condition. But he had been smitten with her from the first and despite being a nobleman of Norman blood, he had loved her and wanted to marry her and call her bairn his own. My mother told me so."

Isobel wiped away tears she couldn't fight. He'd been a good father to her, his only fault in stubbornly refusing to allow her to choose Marcus as her husband. Mayhap because he didn't want to lose her, afraid she'd vanish into the Highlands, live their way of life, no longer an Englishwoman, when in truth she'd never had a drop of Norman or English blood.

"Who else knew? Did my blood father truly know? And Lord Pembroke's people?"

She had wondered why some had not treated her mother or her with the respect owed a countess and her daughter. She had suspected some of the animosity was due to her mother being a Highlander. Now Isobel wondered if everyone had known the truth. That not only was her mother not of English birth, but neither was her daughter. But mostly that she hadn't been the earl's daughter in the first place.

"I canna say." Marcus didn't remark again about her blood father, she noted.

"So if others knew that he was not my father, Mary had to have known then. Why did she not tell me?" She felt her skin chill when Marcus didn't answer right away.

She could never go back there, knowing what she now knew.

If an English or Norman nobleman wished to

marry her and then learned she was not even Lord Pembroke's daughter when he was led to believe she was—what would become of her then?

"Do you think those who attacked my escort thought to convey me to some lord who would marry me for my father's title and holdings?"

"Aye, lass, that I do."

Frowning, she said, "Then we shall let the world know that I am the daughter of Ciarda of the Clan MacArthur and Laren, the MacLauchlan. No Englishman would be interested in marrying me then. King Henry can give the title and properties to someone else—hopefully my cousin, John, though I know very little about him."

"I see only one problem with this notion of yours."

"What is that?"

"Laird MacLauchlan and I do not see eye to eye. What if he knows you exist? But he did naught because he thought he could get his wife with child, and he hasna been able to. What if he knew he could never claim you once Pembroke had, who also had King Henry's support? If Laren learns Lord Pembroke no longer lives, he may feel he is the one to decide who you should wed because he could use you for an alliance with another clan, especially if you are still unwed and now in the Highlands."

"He cannot," she adamantly said. "He gave that right up when he did not marry my mother. Nor did he recognize me as his daughter."

"He had a wife already," Marcus reminded her.

Isobel frowned, not understanding how her mother could have done such a thing. "Why would my mother—"

"She didna ken. He visited her clan and made her believe she was the only lass who mattered in the world to him. Then he was gone. Her da was furious, but he was only a minor chief. What could he do? He couldn't force the laird to marry his daughter when he was already wed. Then Lord Pembroke saw her and continued to return to see her. He truly loved her, my mother said. He was willing to wed her and say he was your da. That you were his bairn."

"They never had any other," Isobel said sadly.

"He adored you though."

"What do we do then, Marcus? You know I have pledged my heart to only you."

"You will marry me."

"If Laird MacLauchlan objects?" She wasn't about to pretend she cared, except that she didn't want Marcus and his clan to be in trouble for it.

"He objects. But he will have naught to say about it."

"We marry then." She had wanted this forever. Though she wished more than anything that her father was still alive. They would deal with whatever they had to later.

"Aye. We will handfast until we wed in the kirk at my castle."

Someone knocked on the door and Isobel leapt off Marcus's lap. "No one can see you in here with me like this."

Marcus rose from the bed and frowned down at her. "We are to be wed."

"But we are not *now* wed!"

"The Clan Kerr believe so. Or at least we have told them so."

"*You* have told them so."

"Because it had to be, for your protection." Marcus strode to the door as if she had not objected and opened it just a wee bit. "Rob, what is wrong?"

Fearing more trouble, she tensed.

"We need to leave. I overheard Kerr say something to a young man about taking word to MacLauchlan. Do you think he kens who the lady is?"

"Aye, it sounds to me that is so. As much as I hate to take Isobel out in this weather, I dinna wish to be caught here should MacLauchlan send his men to fetch and bring her to him. Kerr will tell him how many strong we are and MacLauchlan will send more than enough of his men to outnumber our own."

"I will see if someone has anything for the lady to wear so that she will be warmer when we travel again in this rain. It hasna let up in the least."

"Do so then."

"I will wear my own things. 'Tis mostly just my cloak that is wet," she said, not wishing to delay them. She did not want to end up being her real father's pawn next. She felt only animosity toward the laird for getting her mother with child when he was already married and denying that Isobel was his own flesh and blood.

Rob didn't make a move to leave and Marcus didn't shut the door. "Is there something else you wished to speak to me about?"

"Did she agree to marry you?" Rob sounded hopeful.

"Oh, aye, willingly." Isobel heard the smile in Marcus's voice before he added, "Go. Tell our men to be ready. We will tell Kerr on the way out. I dinna want to leave the lady alone while we prepare to leave."

"Aye." Rob hurried off.

Marcus closed the door and turned. "Will you be all right in this rain?"

She hmpfed and grabbed her chemise. "I am all Highlander. So aye, I am ready."

He smiled at her, his expression one of pride, but also he looked like he did not really believe she was that hardy. He nodded, then folded his arms while he watched her.

She raised her brows. "We are not married, yet. You will have to leave so I may dress."

He sighed. "I will turn around." He did indeed turn then and faced the door and continued to speak. "But we are as much as wed as you and I both have agreed to it. We dinna need witnesses, parents' consents, a kirk, or banns to be posted, my lady. We dinna even need to consummate the marriage for it to be legitimate. You and I both agreed. As we have always wished this. And that is all that is necessary."

"Oh." She wasn't sure if this pleased her or worried her more. She thought there would be more to it than that. Something that would legitimize the marriage so that no one would say later that they were not man and wife—like King Henry possibly. Her Norman suitors also.

As soon as she was dressed and her damp cloak covering her, she hurried for the door. "I am ready."

***

Marcus hated taking Isobel out in the cold rain again, disappointed that they could not stay at the Kerr hunting lodge at least until the morn. But he would not risk getting into a fight with MacLauchlan should he learn about Isobel's father's death and that Marcus was taking her to his home. MacLauchlan would be dastardly enough that he would try to take her from him. Until now, Marcus hadn't concerned himself with the notion, because he was certain if he could have gotten Lord Pembroke's approval to wed his daughter, Laren wouldn't have taken any steps to fight him for her.

But Marcus was glad Isobel had agreed to wed him, as he had always hoped it would be, and somehow he was determined that they would make it work.

She shivered in the damp clothes and he wrapped his arm around her shoulders and headed out into the corridor. "Hopefully, they willna try to detain us. I suspect they willna wish to fight us, but rather warn MacLauchlan that we have you and then let him deal with us. I also suspect Kerr wanted us to hear of what was happening and give us the chance to leave so that we would run into MacLauchlan's men on the road and not within his minor fortifications."

"So what do we do?" She snuggled up to him.

At that moment, he wanted her as a man wants a woman—as he'd always wanted her and now he could have her. If only they had the means.

"He will ken where we are going. We willna go that way." That was all he would whisper to her. Castles had ears and he didn't want to alert the laird as to their change in plans.

He hadn't made it far when Rob joined him and the laird's steward headed for them, his red brows furrowed deeply. "Ye are leaving, Laird McEwan? Ye are no' staying the eve? We thought ye would at least break your fast in the morn before ye left. Ye have not even eaten the meal with us that should be ready soon."

"'Tis trouble we will cause you if we stay," Marcus said shortly.

"But the lass," the man implored. "She shouldna be out in this weather." He hurried after them as Marcus didn't slow his stride with Isobel still tucked under his arm, trying to keep her dry as best he could.

Maybe Kerr *hadn't* intended for them to overhear that he was sending word to MacLauchlan that Isobel was here. And now Kerr would fear Laren's wrath once he learned the lass and her party had left.

Before even Kerr himself could see them off in the drenching, chilly rain, Marcus lifted Isobel onto her horse. Then he, the lady, and his men were off as the steward stood in the downpour before he hurried back to the keep.

"Will they attempt to follow us?" Rob asked.

"They are welcome to try," Marcus said.

At first, Marcus headed in the direction north toward his hunting lodge, though it was four days away. He knew his men would be watching to see if anyone was following them. It seemed Kerr's men would not try to stop Marcus and his men, but he presumed they would tell MacLauchlan where Marcus was headed.

"They will know we are going this way," Rob warned.

"Aye. That is why we are headed this way. At first. He is the one who worries for us all," Marcus told Isobel.

She gave him a wan smile, and he noted she was shivering even more. "Do you wish to ride with me?"

"Nay." Her voice was shaking with the cold, the rain not letting up. "I would tire your horse overmuch."

"It willna be long," he promised her. But if she looked too cold, he was making her ride with him.

When they headed west, Rob brightened. "'We will stay with our kinsman in the mountains."

"Aye," Marcus said. "It willna take us too verra

long." It was still half a day's ride. "But no one will ken we are distantly related to Ulicia and her brood. 'Tis the perfect place to stay."

"Will she remember us? She left so long ago, when she was but a wee lass herself, way before she had four bairns."

"Aye, she will remember us." At least Marcus hoped. And he hoped she had enough room in her shieling to house Isobel and the rest of the men while some of the horses stayed in the attached byre.

For five hours, they rode over grassy glens, rocky terrain, moving around a loch, spying mounded cairns used as a burial ground, and crossed several streams when they neared the narrow trail they would have to navigate to reach the valley on the other side.

Rob had been riding to the left of Marcus until the trail up the mountain became too narrow, and then he rode behind. Marcus had to allow either Isobel to take the lead or himself. He wasn't sure what to do. She didn't look steady in her saddle, but the horses would have a hard enough time making it up the mountain without having to carry two passengers. Still, he worried she might fall. He took a deep breath and dismounted.

"What are you going to do?" Rob asked, hesitating to dismount.

Isobel was so cold she didn't even seem to notice they had stopped.

"She is going to fall."

"Nay." Her voice was merely a whisper, the shake of her head so slight it was barely noticeable.

Marcus couldn't carry her all the way to the shieling, but he had no other choice. She was too cold and needed his body heat.

"We can take turns carrying her," Rob said, as if reading the doubt in Marcus's thoughts.

"Come, lass." Marcus held his arms up to her, and when she turned slightly and she leaned toward him, looking frozen to the core, he lifted her from her horse.

"Take our horses, will you, Rob?"

"Aye and when you need a respite, let me ken, and I will take the lady off your hands."

Even if it killed him, and Marcus knew it was madness, he didn't wish his men to hold the lovely lass close like he would.

For what seemed an eternity, he trudged up the narrow winding path as the horses faltered and the men walked them along the ridge. Then through the gray sheets of icy rain, he spied the shieling down below. After what seemed like forever, they finally reached the abode. But there was no smoke in the chimney, no smell of peat mixing with the rain, no children laughing or talking inside as he would expect.

He glanced back at Rob who gave him just as wary a look.

Isobel had actually fallen asleep in Marcus's arms. She might be light under normal circumstances, but with gowns sodden with water and the ground slick and muddy, he was having a devil of a time making any headway. His arms and back ached, but he was no longer cold. Isobel was still shivering, but not as badly now.

"Let me get past you and check out the shieling," Rob said.

Marcus nodded. "Aye, go." He leaned against a tree and waited while the rest of his men remained with him, wary and watchful.

Rob left the horses with one of the other men, then headed the rest of the way to the shieling, nestled against a cairn.

Rob had already pulled his sword out and crept toward the house, keeping to the rocks until he reached the door and listened. Then he turned to Marcus and shook his head.

He pushed the door slightly, his weapon readied. And was attacked by a young boy slicing the frigid, rain-soaked air with his sword, screaming like a banshee.

"Whoa, laddie, we are kin," Rob said, fending off the shrub-sized warrior. "He has a good swing, dinna you agree, Marcus?"

"Aye," Marcus said, smiling. "His da has taught him well."

The boy stopped attacking and looked in Marcus's direction.

"Is Ulicia here? I am her cousin, Laird Marcus McEwan," Marcus said. He was her distant cousin, but the lad didn't need to know that. He hoped his cousin had told her children of their relationship. "I must get the lady out of the rain. Will you permit us to enter?"

The boy's jaw dropped and he quickly made a clumsy bow. "Aye, my laird. Come in." He sounded so young, Marcus didn't remember a time when he was so small and would have defended his home single-handedly like that against an armed Highlander. The lad would someday make a fine warrior.

"I was worried about you, Rob," Marcus said as Rob gave him a small smile, then helped the others move the horses into the covered shelter next to the shieling.

When Marcus entered the one-room building with a soaking wet Isobel cradled in his arms, he hadn't expected to see three little faces peeking out at him from behind a bed. One of them, a girl about the age of the boy, was holding a *sgian dubh*.

"Where is Ulicia?" Marcus didn't like what he was seeing. The children all looked scrawny, but the place was neat and tidy.

"She went to the village and never came back," the boy said.

"How long ago?

"Seven days."

"Your name, lad?" Marcus set Isobel in a chair. He had to get her out of these wet clothes.

"Druce," he said, holding his head up proudly.

"Your da?"

"Dead."

"I am sorry." He helped Isobel out of the wet brat, and she looked up at him, her eyes tired, and she was still shaking too much. "Let us start a fire. The lady needs to be warmed. She is chilled to the bone."

"Our mother told us not to use the peat too much until she returned," the girl said.

"Your name, lassie?"

"Fiona."

"All right, Fiona. We need a nice warm fire. We have food and will share this with you. But I must warm the lady before she becomes ill."

"Aye," both the girl and her brother said.

His men soon walked into the shieling and noticed the urchins hiding behind the bed.

"Rob, start a fire, will you?" Marcus needed to get Isobel out of her wet clothes, but he didn't wish to do so in front of so many eyes.

"Aye, what about the lass?" Rob said, again as if he knew the dilemma Marcus was facing.

Finbar said, "We can take the wee lass and lads with us to help with the horses."

Marcus knew the men would have already taken care of them.

"We have food that we will need you to help us carry into the shieling," Finbar continued.

The youngest lads looked to their older sister, Fiona, for counsel.

"Go with them." She sounded like she was their

wee mother.

"You and Druce also," Finbar said.

"I will help." Rob soon got a flame going in the hearth.

All of them went to see to the horses and packs.

With the sound of the rain pouring down heavily on the thatched roof, all else was quiet. Except for Marcus's labored breathing as he hurried to strip Isobel of her gowns, then tucked her into the bed that had to be Ulicia's and her deceased husband's. The children had made straw mats on the floor with thin wool blankets to cover them.

He wasn't sure how his men would manage, but Marcus had to warm Isobel in any way that he could. Modesty aside. After all, they *were* married.

Before the others returned to the shieling, he heard his men telling all kinds of tales and was certain the children were already eating some of their foodstuffs while they waited for Marcus to let them know when it was all right to return to the shieling.

In some smaller keeps, the laird and his lady had naught but a curtain to separate them from the rest of their people, though he had a chamber of his own as did his lady when he took a woman to wife, and his men who were not married slept with the other men in the barracks.

Many did not have much in the way of privacy.

After removing his tunic, hosen, boots, and trewes, as they were wet, he climbed into bed with Isobel and wrapped his arms around her, felt the tremors racing through her body, and prayed she would not become ill.

"We are tucked in." Marcus wanted to warn his men that he was in bed with Isobel and not to make any comments about it.

His men ushered the children back into the shieling and made sure they each ate enough to fill their bellies, then herded them to their beds.

"I am afraid there doesna seem to be much in the way of sleeping space," Marcus said.

"We will manage." Rob looked concernedly at Isobel. "Is she with fever?"

"Nay, but she still trembles without end."

"She willna die, will she?" Druce asked, sounding alarmed.

"Nay, lad. When did your mother leave you alone?" Marcus asked.

"'Twas in the morn, seven days ago. She went for food, and she shoulda been back by now."

"We will talk about it in the morn. Sleep," Marcus said.

"Can he tell us a story?" Druce pointed his finger at Finbar.

The flames in the hearth offered a soft glow as the men laid out their bedrolls and wrapped themselves in their plaids, their swords close at hand.

"Only if it is a really short story," Marcus warned, "and isna scary."

He could envision all four children climbing into

bed with him and Isobel because Finbar had scared them with some horrible recanting of a day of battle. Sure, braw warriors loved to hear his tales, but they were not suitable for the tender ears of the wee lass and lads.

"I dinna ken any stories that dinna have wild beasties in them," Finbar said.

Marcus noticed then all the children turned their attention back to him. God's wounds, he didn't know any bedtime stories either!

"Tell what Lady Isobel did to the Norman lord that had you wanting to make her your wife even at a young age." Rob curled up in his plaid. "No beasties in that story."

The children looked hopeful, though he noticed the youngest lad's heavily lidded eyes, and Marcus figured if he said one word, he'd drop off to sleep just like that.

Marcus gave Rob a look of annoyance. He had never told anyone what had happened that day, although his clansmen had tried unsuccessfully for years to learn the truth. He wondered how Rob had even learned that much.

"Did you have to fight evil knaves to free her?" Druce waved a pretend sword in the air.

"Did you kiss her?" Fiona placed her hands on her heart.

"What *did* happen?" Finbar asked, his tone of voice amused.

CHAPTER 11

To Marcus's astonishment, Isobel snuggled closer, her eyes still closed as she said, "Do you wish *me* to tell what happened?"

She was still shaking from the cold, though he thought she'd fallen asleep. "Nay, lass. You might no' get the story right."

She opened her eyes and her mouth curved up. "Mayhap we will have to tell them both versions, aye?"

"There is only one version to tell."

His men chuckled.

Before Marcus could start the tale, Isobel said, "Laird McEwan came to see my mother because his mother and mine had been friends since the time they were wee lassies. So he would come and visit my mother to tell her all the news from home. The first time I met Marcus, I had just turned one and ten, and he was six and ten. I fell in love with him right at that moment. Not that he saw me in any way other than I was a young lass, too young for his attentions."

"No' true," Marcus said. "Even then I knew you belonged in the Highlands with us. You were no' shy or reserved, but welcomed me with your bright smile."

"You made my mother happy. I loved hearing you speak. You did not treat me like I was a bother. And then later when I met your cousins, they taught me how to use a bow and fight."

"Aye, lass."

"But about the incident with the Norman," Rob persisted.

"I was three and ten and my mother and father had invited some guests to celebrate."

"They were no' *your* friends." Marcus was still disgruntled to an extent by what had happened. He had loved her for her actions, but he had wished he had been the one to carry them out.

"Well, nay. They were suitors, I should say."

"Ah," Fiona said, sounding intrigued by the idea.

"Was there fighting?" Druce asked.

"Aye," Marcus said.

"Good," the lad said.

"Well, one of the Norman lords who was eight and ten like Laird McEwan did not like that a Highlander was in attendance. Marcus was charming and...daring. Daring because he made it a point to show them he much admired me when the others not as interested in making my acquaintance."

"Because you were only three and ten," Fiona

guessed.

"Aye. But when Marcus began to show how much he enjoyed my company, the Norman and English lords did not like it. They thought he should not have been there. They did not know my mother was from the Highlands." She paused, then added more softly, "Nor that my father was."

Hearing her words, Marcus kissed her cheek and pulled her tighter into his embrace. He worried that she had not had the time to grieve properly over her da's death, not when she'd been on the run from her own attackers, and then to learn that he was not even her da.

"So they wanted to fight our laird and he yanked out his sword and—," Druce said.

"Nay," Isobel said.

"There is a time for fighting, lad." Marcus stroked Isobel's soft hair, still slightly damp where her cloak had not covered it properly. "This was not one of them."

"But you said there was fighting in the story." Druce sounded petulant.

"No' all stories can have fighting," Fiona said dreamily.

"But the laird said—," Druce whined.

"Aye, there was fighting. Even bloodshed," Isobel said.

Marcus glanced down at the floor and saw the two youngest lads had fallen fast asleep.

"One of the lords started saying how the

Highlanders were heathens and barbarians," Isobel said. "But another mentioned my mother in the same hateful way."

"And so our laird drew out his sword and slayed the five and ten of them," Druce said.

"Nay," both Isobel and Marcus said together.

"Isobel stepped between us and without even speaking a word, hauled off and punched the Norman lord right in the nose."

"Oh," Fiona gasped.

"Blood ran down his face," Isobel said. "Tears, too, and he shrieked like a wee lass."

Marcus's men laughed.

Finbar said, "Now we ken the real reason why you wanted the lass for your wife."

"Among other reasons," Rob added.

"But why didna you use your sword?" Druce asked Marcus.

"I was a guest. I wanted to see Isobel again and continue to bring her mother news from home. I didna take what the Norman lord said to me to heart."

"Besides, he had a wee lass to defend his honor." Rob laughed. "I wish I could have seen it."

"I was proud of her." Marcus kissed her forehead. "But I would have preferred picking my own battles."

"What became of the Norman lord?" Finbar asked.

"Might he have been the one who sent someone to kill you when you visited last?" Rob asked.

Isobel's gaze shot up to Marcus's. "Lord Fenton?

You think it might have been him?"

"Or anyone of your other suitors," Marcus said. "I would not discount any of them."

"I asked my father daily if he had learned who would have done such a horrid deed. He said they had not discovered who had set the knaves upon you. Then again, my father did not make me court any of the noblemen, so I believe he had some reservations."

"'Tis no' important any longer." He wished Rob had not brought up the incident. Now that Isobel was his, it really wasn't important.

"'Tis no' important?" Rob sounded irritated. "His henchman could have killed you. As it was, one of the men sliced your back, and for a while we didna think you would live."

"I want to hear *this* story." Druce sat up on his straw mattress.

"'Tis no' a bedtime story," Marcus said. "Some other time, lad."

Isobel lapsed into silence and he enjoyed the feel of her, the way her body had warmed and she was no longer trembling, the way her soft hair tickled his chest, the way she smelled of roses and rain and woman. His loins tightened with need, and he wished the circumstances had been different. That he could have made love to her in Kerr's castle in a bed, not surrounded by bairns and his men.

He sighed, knowing he had the rest of his life to spend with her and a few more nights would not kill him. Well, nearly wouldn't kill him. If he kept far away from her, it would help.

He couldn't sleep though, trying to decide what to do about the bairns and their mother. He knew it could not be good if she had not returned in all this time.

When everyone appeared to be asleep, Isobel whispered to Marcus, "What are we going to do about the children?"

"I will send Rob and Leith to look for her in the nearest village. We will wait here for word."

"And if she is gone?"

"I will decide then, lass. No sense in worrying about what might not happen." He did enough of that by himself. He didn't wish to trouble the lass.

***

Laren McLaughlin studied the messenger, his brown hair, trewes, and tunic soaking wet from the storm, his body shivering, and finally Laren nodded. "Aye, get yourself warm by the fire, lad. A wench will bring something for you to eat and drink."

Laren's advisor, Tearloch, was leaning against the wall of the cold stone castle, looking dark and ominous, his straight black hair resting on his shoulders, several days' growth of beard covering his chin. He moved away from there and headed across the great hall to speak with him.

"Find her," Laren said. "If McEwan's got her, kill him. But make it look like the Sassenach took care of him."

"What of the ones who killed Lord Pembroke? They will be after her also, you ken."

"Aye. But the first lot o' them didna make it. McEwan took care of them. So if the Norman lord, whosoever he is, sends more men and you have trouble with any of them, do what McEwan did. Eliminate the threat. Whoever the Norman is who wishes Isobel for his bride will only get a sword in his gut."

Tearloch's black eyes glittered with menace. "Your wife willna be pleased if you bring the lass here. She has oft said if you acknowledge the girl, the lass better never be brought under her roof."

Laren snorted. "You think I am ruled by my wife's whim?"

"Your former mistress has never been found," Tearloch reminded him.

"She has been missing before and shows up when it suits her. I suspect she does thus, so I dinna grow tired of her."

But Laren knew what his clansmen were saying in whispered and not so whispered sentiments behind his back. His mistress would not be returning because his wife had made sure of it. He was sorely desirous of making his wife disappear also. She'd never had any children by him and because of it, he had no heir but Isobel now. Until Lord Pembroke died, Laren had no chance of bringing her home. But Laren's wife was the daughter of Laird Kerr, and he didn't want to have a fight with her clan either should she suddenly mysteriously…die.

Laren stood taller. "Isobel will marry the man I choose, and none other."

"McEwan was welcome at Pembroke Castle. 'Tis rumored Marcus has her heart."

"Mayhap. But he shall not have her for a wife. The lad said the McEwan rode with four men. Take three times as many of our own and ensure she is brought here at once. Leave none of their men alive. I dinna want the word to get back to his clan that we had anything to do with this."

"Aye, my laird." Tearloch smiled, then headed for the door.

Laren knew Tearloch believed he would have Isobel for his wife, but Laren didn't wish it. Tearloch was too old for her and too closely related to Laren and Isobel. Laren wanted a son by marriage who would give the clan male heirs. Davin Berwick had lived with Laren's clan for years, once his own da had tossed him out for fighting with Berwick's eldest son once too often. Davin could be a hot head. But he loved the lassies, and Laren was certain Isobel would fall for his charms. Most of all, Laren could easily manipulate Davin, and so he would be perfect for the role.

He'd set Davin up at his manor in the north so that Davin and Isobel would monitor the land and his people there. Isobel would be safe from his wife's wrath, should she feel any contempt toward Laren's only child. He only wished he had learned earlier of the Normans' traitorous deed to kill Lord Pembroke, then steal Isobel away. Then Laren's men would have rescued her, not Marcus's.

His long blond hair sweeping his shoulders, Davin stalked into the hall and raised his brows and lips in a knowing grin. "You are having Isobel brought here? Can I no' go also? Tearloch believes Isobel will be his."

"Nay, you stay here out of trouble. If no one sees you, no one will believe you had anything to do with this."

"Isobel will ken when she learns Tearloch is with your clan."

"Aye, but 'twill be too late, and she willna have any say in the matter. Just as she had no say about Lord Pembroke wishing to marry her to one of his Norman or English friends."

"What if Tearloch attempts to charm the lass?" Davin acted as though he didn't like being left behind.

"He isna as charming as you are when you are with the lasses. You ken that."

"What of your wife?"

Did everyone believe Laren had no control over her? "My wife will—"

"Your wife will what?" Erskina stalked into the great hall, her red brows raised heavenward, then her green eyes narrowed. She fisted her hands on her hips.

"We were discussing my daughter's return to her home. And who she would wed," Laren said gruffly.

"Your daughter?" Erskina fairly shrieked. "You

have no daughter, nor son either."

She knew the truth of the matter—that Isobel was his—even if Erskina chose to deny it.

"When Isobel arrives—"

"You have *no* daughter," Erskina repeated, as if saying so would make the truth of the matter go away. "If she says she is, she *lies*."

"I am certain she doesna ken she is my daughter." Laren bit back words that he wished to speak, but not in front of Davin.

At his words, both Erskina's and Davin's jaws dropped.

"You havena told her?" Now Davin sounded worried. "What if she doesna believe you are her da and instead believes you have taken her hostage?"

"You have no proof you are her da." Erskina sounded as though she was grasping at any notion that might make the truth invalid.

Laren needed no proof. He had taken the lass's mother, who had never been with a man, and when she was breeding, she had told him tearfully that she was with child. His spies had confirmed she had been with no other man. He knew the trouble was with his wife's failure to have his bairn, not his own.

Ignoring her comment, Laren said, "Davin will take her as his wife."

"He canna. *If* she was your daughter, she should wed someone of consequence. No' just some second son of a clan chief who cast him out and you took him

148

in to feed and pamper him." Erskina motioned to Davin with contempt.

The chilly glower the man gave her could kill, Laren thought. If Laren died before Erskina, and his clan chose Davin to be their chief, he was certain Davin would send the woman out into the cold to fend for herself, despite that she was a clan chief's daughter. She wouldn't last a fortnight, not with as many clansmen as she'd angered.

Laren should, in truth, marry Isobel to Davin's older brother, since he would most likely be clan chief someday. But Laren wanted his daughter's child, if it was a male, to be the chief of *his* clan, someday. He had wondered if he had gotten rid of Erskina early on and had wed Isobel's mother, if she would have provided him with more children.

He also knew Erskina didn't want his daughter here as a reminder of Erskina's inability to have his bairn, and that he'd had an assignation with another clan chief's daughter.

Erskina folded her arms. "But, of course, that would be only in the event you *had* a daughter. Which you dinna. If you had, you would never have allowed a Sassenach to raise her as his own."

If he had known his wife would never produce a bairn, he would have taken Isobel from her mother and raised her as his own. A disgruntled servant working for the MacArthurs had come to him with news of Ciarda breeding—though she had already told him so—and

TERRY SPEAR

Lord Pembroke taking her to wife. Then they were gone, and Laren thought the child would never live anyway. When he learned the bairn was a girl, he decided it didn't matter. Not when he intended to get Erskina with child. When that never happened, he began to think of Isobel, resenting that a Norman had raised Laren's only bairn as his own.

He stroked his chin. The girl would have to learn their ways. He imagined she thought herself to be a haughty English lady. Would she spurn their Highland ways? He was certain he and Davin would have no trouble teaching her how to behave within the clan.

***

In the dark, Isobel woke feeling deliciously warm as she cuddled against her Highlander. The fire had died down and everyone in the shieling appeared to be sleeping. She felt right being with Marcus like this, despite having never lain naked with a man. He was hers, as she always knew he would be. Though she was still upset about everything that she'd learned in the last day—her father, the man she'd always thought was her own flesh and blood, was dead. And a man she never wanted to meet had seduced her mother when he already had a wife. She'd never forgive him. Pembroke had called her his own, and taken her mother in and loved her, loved them both. Isobel would always remember him as her beloved father.

A tear slid down her cheek, followed by another, both dropping onto Marcus's chest. Afraid she might wake him, she remained frozen in place. He stroked her hair and wound his arm around her. So he was awake. For how long had he held her like this, felt her bare skin against his, her body pressed against him as if they were wed? She still couldn't get used to the notion that in the Highlands, they were.

He didn't speak to her, just continued to caress her, holding her against him, tenderly, and she assumed he didn't want to talk and wake the others, remaining silent, soothing her with his touch. Which stirred her desire for him even more. She cherished this moment with him in the dark, holding him close like man and wife, wishing though, that they were alone so that he could love her like she had always dreamed it would be.

She slid her hand over his chest, warm and muscled, but he tensed and she feared she had done something wrong, when he whispered, "Lass," his voice rough.

He leaned down to kiss her in the dark, their mouths sealing the promise that they had committed themselves to one another. Then he moved so that his mouth was against her ear and whispered, "You are stirring a need that I canna quench for now."

"The byre?" she offered.

He chuckled.

'Twas not a laughing matter. She thought if he made love to her, if anyone else thought to take her to wife, they would dismiss the notion.

"Too many horses in there," he explained and she

heard the smile in his voice as he whispered to her.

Someone stirred on one of the makeshift beds. She had no idea who, but that from the direction the sound came from, it was one of the men.

Then more stirring. She was sorry she and Marcus had disturbed them. Marcus whispered, "'Tis time to dress and break our fast. I will get your clothes for you."

She didn't want to let him go, loving the heat from his body and the sensuous feel of him touching her. But she knew they had to get on with the tasks at hand. Learn about the bairns' mother, and then decide what to do.

Finbar lit a fire and in the soft glow, with her still tucked under the wools and blanket, she turned to watch the bairns sleep as the men dressed.

Marcus put her clothes on the bed and said in a hushed voice, "We are going outside to get more provisions to break our fast, and then two of my men are heading to the village to learn what has become of the bairns' mother."

"Aye. What about the man who took the wounded knight home from the skirmish yesterday?"

"He will catch up to us when he can. He knows to return home if he doesna."

She'd fretted about him, that he'd be alone. "What will we do with the bairns?"

"Naught to worry about for now, lass." He fastened his cloak over his shoulders as the other men slipped out into the dark of the early morning hour.

She remembered Marcus always being that way. He wouldn't think on what might be, but what was and had to be done. She tended to agonize about things she had little control over. Which in her world, was much.

"Should I wake the children?" she asked.

"Nay, let them sleep for now. I will be but a moment." Marcus headed outside and she wondered if he was giving his men last minute instructions.

When he returned, she had already dressed, thankful her clothes had dried and it was not raining this morning. She started making the porridge.

Seeing her dressed, he invited the men back inside to eat while she stirred the oats over the fire. Though she didn't believe in warding off evil spirits, Mary had taught her that if she was to make porridge, she was always to stir with her right hand, toward herself from the right side of the cast iron pan and around.

She did it out of habit, rather than to ward off anything.

The bairns were still sleeping soundly. When she finished making the porridge, she served it into bowls and the men ate standing up as if they were in a hurry, though there were not enough chairs to accommodate all of them anyway.

Leith and Finbar thanked her for the food and they bowed their heads a little to Marcus, then headed outside.

They had started out with five men, six, if she

included the one she had not seen who had taken the knight back to her keep. Now they were down to three while Finbar and Leith were in the village. She began to worry again. She couldn't help herself. If Laren MacLauchlan was looking for her and her escort, would they find them sitting here? She didn't like that they weren't on the move, trying to reach a castle with fortifications and fighting men. Not just for herself, but she didn't want to see Marcus and his kin sorely outnumbered and vulnerable either. And what about the men loyal to her father? Or the ones who killed her escort? She tried not to fidget as she wanted to do something, but packing up the bairns and taking them from their home was not a solution either. Not unless something had happened to their mother.

Rob and Alroy, named for his red hair, moved outside and Marcus said, "They are going to guard in case anyone shows up unexpectedly."

"Will anyone, do you think?"

Marcus pulled her into his embrace and kissed her mouth soundly, his arms tight around her back, holding her body against his. She felt his staff, hard and eager pressing against her.

"Oh, Marcus," she said on a half moan, half sigh. On the one hand, she loved this intimacy between them and wished they could do more, on the other, she couldn't quit fretting about what they would learn, concerning the children's mother.

"Lass, dinna fash yourself so. All will be well."

She loved him for saying so, though she was not a child and knew better. She let out her breath. "I wish we could be doing something. Not just...sit here."

The bairns began to stir.

She smiled and rubbed Marcus's back, loving the feel of them close like she'd always dreamed it would be, no longer worried about propriety. Not when they had agreed to be husband and wife. "I spoke too soon."

He chuckled.

"I will get them something to eat," she said.

Fiona quickly rose from her pallet. "I beg pardon, my laird, my lady. I shouldna have slept so long."

"Nay, 'Tis fine. We will eat now."

Fiona looked around and seeing only Marcus and Isobel said, "Have the others gone to the village?"

"Two have. To see to your mother." Marcus gave Isobel one last hug, then kissed the top of her head. "I will be outside speaking to the men."

He left the shieling then, and Isobel dished out the porridge for the children as each of them rubbed the sleep from their eyes and began to dress for the day. The boys excused themselves and left the shieling.

When they returned, Fiona left.

"Where are the men?" Druce asked.

"Guarding."

"I dinna see them when I went outside to wash up."

"Aye, they did not wish you to. That is how they guard."

He glanced out the only window and frowned. "I

want to join them."

"Mayhap after you eat. But Marcus has to permit you to do so."

"I can be a good guard," Druce said.

"Aye, no doubt. But he is the laird, and you still have to do as he says. Like with all of the men, they have different assignments. Mayhap he would wish you to do something else."

The boy's eyes widened and he quickly nodded. He was a good lad. The little ones were quiet while Fiona helped to pour mead for them. Isobel thought Ulicia was blessed to have them and worried again as to what had become of her.

"Did his lairdship intend to steal you away from a kirk when you were marrying another?" Fiona asked, in between bites of her own porridge.

"Nay."

"What will we do if Marcus's cousins canna find our mother?" Fiona asked, tears springing into her eyes.

Isobel realized the girl had been very brave to take care of her brothers all on her own, most likely not giving up the hope that their mother would return.

"We shall not worry about what will be." Even though Isobel couldn't help feeling alarmed about their situation, she knew that repeating Marcus's words of wisdom were the only way to deal with this as far as the children were concerned. Then she wondered if the children had other relations in the area. "Was your father from here?"

"Aye," Fiona said. "But his mother and da have died and two of his brothers have gone somewhere else."

"Two? Has he any others?"

"One, and he is married, but he has four bairns of his own," Fiona warned, as if she feared Isobel wished to leave them with their uncle.

Orphaned children were often taken in by family members as a necessity and family was everything. Even her cousins, when their parents died, were taken in by another relation who had eight children. Two more mouths to feed were of no consequence. And they helped to farm the land.

She thought it would be safer than if the children followed them to where they were going with the problems they may face. They could even send for them later, if things were not acceptable here.

They had washed up and the lads had gone out to see if Marcus would allow them to guard, and as good-natured as he was, he kept them outside with him.

"Are you in a lot of trouble?" Fiona asked.

"I pray that everything will work out as it should."

The sound of horses clopping closer sent a shiver down Isobel's spine. She and Fiona strode to the window and looked out, hoping that it was Finbar and Leith with news about the bairns' mother. She saw men she had never seen before.

She quickly drew out her *sgian dubh*.

CHAPTER 12

"What are you doing here?" Not believing his eyes, Marcus hurried out of the woods to greet Angus MacNeill, Angus's cousin Niall, and Gunnolf, their Viking friend who had been raised by the MacNeills since he was two and ten. Angus was dark-haired and dark-eyed, more muscular than Niall, whose hair was curly, but he had the same coloration. Gunnolf was blond-haired and blue-eyed, muscular and tall. All three men were a welcome sight.

Angus hurried to dismount. "As soon as we had word that Lord Pembroke was dead, we knew you would be going to Lady Isobel's aid. We intended to locate you, assuming you might go this route. We met Finbar and Leith in the village. They found the bairns' mother. She has been too ill to return to her shieling, so delirious with fever that she didna ask about her bairns. The woman who was caring for her thought she had made other arrangements for them. Leith said they are fine. They will bring her home in a bit, but they bid us come see you and let you know we are here to help."

Marcus couldn't believe their good fortune. "Did he tell you the trouble we could have?"

Angus smiled a little. "Aye. I thought only we got into such predicaments."

Marcus shook his head.

The men dismounted and stalked toward the byre to take care of their mounts.

"What are you planning to do?" Niall asked, "with regard to the lass?"

"She is my wife."

The men all smiled and offered him heartfelt congratulations.

"The problem is that MacLauchlan should have received word by now that we are traveling with the lady," Marcus said, the men all well aware of the lass's parentage.

"You have our sword arms at your disposal," Angus said.

Gunnolf was watching something at a nearby stream, and Marcus turned to see what it was he was observing.

The lads.

"I have had word that you have wed Edana of the Clan Chattan and so that makes you my cousin by marriage, Angus." Marcus glanced at Niall. "You have gone and wed a French countess. What of you,

Gunnolf?"

He folded his arms and smiled. "'Tis a warrior's life I lead. You will see that Angus and Niall are fretting about leaving their wives behind. Me? I have naught to worry about except for getting them home safely. If I dinna, I would be in the most grievous trouble with the lasses."

Angus and Niall laughed. Angus said, "He wishes he had someone to go home to. Dinna listen to his tales."

Marcus smiled. "A Viking lass? A Highland lass? Which do you prefer, Gunnolf?"

Gunnolf chuckled. "I tell you, this is the life for me." Then he frowned. "But if I had someone that I had cared for all my life as you have cared for Isobel, then things would be different. Will you have trouble from her family in England?"

"I hope no'. I wish no fighting between us. MacLauchlan, now that is a different story. 'Tis inevitable if he is of a mind to claim Isobel as his daughter and his to do with as he wishes."

Marcus led them inside where Isobel smiled broadly at them. "Greetings. I am glad you are here to aid us."

"We would do no less, my lady." Angus took her hand and gallantly kissed it.

Niall punched him in the shoulder. "Marcus looks to be ready to take you to task if you dinna let go of the lass's hand."

She smiled at them. "I will fix you some of the porridge if you would like."

They heard horses again and Finbar shouted, "'Tis only us."

They went outside to see Ulicia as Leith handed her down to Rob, who carried her into the shieling.

"She is better, but canna take care of her bairns until she has fully recovered," Leith said, joining them.

"We will take care of her," Fiona said fiercely.

Her brothers hurried inside with a few fish they had caught in the river and Druce said, "Aye. We will care for her."

"If Ulicia is well enough and her children can aid her, we need to leave. But if you wish to rejoin our clan, we will send men to move you there," Marcus said to his distant cousin.

"I am happy here." Ulicia tucked a brown curl behind her ear as she sat on one of the chairs at her table, and Fiona hurried to get her mother some porridge to eat. "I just need to get my strength back. And my bairns will be help enough."

"Are you certain?" Marcus asked. "I would leave a man to help out until you are better."

"What if MacLauchlan recognizes him and believes you have been this way?" Ulicia looked worried for his safety and most likely for her own as well as her bairns.

"He doesna know I am kin to you. And he doesna know all of my men." Marcus motioned to one of them.

"Leith has only recently joined our clan."

Leith nodded his assent.

"He will stay. I would have more peace of mind if I thought he could help and then follow us later."

"Aye, if you feel he must," she said reluctantly, but Marcus saw the relief in her light brown eyes and was glad he was leaving one of his men behind.

Leith was already helping the older lad and Fiona prepare the fish for a meal.

Marcus patted Ulicia's shoulder. "We must be on our way then. Have your mounts rested some?" he asked Angus and the others in his party.

"Aye. We arrived in the village last night and we were trying to learn where your distant cousin lived when we had the good fortune of seeing Leith fetching water from the well and knew then we were in the right place," Angus said.

"Good, when you are finished eating then, we will leave."

Marcus was surprised when each of the bairns hugged him.

Druce said, "When my mother no longer needs me, I will fight for you."

Marcus very seriously nodded. "Aye, I would have you on my side. Any man who can take on Rob and survive the encounter, is a formidable opponent indeed."

Rob grinned as all gazes swung to him. He shrugged. "Aye, what can I say? The lad has a mighty swing."

The men quickly finished the porridge Isobel had served them.

Druce beamed and then the bairns hugged Isobel and she looked sad to be leaving them behind. That made Marcus think of her with their own bairns someday and that gave him a good feeling.

"You know we are closer to the Chattan's castle now," Angus said. "Mayhap we should go there. Edana wished to see you."

"Aye, we shall do that then. My hunting lodge is closest, but affords very little protection and MacLauchlan may no' guess we are headed for the Chattans' and not to my own keep."

"Aye. I am curious about this ward you were caring for that you wished the Chattan brothers to meet and hoped one would wed her. The brothers returned home, wouldna speak of the matter, and none had a bride in hand," Angus said, as they left the shieling and mounted their horses.

Isobel rode beside Marcus and turned to look at him, curiosity in her expression.

"'Tis a long story," Marcus said. "The Chattan brothers were delayed so long, by the time they reached my keep, the circumstances had changed."

"How so?" Angus asked.

"My ward is no longer my ward, but I am still trying to rectify that." Marcus hadn't told anyone the details because he thought that best left up to the man who wished to wed the lass, the daughter of a friend who had died and left her in the hands of an unscrupulous uncle. Although Marcus had planned to tell Isobel when they reached his keep so that she would know why this was so important to him. He wished she could meet her and be her friend.

"How goes married life between you and my cousin?" Marcus asked Angus. Edana had a strange gift of knowing things she should not and he had been afraid she'd never find a man who could love her like she deserved. He was glad she married Angus, the two of them appealing to each other from the time they were young, very much like Marcus and Isobel.

Angus smiled. "She is a delight. I should have wed Edana long ago."

"Aye, I agree. And you, Niall? No trouble with the French aristocracy over wedding the countess?"

"Nay. They were happy that I married the lass."

Gunnolf snorted.

Everyone looked in his direction. Gunnolf shrugged. "In the end."

Marcus wasn't surprised. If he hadn't been away at the time, he would have offered to go with Niall and Gunnolf and aid them in locating the countess. Especially after he had learned of all the difficulties they had gone through.

"And you and Isobel?" Angus asked.

Isobel flushed a pretty pink.

Marcus smiled at her. "She is the best thing that

has ever happened to me. But we have no' had the pleasure to get to know each other like we will."

The men chuckled.

She looked beautifully embarrassed. But he knew she did not mind the attention. She was used to his cousins teasing the two of them, and she was always good-natured about it.

**

With the land cloaked in fog every morning until nooning, and low hanging clouds covering the sky, they had not had to suffer any further drenching rains, just light mists, which Marcus was glad for. It took them two days to reach the lands of the Clan Chattan. They had not even gone far when Edana's brothers rode out to meet them and everyone halted to speak for a moment before they continued the rest of the way to the castle.

The brothers were a lively lot and when Marcus had been but a lad, he'd spent many a day hunting, sparring, and even swimming with his cousins in the loch.

Gildas, the second eldest of the brothers, his blue eyes sparkling like the waters of the loch were narrowed a little when he said, "We have had travelers since Angus left to find you." Gildas's tone of voice warned it was not welcome news.

Marcus growled, "Laren MacLauchlan—"

"Nay, no' him."

"Pembroke's men?" Marcus was surprised they

would be there and not storming his own castle.

"His nephew."

Isobel's eyes were wide with shock. "John is here?"

"Aye. He suspected Marcus had found you after one of Marcus's men took the knight home and left him there to tend to. Marcus's kinsman came to Rondover Castle and John and his escort followed him there, thinking that you would be there already."

Marcus didn't like the worry in Gilda's expression. "And?"

"He wants Lady Isobel returned home at once. That he means to return her, I should say."

"Nay," Isobel said. "He can have my…my father's title now. His lands. I have agreed to be Marcus's wife."

"It seems that isna enough," Drummond, the youngest of the Chattan brothers, said. "We would ride with you to your keep, Marcus, if you wish it so that you can keep the lass from the likes of her cousin."

"Nay," Isobel said. "I will speak with him. He must believe I have been taken against my will or some such thing. He does not know the fondness Marcus and I have always had for each other. My cousin has rarely visited."

She rode toward the castle and Marcus caught up to her, not liking this business one wee bit, but he would set her cousin straight at once. He and the lass belonged together and nothing would tear them apart now.

"He willna have you returned, lass," Marcus said adamantly.

"What if John has King Henry's backing?"

"We will mention about your heritage if you agree," he said to her.

She looked ill at ease over the matter.

"'Tis up to you."

"Aye, we will do that. If you think it will make any difference."

"Surely your cousin will see that this is what you want and will agree without too much trouble." Marcus would go to any lengths to fight anyone who wished to take her away from him now. When he was attempting a diplomatic solution with her da, that was one thing. He respected him for the way he normally dealt with the Scots at the border, attempting to keep the peace. She adored her da and he her, so Marcus had not wanted to fight him and upset Isobel, nor had he wanted to have to deal with King Henry, should he have taken the side of the earl.

John was a different matter. The cousin was an unknown quantity to him. It was always important to know one's friends and foes. "What kind of man is he?" Marcus asked Isobel as they drew closer to the gates.

"He has always been standoffish, but I think 'tis because he never lived with us. He would visit every once in a while. Maybe ten times in the last ten years? We were never close. He was rather sullen as a lad, and he never spoke to me, but I attributed that to my being a lass and he was more interested in speaking to the men of my...father's court. He has a younger brother by a year, but I saw him even less."

Marcus wished he hadn't had to tell her who her da really was. Every time she hesitated to refer to him as her da, he felt a twinge of guilt. Though he still felt it important for her to know the truth because her *real* father seemed to want her for his own pawn in securing clan ties, and he wanted her to know that King Henry might not pursue the matter if he learned she was not really Pembroke's daughter.

It was hard for Marcus to know what kind of man John truly was from the little Isobel knew of him. He turned to the Chattan brothers. "Have you a feel for the situation?"

"Aye," Kayne said. He was the third eldest brother. "The man is adamant that he wants Isobel returned at once to her rightful place."

"And then married off to someone that King Henry approves of so John can win favor with the king?" Isobel asked, sounding bitter.

Marcus didn't blame her. He wasn't about to allow her cousin to return her home. "We are wed," he reminded her, in case she needed reminding.

She smiled at him, then frowned. "Under your laws. John may not agree to yours."

"You are no' leaving with him." Marcus had not expected this development at all. Once John had her da's title and lands, Marcus assumed that's all he'd care about as long as Isobel was happy. The greedy bastard.

Kayne said, "We have disarmed his men, the

twenty he brought with him as we would do any that are no' our allies or kin. We back you in this, Marcus."

"Many thanks to you and your kin," Marcus said.

As soon as they reached the gates, two of the Chattan brothers led the way, the rest of the party following. Several men hurried to take their mounts, while Marcus helped Isobel down from her horse.

He took her arm and strode with her and the others toward the keep, but before they reached it, Edana rushed out, always the family greeter, and hurried to see him and Isobel. She beamed, her dark hair shimmering with red as she looked like she wanted to throw her arms around Marcus and give him a hug, but because he was holding onto Isobel's arm, she hesitated.

He let go of Isobel and gave Edana a hug. "Cousin," he said, with great affection. Then he turned and took Isobel's arm and introduced her. "My dear wife."

Again, Edana hesitated, and then she smiled broadly and wrapped her arms around Isobel in a warm embrace. "Cousin," she said, fondly. But then she whispered, "Forgive me for saying so, but you are no' at all like your cousin John. He is a pompous bore. He has only just attempted to claim your da's title and hasna even earned it."

"I agree," Isobel said. "I will tell him what I intend to do."

Edana again smiled brightly at her, and said to Marcus, "If you will release Isobel long enough, I will take her to the guest chamber and have a bath prepared for her. She can come down when she is ready to see her cousin."

"I will go with her," Marcus said.

Edana lifted a brow.

"In case anyone has any ideas about trying to run off with her."

As they entered the keep, Edana smiled again. "For protection, aye. I will ensure you have more time to clean up then," she said to Isobel.

"Where are John and his men?" Marcus asked.

"In the great hall, feasting. They wanted to come out to see you, but my father said no. He is sitting with them still and sent my brothers instead."

"Good."

Edana led the way up the narrow, curving stone stairs until they reached the fifth floor of the tower. "This chamber looks onto the loch and you will have enough privacy on this floor. I have already instructed the servants to bring up a bath, and," she said, motioning to the bed, "I have set out one of my gowns for your use, Isobel, suspecting you had naught with you when you had to flee from the men who killed your escort."

"Did the knight live that Marcus's clansmen took back to my father's keep?" Isobel asked.

"Aye."

"And my kinsman?" Marcus asked.

"He is here, eating with the others. Like John, he

wished to see you, but my father asked that he remain at the table. He didna want anyone to leave but my brothers."

Several men suddenly entered the chamber, some carrying a wooden tub, others carrying buckets of water to fill the tub.

As they continued to parade in, deposit their water, and then leave again, Edana, Marcus, and Isobel remained silent. When the tub was filled, the servants left the room.

Edana asked, "Will you need a maid to help you?"

Marcus shook his head.

Edana chuckled. "You are so much like Angus. I canna decide if he gets it from you or you from him." She paused at the door. "Would you prefer to eat here? I can send up food for you, if you would rather eat in the chamber."

"Aye," Marcus said, then looked at Isobel to see her preference.

She looked frazzled now that she'd removed her cloak and set it aside, half her dark brown hair in curls about her shoulders and trailing down to her hips.

"Aye," she said, nodding as if saying the word was not enough. "I am tired from all the traveling. If it would not appear too ungracious, I would prefer to see everyone on the morrow when we break our fast."

"Aye, I will tell my father what you wish. He said 'tis up to the two of you, and he said that he wants to know why his favorite cousin hasna visited in so long.

Though, of course, he says so in jest, knowing how busy you are with taking care of your clan."

"I will come down and visit with him...after a time," Marcus said.

Edana grinned. "I willna tell him in case you change your mind." Then she gave Isobel and Marcus another hug and quickly left the chamber, closing the door as she departed.

Marcus strode across the floor and bolted the door, then turned and saw Isobel struggling to pull her gown over her head.

"Let me help," he said, hoarsely, the thought of seeing her naked and in the bath already stirring his loins. He couldn't have asked for a more perfect way to end their journey today, no men and bairns in the same room as them. All alone and finally able to make love to his beautiful wife like he'd wanted to as soon as she was old enough to do so. Now all that had changed, not in an entirely good way as he wished her da had lived and given Marcus his permission freely to wed the lass.

***

Angus, Gunnolf, and Niall backed up Angus's wife's brothers as John Pembroke stood behind the table where he was to be seated, looking for any sign of Isobel, no doubt. Angus couldn't have been more pleased that his cousin by marriage and good friend, Marcus, had taken his beloved Isobel to wife. The man had piercing blue eyes, his dark brown hair curling at his shoulders, a beard making him look older than

Angus thought he was. Mayhap five and twenty.

John's men had taken his cue and also rose, but Tibold, chief of the Clan Chattan, asked them to please take their seats, though the men did not.

Edana quickly entered the great hall and joined her da, leaning down to whisper something in his ear.

Tibold nodded. "Lady Isobel will see us in the morn. She is weary from her journey and—"

John scowled. "I wish to see her now."

"That willna be possible. She is in her bath by now." Tibold smiled.

"Where is this McEwan who was said to have saved my cousin?" John looked over the other men that had joined them, Marcus's kinsmen, but Angus was certain Marcus would not leave his wife for the rest of the night.

"He has other matters to attend to." Tibold's determined look told the man he would send him and his men from the keep if he did not abide his rules.

Angus and the other men would back him up with might, if necessary.

For the longest time, John remained standing as if he couldn't decide if he should push the issue or give in.

Then, in a hostile way, John dropped to his seat and bumped the table with his abruptness, a scowl still plastered on his face. "We will take our leave in the morn after we break our fast. Mayhap after she has slept the night, she will feel rested enough to travel."

If she was rested enough, she would travel to

Marcus's castle, Angus thought, as he watched John's men take their seats. Angus suspected that Marcus would prefer that Isobel stay here a while longer and when they were ready to go, Angus and his cousin, Niall, and their friend Gunnolf, and his wife's brothers would also ride as escort to ensure Marcus and Isobel and his kin arrived safely.

Angus and Edana took their seats on the other side of her da while they listened to John complain. "I do not know why the man would bring her here and not return her to her own people."

Tibold said nothing, just continued to eat his deer and drink his ale. Angus knew his da by marriage wasn't about to explain anything to the Norman that he didn't wish to.

"Mayhap he didna believe she would be safe if Lord Wynfield had it in mind to send her again to serve the English queen," Angus said.

"Lord Wynfield is a fool. Once I return, he will have to find work elsewhere. It is my duty to ensure my cousin has a proper husband."

To earn favor with the king, Angus thought cynically. John didn't care one whit what Isobel wanted. Now that her da's nephew had taken on the title, there was no real reason for Isobel not to wed Marcus, except because John wished to use her as his pawn.

"You know that Isobel has pledged her heart to Marcus." Angus was not sure how much John knew about the situation, but he wanted to make John aware that they weren't about to turn her over to him.

John gave a disgruntled laugh. "She knows it is not her choice. Just as when her father was alive. But aye, I was in attendance at one of her dances and saw the way she looked at him and the way he looked at her. 'Twas obvious they had feelings for one another."

"One of her suitors sent men to kill Marcus. Now he has had her father murdered and slain her escort before they could reach Winchester. Think you, if you decided some other husband for her, that you wouldna be marrying her to the villain? Although, now that you have stepped in to take your uncle's title, mayhap none of her suitors are that interested in marrying her." Angus hoped that would be the case and then John would give up the notion of marrying her off to someone else. If he had to give away some of his newly acquired property, would he decide he'd rather not and just hand her over to McEwan?

"She has a substantial dowry," John said coldly, as if it bothered him that she still had means and that he had not gained all her da's properties upon his death. He fingered the brown bread disdainfully. "Where is this McEwan? I wished to thank him personally."

Tibold said, "With his wife, I suspect."

"He has a wife? Here?" John sounded shocked.

"Aye, here," Tibold said.

Angus smiled at the laird.

"Then why would Isobel wish to wed him?" John asked.

"She loves him," Angus said.

"But he is married."

"Aye," Tibold and Angus said at the same time.

Gunnolf and Niall chuckled.

But Angus suspected they would have trouble once John learned that Marcus's wife *was* Isobel.

CHAPTER 13

Marcus helped Isobel out of her garments, though he was not a practiced lady's maid and he had a lot to learn. He was trying hard not to pull her hair or fumble with her ties, and he felt like a green lad.

She smiled up at him, her expression lighthearted and affectionate, just the way he loved for her to be. She pulled at his tunic and gave a little tug.

"Your bath first, lass. If I strip out of my clothes first, you will never have your bath."

She chuckled wickedly and helped him with removing her clothes. And then, naked, her hair covering her breasts, the rest of her skin bare to him, she seemed a wee bit shy, as she quickly climbed into the bathwater. It was a small bath, only one person could fit in, and he was wondering if one of his men could create something larger for two to bathe in when he returned to his keep.

He took the cloth from her that she had started to use to wash her arms, the water high on her chest, her long hair floating on top of the water, some of it wet enough to cling to her breasts. He started to wash her back as she pulled her hair forward and she leaned over a bit.

"You are beautiful, Isobel," he said, his voice already turning husky with need. Just the sight of her naked, the desire to brush the hair away from her breasts, to see the dusky nipples that he'd barely glimpsed, peeking between strands of her silky hair.

"You are also," she said.

He smiled at her declaration, no woman having ever said that about him, though only Isobel's comment would have interested him.

Then he washed her hair with the soap Edana had left for them. Once he was finished with Isobel's hair, he swept the cloth across her breasts. She leaned back against the tub, closed her eyes, and purred.

He was done in, his groin tightening with need, his blood hot with desire. He slid the cloth over her breasts again, his hand feeling her nipples grow erect, as he paused to enjoy them. He couldn't touch her and see her like this without wanting her with rampant longing.

Then he ran the cloth lower, over her legs and pushed them apart to see her dark curly hair at the apex of her thighs and washed there.

"Ahh," she groaned and started to rise from the tub. He quickly dropped the wet cloth and grabbed a much larger one to dry her. He wanted to wrap her in it and carry her to the bed, but he needed to wash the dirt and mud off himself from all the traveling through the wet region before he joined her there.

He helped her out of the tub and guided her to sit by the fire. "I will wash up quickly and then we will retire so you willna catch your death."

"Aye, hurry." She looked sweetly at him, her skin so soft and clean.

"Aye, of that you can be sure." In no time at all, he had discarded his sword and scabbard, *sgian dubh*, boots, his plaid, and tunic on the floor, then got into the bath, noticing that she was watching him the whole time, appraising him, seeing just how aroused he was, which had the effect of making him even harder.

She was attempting to dry her hair without showing off her body too much or at least trying to keep herself covered so she'd remain warmer by the fire. She kept revealing a slim leg, a full breast, a nipple as she toweled her hair with one edge of the cloth.

He would have sat in the water longer, but he vigorously scrubbed himself down as quickly as he could, then surged up from the tub and grabbed the lengthy bit of cloth to dry himself. Once he had managed that, he joined her at the fire, pulled the cloth from her hands, and began to dry her hair. He kept the front of his body against her back to warm her. The fire helped to warm her front, while he attempted to dry her hair the best he could.

He wrapped his arm around her shoulders, still drying her hair, but holding her close. "I love you, Isobel. I always have."

"Oh, Marcus." She turned in his arms, wrapped her arms around his waist, and pressed her luscious, naked body against his. "You know I have always loved you. Even when you were impossible."

He chuckled and dropped the cloth, then grabbed her up in his arms and carried her to the bed. "I have never been impossible."

She laughed. "Aye, you have."

He set her on the bed, then climbed in beside her and yanked the curtains closed.

"Your wound," she said, with real concern.

"Healed, a scar, but it doesna bother me much now."

"May I see?"

"It probably isna pretty to see."

"Turn over. Let me see."

He really hadn't wanted to. She was beautiful and he didn't want her to see him all scarred up.

She gingerly touched around the scar. "It does not hurt?"

"Nay, no' any longer." He turned then and saw the tears in her eyes.

"Ah, lass." He felt moved by her tears, but he didn't want her to feel bad again over what had happened to him.

He kissed her mouth, raking his hand through her

damp hair. She touched his arms, his back, his waist, exploring like she wasn't able to earlier, just like he had never been able to with her.

Her lips were sweet on his, her mouth softening against his. He treasured her, had loved her for her smiles and flirtatious ways directed only at him, how witty and clever she was, and how she never shied away from work or duty. But mostly the way they had shared a secret love for one another, when they were permitted naught more.

But now…now she was his.

The urge to plunder her was great, as much as he burned to have her, but he attempted to slow his racing heart, to drink in her sweet scent from the soap made from the aromatic herbs of fennel, lavender, and lime, to enjoy this first moment of bliss that he had feared he'd never experience.

He cupped a breast and ran his thumb over the nipple, already taut with expectation. She shivered a little, and he leaned down to lick the nipple as her hands moved to his head, her fingers raking through his hair. His touching her and her touching him made him steel hard for her as she moaned a little when he swirled his tongue around her nipple.

She rubbed her foot against his leg and he smiled to see her unafraid and eager to touch him. He hadn't known what to expect from the lass who was inexperienced in the art of lovemaking, but she proved to make his blood heat and his heart pound with her sizzling touches. Though he was certain she didn't realize just how much she did.

He groaned as her leg moved higher on his leg, and he pushed it back against the bed, then ran his hand down her hip, and over her dewy curls at the apex of her thighs. He began to stroke her, to ready her for him, to make her even wetter, to soften, to accept him before he made the plunge that would claim the lass for his own.

Her hands had stilled on his waist, her breathing nearly ceasing as she gave into the feel of his stroking her.

He smiled at her, loving that she was so caught up in the moment, that naught else seem to exist. Then he began kissing her again, stroking her at the same time, her hands again moving over his muscles, touching, kneading, drawing him even further under her spell.

"Oh, oh," she panted out and he smiled again before he inserted a finger into her wet sheath, feeling as deeply as he could go, enjoying the sensation of her body rippling with pleasure. "'This might be uncomfortable for a wee bit as you welcome me in," he whispered against her ear, not wanting to frighten her, but he didn't know if her mother or Mary or some other woman had warned her what the first joining would be like.

"'Twill burn and hurt and then I will be sore," she said, "but later, 'twill be joyous." She smiled up at him, willing him to bury himself in her.

"I wish the first time wouldna."

She reached down and touched his length, making it jump under her soft hand. "'Tis only natural when you are so big and I have never been with a man before."

"Aye." Still, he didn't want to hurt her and he feared she would be afraid to make love again with him if this was not done well.

He moved her legs further apart and lined himself up, pressing gently into her. She sucked her breath in and he said, "Breathe and relax. 'Twill be easier that way."

She relaxed considerably and he pushed in, took her maidenhead, saw the shimmer of tears in her eyes, and he immediately held himself still.

"Do not stop," she implored him. "I just never thought this moment would come. Love me, Highlander, like I have always loved you."

"Aye, lass." Though he suspected the tears were not strictly of a sentimental value, but that she was hurting. He pushed all the way in and once there, she finally truly relaxed. He began to thrust, enjoying the coupling, but also hoping that their joining would be fruitful soon.

He loved her with all his heart, and no one could take that away from him.

Isobel couldn't believe how Marcus had moved the world for her as he'd pleasured her and made her feel like the earth had shifted. She had never expected him to kiss her breast, or tongue her nipple. Or touch her between her legs and make her feel so exquisitely. She had only thought he would tup her like a ram did a ewe. But this…this was so wondrous, she wanted to do it over and over again.

Now, he was filling her with his staff and she couldn't believe how big he felt inside her, and how amazing that felt as well. She felt connected, as though they were meant to be together, and now they were. That they could no longer be torn apart. He began to kiss her as his thrusts slowed and she kissed him right back, her tongue sliding around his in the most delicious way. When she did that to him, he began thrusting deeper, harder, faster, and she could feel his heart beating hard, just as fast as her own was pounding.

He held himself still for a moment and then thrust again. She felt her own body climbing to that other sphere where she had felt the earth move for her before. A wash of warmth spread through her as he thrust one last time and settled on top of her.

She loved the feel of him against her, his body so hard and strong, and muscled. She wrapped her arms around him, not having known what to expect, but it was amazing beyond measure.

"Are you all right, lass?" Marcus whispered to her as he moved to get off her, and she felt him slide out of her and wondered when they could do it again.

"Aye."

"Sore?"

"A little," she admitted.

"Come, let me wash you and then I will dress and let a servant know we wish some sustenance."

She nodded, and he climbed off the bed, then took her hand and waited for her to leave the bed. She was no longer a virgin, an unmarried maid. She loved Marcus for it.

She wasn't certain if it was something a husband or wife should talk about, but as he pulled her over to the cool bathwater, she said, "Did I give you pleasure?"

He smiled down at her with such tenderness, she felt her eyes prick with tears.

Then his smile faded. "You are feeling bad?"

"Oh, Marcus." She threw her arms around him and hugged her naked Highlander to her chest. "'Twas wonderful. Naught that I could ever have imagined, though I must admit, I tried many a night after I saw you and you had to leave me behind. Or in between the long periods when we could not see one another."

He kissed her cheeks, her eyes, and her mouth again, his tongue seeking entrance. She felt deliciously wicked when they kissed in such a manner, yet she reminded herself they were well wed, in the Highland way, and it was the only thing that mattered. She was a Highlander, just like Marcus, after all.

She felt his staff coming to life and she raised her brows as she looked up at him.

He grinned. "You must rest."

She sighed, certain he knew what he was talking

about and he pulled away. Grabbing a dry cloth, he wiped her between the legs, then set the cloth tinged with blood aside. He seized the wet one, and washed her gently. Then he took it and rinsed it in the bathwater and washed himself.

Once he'd carefully dried her, he dried himself, then took her back to bed. "Rest and I will return with something to eat."

"Aye." She settled into bed, glad he was the one to bring them food and not her. She felt perfectly boneless and didn't want to move an inch from bed anytime soon. "Do not be long."

"Aye." He smiled and tucked her in. "You are beautiful."

She looked over his nakedness, the way his staff was already half aroused, and the rest of him hard and toned and braw. "You, as well."

He chuckled, leaned down and kissed her enticing lips, and then shut the bed curtains.

"If you are sleeping when I return, do you want me to wake you so you can eat?" he asked as he began to dress.

"Hmm, it depends on what you bring to eat." She nestled against the pillow, and already felt sleep overwhelming her. Between the long day of traveling and the one before that and everything else going on in her life, she was tired. But after making love to Marcus, it was a different kind of tired. A satisfying, happy kind of tired. She listened to him dressing and waited for him to unbolt the door and step out, then close the door.

***

Before Marcus left the chamber, he pulled the bed curtain open to see if there was anything else Isobel would really love to have to eat if Cook had it and give her a kiss. Isobel was already sound asleep, her eyes shut, the blankets covering the lower half of her breasts, and she looked angelic and happy. He could only smile at the lovely sight of her and wish that he didn't have too long to wait before he could make love to her again. But he wanted their lovemaking to be good for her and he didn't want her to suffer if she wasn't ready for it for a time.

He kissed her cheek, closed the curtains, and left the chamber. Under normal circumstances when he visited the Clan Chattan, he wouldn't have given it any thought about joining the family in the great hall and greeting them, then hieing himself off to the kitchen to see if the servants could spare them some food. But this time, he was reluctant to deal with her cousin John, as Marcus wished only to ensure Isobel had something to eat if she could wake long enough to do so.

Still, he wished John to know that Isobel was his wife and if the man had issue with it, Marcus wanted to deal with it now. So he headed straight for the great hall.

When he stepped inside, the conversation slowly died down until not a man or woman in the hall was speaking, all eyes turning to see him.

He bowed his head to Tibold, chief of the Chattan clan a little in greeting and then his gaze shifted to the man seated to the right of him, John, Isobel's cousin, dark brown hair tinged with red, a scruffy beard, and glacial blue eyes. The man was observing him, not that everyone else in the hall wasn't, waiting to see what he would do next.

Marcus caught a servant and asked him to take a meal up to Isobel in their guest chamber. The servant bowed his head and hurried off to do as he asked and Marcus suspected Edana had already made her staff aware that they needed to prepare a meal for Marcus and Isobel when they were ready for it.

Then Marcus strode to the dais and Tibold rose from the table. Nearly everyone else rose as well as a courtesy to the chief.

Marcus gave him a warrior's embrace. "Good to see you again, Uncle."

"It has been too long." Tibold motioned to John, who belatedly rose from his seat.

Marcus wondered if the newly turned earl felt the Highlanders were beneath him, and he didn't need to stand in the clan chief's presence. Since he was partaking of the chief's food and good hospitality and he didn't owe this man anything, Marcus thought even less of Isobel's cousin.

Tibold made introductions and John said, "Then 'tis you that I owe thanks for saving Isobel from the men who murdered her escort. They said you were with your wife."

Marcus glanced at Tibold and the older man smiled at him, a twinkle of mischief in his eyes.

Marcus suspected that the way John spoke of the circumstances, he didn't believe Isobel was that wife. "Aye, she is sleeping now, but I would be remiss if I didna ensure she had something to eat."

"Tibold said Isobel had a fondness for you. Is she too upset about you marrying another? Though as soon as I see her, I will assure her she will soon find a suitor whom she is completely satisfied with."

"She need not look any further. My wife and Isobel are one and the same," Marcus said, wanting to make the matter clear.

"You lying whoreson!" John reached for his sword, then recalling he was unarmed, he threw a punch at Marcus.

Marcus quickly defended himself, deflecting the blow that had it succeeded in finding his face would no doubt have given him a bloody nose. John grabbed up his dirk that he'd been using on his meal, and Angus intervened, seizing his arm and yanking the dirk free.

"If you wish to remain here as my guest," Tibold said, "you must behave civilly."

"Have you sullied her?" John roared, jerking his arm away from Angus and directing the comment to Marcus.

"We are husband and wife," Marcus said, then showed the bloodied cloth from their guest chamber, "duly consummated."

In the English way in royal households, they would oft have witnesses to the deed, stripping the newly married husband and wife before they watched them consummate the marriage. This was a way to ensure the marriage was truly consummated, but instead, this would have to suffice.

"You cannot have her," John said.

Marcus smiled. "She and I pledged ourselves to one another years ago. Then her da died, and we knew you would take the title. Once her escort was killed, there was naught else I could do, but rescue the lass and wed her."

"And if you had her father killed for just this reason?" John accused.

"Speak your words carefully," Tibold said. "Marcus is the most honorable of men and has always had good relations with Isobel's father."

Rob spoke up, "Marcus wouldna have ever killed the man as much as he respected him and cherishes his daughter. He knew her da and Isobel loved one another deeply. How would that have set with the lass if Marcus had killed him? Save your tale for the Norman who did the deed. Even Wynfield has said the man was a Norman who killed Lord Pembroke."

John ground his teeth and glowered at Marcus. "This does not end here."

"You have the title and her da's estate, aye?" Marcus folded his arms, irritated with the man. "What difference does it make if the lass weds someone she loves?"

"She has no head for such a matter. She sees you as something different, but you will not provide her with the kind of place and comforts that an English nobleman could offer her."

"And you know this how?" Marcus asked.

"She is my cousin, and you are a..." John paused. He was surrounded by Highlanders and he must have realized his folly before he spoke any further words.

"She may be your cousin, but she has known me longer. When she has rested, she will tell you how she feels. I am sure you will understand and agree this is the best for all concerned," Marcus said, his voice congenial, but his look was not. Then to Tibold, he said, "I bid you good eve. My lady wife awaits me and a meal."

John's face was red with anger, but he kept his mouth shut and didn't agree or disagree. He wouldn't win this battle no matter how much he might wish to.

CHAPTER 14

Isobel woke to the sound of someone coming into the chamber. She expected to smell baked bread or something else to eat, but she smelled nothing.

"Marcus?" she called out.

A woman said, "Selice, my lady. He wishes you to come down to eat."

"He was having someone bring food here." Isobel frowned at the closed curtain.

"Aye, my lady. But the chief wishes to greet you."

Isobel was torn between not wanting to appear ungrateful to the chief of the Clan Chattan, and doing what she wanted to do—which was stay right here in bed until morn. "Tell him I hope he can forgive me for remaining here, but I could not possibly come down. I am too weary from my travels." Which she was, but also, she didn't want to have to see John just yet. In the morn when she went down to break her fast, she would be rested enough to handle it.

"He willna like it, my lady. He...wishes you to tell your cousin that you are happy to be married to Laird Marcus McEwan. That he hasna kept you from your cousin in an attempt to prevent you from telling him the truth."

"Very well. When Marcus returns, I will go with him."

"I will help you to dress."

"Thank you. I will wait for my husband." Isobel felt something was wrong with the way the servant was acting. She was certain Marcus would have come to her with word, and not sent some servant. Not only that, but that she was so insistent that Isobel do her bidding.

The woman gasped in surprise or fear. Isobel scrambled to the other side of the bed in a hurry, realizing if something was really untoward, her *sgian dubh* was on the floor with her soiled garments near the bathing tub. And she could not reach it quickly.

The curtain on that side of the bed was jerked aside and a dark-haired man, with eyes just as dark, whom she didn't know, grabbed for her. She screamed, but as thick as the walls were and as far away as the great hall was from the bedchamber, she was certain no one would hear her.

He attempted to tie a piece of cloth around her mouth as another man suddenly appeared next to the bed and tried to pin her flailing body down. Her heart thundering, she was frantic, fighting the one who tried to silence her tongue, kicking at the other, knowing if they carried her away, she could be in the worst danger. She wasn't even dressed, for heaven sakes!

She must have connected with a part of the man's body that caused him great pain, as he was trying to grab her arms and keep them from swinging at the other man because wherever she slammed her foot made him curse out loud and fall backward.

She screamed, yelling for help, still fighting the other and managed to swing her fist hard and hit him in the eye. He dropped the cloth and fisted his hand, but before he could do anything to her in retaliation, the door banged against the stone wall, startling her and him. Running footfalls headed in her direction, and maneuvered around the bed. She prayed it was Marcus coming to aid her.

As soon as she saw Marcus, she witnessed his mask of red-faced fury. He seized the man who had twisted around to tackle the real threat, grabbing for a dirk sheathed at his waist. He didn't have a chance to remove it. Not when Marcus was pummeling him half to death with his mighty fists.

The man fell and before the other could run away, Marcus grabbed him up and with one swing, knocked him out cold. The villain crumpled to the floor while the other lay there bloodied, clutching his stomach, groaning in pain.

Marcus quickly joined her at the bed. "Are you hurt, Isobel?" He was altogether a changed man.

Protective, endearing, concerned, loving, not anything like the warrior she had just observed.

Still shaking, she nodded, pulling a coverlet around her nakedness.

"God's wounds, if your cousin sent these men to the chamber while I was speaking with him…"

"Did you see a maid?" She couldn't see around the curtained bed, the curtains still closed on the opposite side where she'd been sleeping.

"Nay. When the men attacked you, I am sure she ran away."

"She did not go for help?"

"Nay. I saw no one leaving the room. Only heard you scream as I was returning to the chamber. Unless she scurried down the servants' stairs. Lass, I am so sorry. Had I no' left the chamber when you were sleeping, or insisted you bolt it after I left, none of this would have happened."

"'Tis not your fault. 'Tis the fault of the man who sent them."

"John, your cousin," Marcus said, sounding angry.

"Aye. No one on the Chattan's staff would have done so."

"Nay. These men have to work for your cousin." Marcus used the rope to tie up one of the men, who had intended to use it on Isobel. He tore the other man's tunic into shreds and tied him up with the remnants.

"What are you going to do with them?" She hated how shaken she still felt, her heart racing and her skin chilled.

"I canna leave you alone again, but I need to tell Tibold of this deception."

"I will dress and go with you." She wasn't about to be left alone again.

"Let me get the clothes Edana left for you."

Isobel moved to the other side of the bed where the curtains hid her from the bound men. Then when Marcus handed her the chemise, Isobel dressed as quickly as she could. Once she had finished dressing, she found a comb that Edana had left for her, and combed out her tangled hair. "I am ready." She noticed then that Marcus was watching her, his look concerned.

"They did naught." She took hold of his hand. "You stopped them before anything could happen."

"What I dinna understand is what they hoped to accomplish. They would never have gotten you out of here before I discovered you were gone. Nor could they have moved you off the grounds that easily." He ran his hands down her arms, then he pulled her against his warm body and held her tight.

She cherished the way he cared for her, wrapped her arms around his waist, and hugged him back just as tightly. "I love you, Marcus McEwan. No one will separate us now."

"Aye. If I didna need these men for questioning, I would have dispensed with them forthwith."

He glanced back at the men. "I will wake the unconscious man and make them walk with us to the great hall and turn them over to Tibold."

Before he could make a move in that direction, they heard heavy footfalls running their way.

Marcus moved Isobel behind him and stalked toward the door, grabbed his sword, then poked his head out. "Angus and Chattan's sons," he said, sounding relieved.

Isobel sighed with relief. "Then the maid must have warned them."

"Mayhap she was coerced to come here." Marcus turned to the Chattan men. "The bastards are over there. If it hadna been for needing information from them, they would be dead men."

Angus and the other men entered the room and Angus clapped his hand on Marcus's shoulder. "Aye. We will take care of this."

"The maid who came to say I was needed below stairs, did she give you word?" Isobel hoped the men had forced her to come with them.

"Only after one of the other servants saw her running down the stairs, and he knew something was amiss as she should have been helping with the serving of the meal. She finally broke down and told us what was happening," Angus said. "We believe she had been pressed to do it, and then feared she would be severely punished for aiding them."

Isobel understand the dilemma. "I wish to speak with her." Instead of the men interrogating her and making everything worse.

"As you wish if Da agrees, but you will have an armed guard," Kayne said.

Kayne and Drummond splashed water from the tub on the unconscious man's face. Then they roused him enough that the other brothers were able to get him to his feet.

"Who do you work for?" Kayne asked the man whose face was swollen and bruised by Marcus's fists.

"Lord Pembroke, the new earl. She is his cousin, and 'tis his decision to wed her to whomever he wishes," the man said.

"He is wrong," Marcus said.

Then the Chattan brothers hauled the two knaves out of the chamber.

Angus said to Isobel and Marcus, "The servants prepared a meal to be brought up here. Did you still wish it?"

"Nay," Isobel said adamantly. "I wish to see my cousin, eat in the great hall with everyone else, let them know that Marcus is my husband, and I will claim no other."

Both Marcus and Angus smiled at her, and then escorted her down the corridor after the other men. She knew that their amusement was due to the fact that she said she claimed Marcus and not the other way around. But it was true. From when she was a lass of one and ten, she had decided that he would be her husband. She'd only had to get her father to agree.

Feeling sad again about her father's death, she

wished with all her heart he had been the one to grant her permission to wed Marcus and that her dear father was still alive.

"Are you all right?" Marcus took her hand in his until they reached the stairs.

"Aye, Marcus. They surely gave me a fright." She was still trembling some from the scare. "But they did not get off with me and that is the most important thing."

Once they were on the narrow stairs, they had to walk single file, the curving stone stairs a way for those defending the castle to have an easier time of it, the ability to swing a sword when the man attacking from below couldn't. The defender of the castle would only have to fend off one man at a time.

When they reached the ground floor, she felt apprehensive, worried how this would all play out.

As soon as the Chattan brothers hauled the beaten men into the great hall, all conversation stopped instantly, and all eyes were upon them. Then the gazes shifted to Marcus and Isobel as they made their way past the men to see Tibold.

He rose from the table, his face barely suppressing anger.

Edana joined Isobel and took her hand, though Marcus had his arm around Isobel's waist.

"Are you all right, Isobel?" Edana said, her voice shaken.

"Aye, I am fine. If Marcus had not come when he

did..." She turned her fury on her cousin. "You had these men attempt to take me hostage while under the Chattans' and my husband's protection? You must be insane, John."

"Laird Pembroke to you, dear cousin. I do not recognize this marriage between you and the... the Highlander. 'Tis plain to see that you have not the sense to make such a decision on your own."

Marcus released Isobel and took a step toward the earl.

Tibold quickly held out his hand in a gesture to stop Marcus. "Hold, if you please, Marcus. I will have a word alone with you, Isobel, my sons, and Angus."

"Niall and Gunnolf also, if you would permit them to join us as well," Angus said.

"Aye, it goes without saying."

"As to you, Lord Pembroke, you will remain here," Tibold said.

"Or?"

"You wouldna like the alternative. First, Lady Isobel, Marcus, eat and we will finish this business in my solar."

"Aye, thank you, Tibold," Isobel said.

Tibold smiled warmly at her and then Isobel and Marcus were seated next to Tibold, while John fumed on the other side of them.

To Isobel, Tibold said, "My lady, my condolences for your loss. I wish we were meeting under better circumstances."

"As do I."

Tibold's expression turned dark. "For the rest of your stay, you willna have any more difficulties."

"I thank you for your kindness." She truly liked the chief of the Clan Chattan and could see why Marcus cared for his extended family. And she realized they were hers now also.

"You have married my favorite nephew. 'Tis befitting that you stay with us a time."

She cast him a smile and bowed her head in thanks, though in truth, she wished to see Marcus's castle and his people. She hoped they would be happy with her there and not see her as a Sassenach, even though she was not one. But she had lived as one for all her life. She wasn't sure what Marcus would tell his people about her heritage. And then she realized she had a new dilemma. It would not be good to be considered a Sassenach, and since he and his people didn't have a fondness for Laren MacLauchlan, her true father, Marcus's people would most likely be wary of her for that reason.

She sighed and ate her food, hoping they could work it all out to everyone's satisfaction. She loved Marcus with all her heart, and his cousins whom she'd known for years also, but she just hoped the rest of his people would welcome her, too.

She was surprised that Tibold didn't force John and his people to leave after what had happened. Why didn't John just leave? She suspected he would attempt to stay there until she and Marcus left to continue traveling to Lochaven and then try to take her from Marcus when they didn't have all of Chattan's clansmen to deal with.

When they finished their meal, Tibold spoke with some of his men in private. She noted they were armed, unlike John and his men, and they kept them confined to the great hall while the servants cleared away the remnants of the meal.

"May I speak with the maid who came to my chamber afterward?" Isobel asked Tibold.

"Aye," he said, "as you wish."

In the solar, she took a seat on a bench while Tibold sat on another and the rest of the men stood, though Marcus rested his hand on her shoulder in a tender way. Which everyone noticed.

"You might be wondering why I have not thrown the earl out of here as angry as his actions make me, but I wished to ensure that when Isobel and Marcus leave here with my sons and son by marriage, John and his men wouldna give you any trouble. They will remain here, incarcerated, if necessary, but they willna leave until I am certain you have had time to reach Lochaven," Tibold said.

"We thank you for your aid," Marcus said.

"I can never repay you for saving Kayne's life, Marcus, when you were lads in the heat of battle. You are as much a son to me as my own."

Marcus bowed his head a little in acknowledgement.

Kayne grinned at him. "If you had moved a little to the left of me, I would have been saving you instead and then you would have been thanking me."

"Aye," Marcus said smiling.

Isobel wondered about that story, and about the lass Marcus had taken in as his ward. How she wished she had lived close by them and shared in more of his life all these past years.

"Dinna tell me you havena regaled the lass of all these tales already," Kayne said as he looked down at Isobel's clueless expression. "I see you havena. Well, suffice it to say, he was heroic."

"He is," Isobel said. "Always."

Tibold said, "When you feel rested up enough—"

"We leave on the morrow at dawn," Isobel said.

Tibold eyed her with suspicion, while the other men watched her, probably trying to figure out her reasoning. Maybe they thought she was afraid John and his men would try something further, when she was not. She just wanted to leave as quickly as possible so they could be at Marcus's castle, and she could get to know his people and begin some kind of routine. She realized how important that was to her. Having a schedule she was familiar with. And even more so, settling in the chambers with her husband.

"Your reasoning, lass?" Tibold asked.

"I thought we could leave before you had to put up with much more of John and his men. But also, I want so to be settled at Lochaven with Marcus and become acquainted with his people. I want to feel useful."

The men all smiled at that. She felt her cheeks heat, thinking the men thought part of her usefulness had to do with bed play when it was the furthest thing from her mind. Not that she hadn't thought of being with Marcus at night in his chambers, *their* chambers, and being at home, but she had not wanted the others to think of that.

Marcus cleared his throat. "If you are certain?"

"Oh, aye. I am much recovered already. A good night's sleep and by morn, I will be ready to travel again."

Again, the smiles. She was fairly certain Marcus had no intention of making love to her again during the night, worrying she might be too sore. She hoped she wasn't and it wouldn't be too long before they could share in that blissful state again.

"What say you?" Tibold asked his sons, Angus, Niall, and Gunnolf.

"We will ride when the lady wishes it," Halwn, next to the youngest brother, said. He was the closest of the Chattan brothers to the youngest the way the two always paired up, Isobel thought. She already liked him for agreeing with her.

"Marcus?" Tibold asked.

"Aye, if that is what the lady wishes. If she feels ready to ride by tomorrow morn after we break our fast, so be it." Marcus looked a little skeptical though.

She didn't know why. She felt fine. Well, tired still

as she'd only slept a wee bit, and now that she'd had a meal, she was ready to sleep the rest of the night away. But by morn, she would be ready to leave.

"All right. Then that is what we will do." Then Tibold proceeded to tell them what to do in any eventuality and Isobel nearly drifted off to sleep as she leaned against Marcus still standing behind her. "But Egan, I wish you to stay here. You will ensure we have no trouble with John and his men."

Egan, the eldest brother and the quietest, nodded, though she wondered if he was disappointed that he could not ride with them.

At one point, the conversation between the men all ceased, and Isobel's eyes popped open. They were smiling at her.

"Why dinna you take your lovely wife to bed, Marcus. And then she truly will be ready for tomorrow's ride," Tibold said.

"The maid," Isobel quickly said.

"Drummond, have the maid brought up here for questioning," Tibold told his youngest son.

"Aye, father." Drummond stalked out of the solar.

The men talked of other matters—about cattle, sheep, and horses, nearly putting Isobel to sleep again. Once she heard footfalls headed for the solar, she sat up straighter.

Tears streaked the maid's face and her eyes were red.

Isobel knew, as the lady of her own father's manor,

that she could not be swayed by the woman's tears here either, and had to keep her own emotions out of it.

"Tell me what happened." Isobel figured that was the best approach.

The woman's face was so pale, she looked as though she would collapse at any moment. It was bad enough that her chief was there listening in, but with all his sons and Isobel's husband and the others looking so fierce, Isobel suspected the woman was terrified.

"I beg your forgiveness, my lady," the woman said, in a choked voice. "The Sassenach said you hadna come here willingly with Laird McEwan." She glanced in his direction. "He said King Henry and King David would have the McEwan's head for bringing you here."

She lowered her eyes. "I didna want his lairdship to get into trouble."

Over a Sassenach? Isobel wondered if that's what the woman meant.

"But then you wouldna leave without his lairdship's say so and I assumed the men had lied. They said you wished to go home. When you wouldna cooperate, the one man shoved me aside and they tried to grab you without your consent."

"You brought them to the chamber willingly?" Isobel asked, surprised. She truly had thought the woman had been forced to do it.

"Nay, my lady," the maid said quickly, her eyes widening. "They forced me to go with them. 'Tis just that I wanted you to know what they said to me. I was a'feared for my life."

"You did not tell anyone else on the staff that I was in trouble?"

The woman looked down at the rushes on the floor. "I was afraid of the men, and then for taking them to your chamber, I was afraid of the punishment I would receive."

She dropped to her knees and begged Isobel, "Take pity, my lady. I didna mean you any harm."

Tibold raised his brows at Isobel and she sighed. "If you were faced with the same circumstance and had it to do all over again, what would you do?"

"They showed me their dirks. And I...if I had not done as they asked, they would have killed me to silence me. Then they would have grabbed another maid and forced her to do their bidding. Had I to do it all over again, I would have run screaming from the chamber as soon as they grabbed for you."

"Thank you." Isobel had nothing further to say to her.

"Drummond, take her from here. I will deal with her in a moment," Tibold said.

When Drummond led the maid out of the room, Isobel asked, "What will you do with her?"

"She will be punished for her complicity. She had ample time to warn my staff that you were in danger."

Isobel bowed her head. She had felt the same way. And it was the chief's decision, but she had to know for herself why the maid had helped John's men.

"Are you ready for bed?" Marcus asked her, and she felt her cheeks flame anew. He smiled down at her, then took her hand.

She bid everyone good night as they bid her the same, and then he led her out of the solar.

"I only just closed my eyes," she said.

He chuckled. "Aye, lass. I am sure of it." But he knew differently. He'd had to reposition his body behind hers to ensure she did not fall over, she was sleeping so soundly. He loved her.

He was still beyond enraged concerning John's tactics.

Although if he had been John, he might have felt the same need to possess everything his uncle had, including Isobel. The nephew, who had nothing, hadn't earned any of it, but suddenly had it all.

Everything, except the most important thing in the world—at least to Marcus—Isobel.

Marcus knew Tibold would put the two men, who had accosted her under his own roof, in the dungeon. Marcus was glad his wife had been such a hellion and managed to disable the one man. By the looks of it from the way he'd been holding his groin, she'd kicked him there. And the other man was already sporting a punch to the eye before Marcus got hold of him. The villain had been about to hit her and knock her out when Marcus grabbed his arm and let him have it.

Marcus wanted to sleep with her now, but he also wanted to make love to her again. However, he would wait. He was afraid she would be too tender, and then she still had to ride horseback for hours on the morrow and he didn't want her to be even sorer.

"You look so serious," Isobel said as he shut and barred the door.

He smiled then, and began to help her out of her borrowed clothes. But he couldn't help frowning again as he removed her brat. "You are certain you were no' injured?"

She shook her head.

When he pulled her *léine* over her head, he noted bruises on her wrists and arms. He growled. "I will kill those whoresons for laying a hand on you."

"Nay," Isobel said, pulling at his tunic. "Let us retire to bed and think of naught but each other."

He took her small hand and kissed her arms between the bruises.

"I love you, Highlander."

Her declaration melted away some of his hostility. He would ensure Tibold knew that the men were so rough with her that they had bruised her. Before he could remove her thin, nearly transparent chemise that revealed her glorious breasts, the curve of her hips, and the dark curls between her shapely legs, she tugged again at his tunic.

He smiled and yanked it over his head, and then unfastened his belt and plaid. Sitting on the bed, he leaned down to remove his boots, but she knelt before him and removed them instead.

He ran his hand over her hair and again wished he could make love to her this eve, but he was just glad he could sleep with her in a bed and hold her in his arms the night through.

He rose then, and pulled her from where she was crouching before him. He helped her out of her chemise, and then sat her on the bed so he could remove her shoes. She took him in with her hot-blooded gaze, his body reacting accordingly. She smiled when she saw his staff growing.

"You do that to me." He encouraged her to climb into bed. He blew out the candles and joined her on the mattress and pulled the furs over them. "Often, lass. When it isna always a good thing."

"Nay?"

"Nay, no' when I am about ready to ride a horse, walk, or any number of other things."

She laughed and ran her hand over his chest as he slid his hand down her side. "Come, move against me. We must sleep."

She sighed and nestled against him, and he thought he could not have been more pleased, except if he could have made love to her.

"We can, if you wish it," she said softly against his chest, as if she knew his private thoughts.

"Nay, you must rest and we must ride for far too long on the morrow. When we are home, I will ravage you every chance I get."

She smiled against his chest. "I will insist you keep your promise."

He chuckled. "Of that, you can be assured."

CHAPTER 15

The next morn, they broke their fast and found their horses already saddled, provisions packed, and everyone ready to ride. Despite being half to fully aroused last night due to Isobel's soft, naked body pressed against his, Marcus was glad they had waited to make love because of the long ride ahead of them, and he wanted Isobel to always cherish their lovemaking.

He'd privately remarked to Tibold about the bruises on her arms and how violent the men had been with her when they had tried to remove her from the chamber. Tibold assured him he'd mete out the punishment. As to the maid who had led John Pembroke's men into the guest chamber, Tibold had not banished her from the clan, but had counseled her firmly, and she was given extra work to perform, to Isobel's relief.

With well wishes from Edana, Tibold, and several others on the staff—while John and his men had been noticeably absent at the meal—Marcus and Isobel and their party were off with an additional half a dozen Chattan clansmen to protect them.

Angus moved up alongside Marcus. "Tibold confined them in the dungeon for the night because of the fights between his men and John's last eve. Tibold figured a stay there would impress upon the earl to keep his men in line. They willna be released from there until later this morn, and not from the grounds until Tibold is certain we have time to arrive safely at Lochaven."

"Good, because if I see him while we are on our way, I will likely kill him," Marcus said. "And I would rather not if I can help it."

The first day of their journey, they met with no difficulties as gray clouds filled the sky and a chilly, stiff breeze continued to blow as they made their way across streams and glens, through forests, and managed to cross one river. But the second day, the rains started again and visibility was obscured. They paused at the edge of a stream flowing over rocks from the mountains in the distance and gave their horses a rest.

"How are you holding up, lass?" Marcus asked, helping Isobel down from her horse. She was stiff and quiet, keeping her brat secured over her head to shelter her from the pouring rain.

She smiled brightly at him, albeit he could see she was tired and the way she moved and grimaced she was sore from the long ride, but he loved the way she could make him feel warm all the way to the marrow of his bones just with that one bright smile.

"I am going home with you," she said, "and that makes me feel as good as when we made love last eve."

He grinned and pulled her into a warm embrace. "We will be getting in verra late this eve if you can manage."

"Aye. I can."

Still, he worried about her. She was a lady, raised in an English household, and he was certain that traveling for days like this was not something she had oft experienced, if ever. He admired her for her drive to continue on. But he didn't want her growing ill.

"We will see. If the journey takes us too long, we will stop and—"

Her brows rose as if she would challenge him if he mentioned her condition and he continued, "Rest the horses. We dinna want to push them too hard and overtire them. Especially with the weather such as it is."

"Aye, true." She looked like she stubbornly resisted the idea that *she* would be overly tired and hold them up.

Though Marcus truly wished to get her to his castle where she would be better protected.

By gloaming, they still had about two hours to ride and that was entirely too much time left for either the horses or Isobel to travel.

"We will stop," Marcus said to Isobel and the men after putting in seven hours of traveling already.

"Aye," Angus said. "My horse is tired. I fathom he

would collapse if we tried to make the rest of the journey."

"Mine as well," Gunnolf said.

"We will rest a few hours and then head out again," Marcus said.

Isobel shook her head as Marcus helped her down. She was certain that the men's concern was not all about their horses.

The rains had stopped, but a dense fog had settled over the area. And she surveyed the boulders surrounding them, recognizing the crannog as a form of defensive enclosure on a peninsula surrounded on three sides by the loch. Both Marcus's cousins, Rob and Finbar, had ridden well ahead of them, and then returned shaking their heads as they set up their bedding in the crannog, the southeast portion enclosed by an arc of boulders standing six feet tall, with irregularly spaced gaps to use arrows in defense. The space was forty square feet, the ground level and two feet above the surrounding area with the loch behind them.

It appeared that both ancient peoples and more modern ones after that, most likely Marcus and his clan, had worked to fortify it. It was a better defense than nothing, and it meant they were getting closer to his keep. She noted the saddle quern and the cylindrical hand stone used to grind grain and the hearth that had been used for cooking and heat. She realized some of Marcus's clansmen must stay here for days at a time.

The Chattan brothers had been trailing way behind and had spread out. Now they all came into view, and again, they were shaking their heads, confirming they had not seen any trouble behind them.

She was glad to see the brothers rejoin them and fill out their defensive numbers again, but the fact that they were ensuring no one was following them, or ahead of them, made her believe Marcus had some concern.

"Do you suspect Tibold would have let John and his men go and they are following us?" Isobel asked Marcus.

"Nay, lass. My uncle is good at his word," Marcus said.

"Aye," Kayne said. "Da wouldna let the swine— beg your forgiveness for saying so, Lady Isobel—but he wouldna let the men leave until he was certain we arrived. Mayhap two days from now. He would give us more time than necessary in the event we ran into difficulties."

She realized that John was not truly any relation to her. Not a cousin at all, since he was Lord Pembroke's nephew and she was no longer Lord Pembroke's daughter.

So who were they concerned about? The villain who had paid men to attack her escort? Would he send men this far northwest into the Highlands?

Then she wondered if the concern was about her real father. Though she hated to imagine him as such, just as he had not claimed her either.

"You are concerned that someone else could be following us or lying in wait ahead?" She wanted to know the truth.

"Aye." Marcus offered her bread and porridge. "Laren MacLauchlan's men. I doubt he would lead them. But he wouldn't hesitate to send his men to bring you back, if that is the case. Instead of trying to locate us, he could verra well have come here instead, waiting for our return. Except we have more numbers than he would suspect if he believed we were still traveling with the same amount of men as when we stopped off at the Kerr's hunting lodge."

She was glad they had more numbers than before, but unsettled with the notion that Marcus and the others would have to fight any men, particularly when they had no claim to her.

After they ate, the Chattan brothers took first watch as everyone else settled down to sleep for a few hours.

"We will leave at the first hint of light in the sky." Marcus wrapped Isobel in his arms, a spare plaid securely around them. "It willna be much longer after that."

"Will your clansmen accept me?" Isobel asked quite sincerely. She still worried that they would either see her as being from the enemy clan, or they would see her as a Sassenach.

"They will adore you." Marcus kissed her forehead and snuggled closer to her. "You know how my cousins are."

"Aye, but they are used to me. They have known me since we were young. But…"

Marcus sighed. "Sometimes I have been a tyrant when I have returned from seeing you and knowing I was unable to have you for my wife. My people will be more than happy to learn 'tis now so."

She smiled a little at his saying so. "But I am…"

"My beloved wife, lass. That is all that anyone cares about. They will love you as much as I do. Have I told you that you worry overmuch?"

She smiled and snuggled closer to him, loving his warmth and strength. "Once," she said, "mayhap."

He chuckled for he had told her numerous times that she did.

"When we reach the keep—"

"I will have a bath prepared for the both of us, then we will meet in the kirk to be wed."

She suddenly felt sad with the notion. She'd always wanted her father to take part, and she wanted Mary there to share the experience with her, and someday hold her bairns. She could not imagine Mary not being there.

When she didn't say anything, Marcus said, "You wish Mary to witness the celebration."

She loved how sensitive he could be where her feelings were concerned.

"Aye. 'Tis not that I wish to delay a kirk wedding, but I only wish Mary to be there with me as she is like my second mother."

"I understand. As long as you dinna mind that we continue to be with one another as a married couple until we can bring her here."

She kissed his mouth. "Thank you, Marcus. I love you."

"I would do anything for you, lass. You only have but to ask. Sleep now, and we will leave soon."

"I am…ready for more," she whispered.

He laughed. "'Tis good to know. I have been ready forever."

She smiled, loving that he felt that way. Someday, maybe, she would share how much she'd thought of him when she was alone in her bedchamber at night.

They slept for a short while and she thought they would sleep longer, or that the dawning daylight would wake her as she was not used to sleeping outside of a keep when she heard shouts off in the distance.

Marcus quickly pulled away from her, the spare plaid they used as a blanket instantly cast aside, and she was chilled at once. He jumped to his feet. In the dark, she heard him unsheathe his sword. Her heart pounding, she quickly sat up now, but was unsure as to what to do. She didn't want to get in the way of the men, who did know what to do, but she remained quiet, as did everyone around her. The only sounds were that of the men quickly rising to their feet and unsheathing their swords.

It was a chilling sound and most likely meant it

could only lead to fighting and killing. She involuntarily shivered.

No one could see anyone in the dark, but suddenly, Marcus was crouching next to her, his hand touching her shoulder as he tried to locate her, and she jumped a little. He whispered, "Stay inside of the fortification, with your back up against the wall, lass. There are no openings against this wall, which is why we slept here."

"Aye," she whispered. "Is there naught I can do?"

"Nay, just stay out of harm's way, lass." Then he kissed her lips and he stood again, his leg against her hip.

She knew then he planned to stay close at hand. She was glad for it as she unsheathed her *sgian dubh*, and then leaned her back against the boulder, ready to stand if she thought she could help. She shivered from the cold and the worry, her heart thundering in her ears.

Horses galloped toward them and she was dying to stand and peek through the openings in the boulders to see who was riding, with the sun just beginning its ascent, a lightening of the sky occurring, and the faint orange glow just appearing.

She wanted to ask if the riders were their men or the enemy's, but she kept quiet like the men did, not wanting to disturb their warrior concentration. Because of the dark and the distance from the riders to the crannog, Marcus and the others probably couldn't make out who the men were anyway.

She thought the horses would have had enough rest

and wished they could ride the remaining miles to Lochaven to avoid a battle, but she knew that the number of miles they had to still travel would be far too great to outride men determined to fight her escort.

The horses were nearly to the crannog and she could now see the men and the horses inside the crannog, swords in hand, tense, ready. Two men had arrows and bows readied as they peered through the slots between the boulders.

"'Tis Gildas," Rob said quietly.

"And Kayne," Finbar said.

The men galloped onto the peninsula and soon entered the crannog. They dismounted and Rob took their reins and led the horses to the other side of the barrier to stay with the others.

"What happened?" Marcus asked, his voice hushed.

"We were attacked. Halwn and the rest of our brothers are coming," Kayne said, then drank some ale.

"We killed a couple of their men," Gildas said, "but there were too many of them."

"How many?" Marcus asked.

"We counted fifteen torches among them. Mayhap more. We targeted two of the men closest to us as they had seen us and we had no choice. We hoped to kill them without alerting the others, but that didna happen. Then we left in a hurry as their men gathered to fight us," Kayne said.

Isobel was now standing, shaken, again wanting to leave this place before they were surrounded.

"Go, Rob, get reinforcements," Marcus said.

Rob immediately mounted his horse and took off.

But it would take two hours or so for him to reach the castle and another two to return with more men.

"We stay here as there isna any way that we could reach the keep before we are engaged in combat," Marcus said.

"Was it MacLauchlan's men?" Isobel asked.

"We couldna tell, lass," Kayne said. "All we know is that they were looking for you, and we overheard their plans to stop us before we reached the safety of the castle. They have been here for some time, and waiting on us, though they were no' sure which path we would take. Then one of their scouts had seen our tracks in the mud and informed them as to our increased number. Though they were no' for sure if the riders included you and Marcus or if they were more of his kin scouting the area for trouble."

"I would send you off with a couple of my men, if I thought you could travel to the keep without running into trouble," Marcus said, "but I fear it would be too much of a risk."

She agreed and was glad that at least the Chattan brothers were all accounted for.

"They could barrage us with arrows, but they would chance hitting Lady Isobel," Angus said.

"They have only the one way in, and the peninsula can only take a couple of horses at a time so they willna be able to reach us en masse," Marcus said. "We will have to wait for reinforcements. They may think to cut us off and not have that ability."

The sun was rising, though a thick gray mist cloaked the area still, and Isobel was glad for that because the men coming for her wouldn't be able to clearly see them any more than they could see the brigands. She was relieved that this location seemed to be defendable by the small force.

"Rest," Marcus said to the brothers, but they looked like they were ready for a fight and resting wasn't in the plans. "You have been on guard duty. Rest. If the fighting begins, you need to be well-rested."

Gildas, the oldest of the brothers here, said, "Aye. Grab your plaids, brothers. Marcus is right."

Drummond, the youngest, grunted. Of all the brothers, he was the hothead and the first ready for a battle.

When the brothers settled down, the others made their horses lie down so the aggressors could not see how many they numbered. And then everyone remained quiet. Four of the men readied bows and arrows at the gaps between the stones or at the entrance to the crannog.

Everyone else took seats and watched out the openings for any sign of movement. Isobel wanted to watch also, but Marcus wanted her away from any of the openings for her own protection. She still wanted to watch, to do something, should she see some sign of the men and help to alert the others if nothing else.

He sat down with her on the grassy floor and took her in his arms. She wasn't sure what he was intending to do until he whispered, "Sleep, lass, so that when we have a chance, we can leave here and continue on our way."

He acted as though there would be no fight and that everything was calm.

"You didna have enough sleep," he said. "I hadna intended for us to wake that early."

Realizing she could do nothing else, she curled up against Marcus's body. He wrapped the spare plaid around them and he closed his eyes.

She noted some of the men casting glances their way, smiling a little. She suspected if they could have been where Marcus was, they would have traded places in a heartbeat.

"Marcus?" she whispered.

"Aye, lass."

"I do not want to go with those men."

"Aye, and you willna."

"But if it means no blood would be shed..."

He shook his head. "I wouldna give you up to keep the peace. What kind of a husband would that make me?"

"I was just thinking that if it would make any difference at all..."

"Nay."

She sighed and for a short while she slept until she felt Marcus tense beneath her, and she heard the sound of horses moving toward them. Her skin freckled with goose bumps. She wished there was some reasonable way out of this.

"Five men are moving out of the fog," Finbar whispered.

"Should we shoot them?" Angus said.

Niall ground his teeth. "I would be done with them, reduce the numbers we have to fight."

"Nay," Marcus said, watching the men. "They have to know they are a target. Let them have their say."

The men stopped far enough away that they were not a threat unless they were armed with bows and arrows.

"Marcus McEwan, hand over the lass, known as Lady Isobel, and we will leave in peace," one of the men said, his hair and beard black.

At once, Marcus recognized the man's voice. "Tearloch, Laren's right hand man. If Laren sent him to fetch the lass, he means business."

"*Now* do we shoot them full of arrows?" Niall asked.

Marcus smiled at Niall, then shouted out to Tearloch, "The lass prefers to stay with her husband. You have come on a fool's errand, Tearloch. Tell Laren that he has no claim to Isobel."

"Since he is her da, he begs to differ with you. 'Twas a travesty that Pembroke claimed her as his own. Now that he is dead, 'tis time to rectify that."

To Marcus's surprise and concern, Isobel joined

him at the entryway to the stone structure. He quickly took a protective stance at her side, hoping she didn't intend to offer herself up to Laren's men in an attempt to protect him and the rest of their escort. One of the men serving as archers, moved to protect her also.

"How can he claim me now when he never did before?" Isobel called out to Tearloch, her tone angry. "My father was and will always be the one who raised me, loved me, and provided for me. I know not who your laird is, nor do I care to. I am wed to Laird Marcus McEwan. So as Marcus has said, you have been sent on a fool's—"

An arrow shot out of the fog toward the opening of the stone enclosure, and Marcus scooped Isobel up in his arms and dove for cover as everyone else ducked behind the boulders. Retaliating, the archers in Marcus's party shot arrows at the quickly retreating Tearloch and his men. Two went down after their horses reached the mainland and the wounded men landed in the grasses. Tearloch and the other three managed to escape.

"The archer was aiming for you," Angus said to Marcus.

"Good thing he is a lousy shot," Marcus said.

"He cannot believe that if they killed you, I would go willingly with the men, can they?" she asked with such incredulity, Marcus had to smile.

"Nay, lass." He frowned then. "They know I lead the party here and if they were able to eliminate me, mayhap the rest would feel leaderless."

Angus and Gunnolf snorted.

"Aye, my feelings also," Marcus said. "Any of the men here would see to your safety. But to Tearloch and his men's way of thinking, it would be one less man that they would have to deal with. They dinna know how many strong we are. Until more of my men can arrive, we will just have to wait them out. They may think of attacking at nightfall, which would be my tactic, but my men will arrive well before that."

"I hate the waiting. I wish we could do something," Isobel said.

"Aye, I agree," Marcus said, sitting beside her again and taking her in his arms to keep her warm. "Sometimes the waiting is worse than the fighting."

Isobel was already chilled again and trembled either from the cold or from the fright of what had just occurred. Thankfully, the stones in the form of walls provided protection from the most chilling winds. But the air around them was still cold.

"What was this building used for?" she asked.

"A place to weather a storm, a semi-defensive structure. At one time it had a thatched roof, but a gale tore it off and no one has had the time or need to replace it. Though if we had a roof like that now, archers could burn us out and that wouldna bode well."

"Aye. You…you dinna mind if we wait until Mary joins us before we have a wedding, do you?"

"Nay, lass. Whatever you wish."

"I wish Tearloch and his men to go away."

"As do I."

"More riders are approaching from the southeast," Angus warned.

"What the devil are they doing?" Marcus said, leaving Isobel and peering between the boulders.

"I canna see who they are as the fog hides them from us. More of Laren's men, mayhap?" Gunnolf said.

"I would think he would have had them with him all this time," Marcus said.

Then the sound of fighting began in the fog.

Everyone inside the enclosure was tense, waiting for an order.

"We come in peace!" a man shouted.

"Lord Wynfield!" Isobel cried out.

Marcus glanced at her.

"He must have come with an escort of men to see if I had been brought here. He has not fought since he was a young man. Tearloch and his men will kill them," Isobel said with tears in his eyes.

Marcus had thought it was Wynfield, but seeing the stricken look on Isobel's face, he knew it was for sure.

"I will take a dozen men with me. The rest stay here and protect Isobel."

"There are at least thirteen of their men out there," Angus warned. "I will go with you."

"And me," Gildas said.

"And however many men Wynfield has." Marcus hoped they were fighting men.

"I will go," Niall said, and Gunnolf was already

getting their horses to stand.

Halwn and Kayne also volunteered, though Drummond wished to go as well.

"Nay, I wish Isobel well protected. That leaves the three of you brothers, two more of your men, and Finbar."

"Aye," they said, acknowledging that their job was just as important.

Marcus mounted his horse and led the party toward the sound of shouting and he and the others rode half a mile into the fog before they could see the men who were fighting. Lord Wynfield had eight or nine men with him, it appeared and he was holding his own.

Marcus rode up to dispatch the man who was fighting him and wheeled around to fight a new attacker. Marcus still had not seen Tearloch, but as soon as he was able, he would fight the man. Marcus was certain that if he killed Tearloch, his men would indeed feel leaderless and scurry home to their laird.

"These are not your men?" Wynfield called out, sounding winded and surprised.

"Nay. They claim kinship to Isobel and want to take her with them. But I have married the lass and she isna going anywhere." Marcus swung his sword at a MacLauchlan clansman, connecting steel against steel in a loud clang.

"Her father would have to approve." Wynfield took another swing at one of MacLauchlan's men.

Marcus struck at the man fighting him and dealt

him a killing blow. The villain fell from his horse and the animal ran off. He turned to fight the man Wynfield was struggling to defeat and saw that the baron had been cut across his leg. Marcus again rode to his aid.

"Go, Wynfield. Directly west, cross the peninsula to the crannog. Isobel is there. She will care for your wounds."

"You need me..."

"Nay. You can protect her there."

Marcus killed the man who had been fighting Wynfield, and the baron said, "Her father lives."

He rode off in the direction Marcus told him to ride and Marcus stared at him in disbelief.

CHAPTER 16

His thoughts in turmoil as he considered Lord Wynfield's words, Marcus watched the baron ride off. He couldn't believe Lord Pembroke was truly alive. Had Wynfield lied about the earl? That Isobel's father, or at least the one who had raised her, had not died?

Marcus had to concentrate on the fighting at hand. He hoped that he, his men, and Wynfield's killed Tearloch and enough of his people that the rest would realize they were defeated and return home. If Lord Pembroke was truly alive, it wouldn't make any difference to Marcus. He had rescued Isobel and married her in good faith, believing Pembroke's nephew would take over the earldom and John had no need to decide matters for her. Marcus and Isobel had done what they had wanted to all along, and he wouldn't give her up for any reason or anyone.

Lord Wynfield shouted off to the east in the

direction of the crannog, "'Tis me! Lord Byron Wynfield. Marcus sent me here to help protect Lady Isobel."

Marcus prayed no one would kill Lord Wynfield by accident, and that the baron would recover from his injuries. Which made Marcus wonder again what had truly become of Lord Pembroke. Had the baron hoped to still wed the lass and used that as a ploy to return her home?

"Nay!" Isobel shouted, her voice frantic with fright.

"God's wounds," Marcus swore, fearing for Isobel's safety, and broke off the fight with another man he had engaged. He turned his horse around and galloped back to the stone enclosure. The man he'd been fighting and another raced after him.

When he reached the peninsula, he saw Tearloch on foot, his sword at Wynfield's throat, the two of them facing the crannog, both men's horses nearby.

Marcus cursed again and rode toward Tearloch as Finbar held Isobel tight in his grasp, not letting her leave the enclosure. Her face was red and frustrated, her eyes narrowed as if she would kill Tearloch herself for threatening Wynfield.

"Tearloch!" Marcus shouted, "Let the old mon go and fight me! A Highlander. Not someone who hasna held a sword in his hand for a good ten years."

"Send Isobel out to me and I will let the Sassenach go," Tearloch snarled.

Two of the Chattan clansmen were ready to release

arrows, but they didn't and Marcus knew they were afraid to hit the baron.

As soon as Marcus was near enough to Tearloch to engage in combat, two men came out of the fog to fight Marcus. The archers targeted them instead and the three brothers charged out of the enclosure to help Marcus fight the new arrivals, leaving only three behind with Isobel—the two archers, and Finbar who was still holding her tight, not allowing her to go to the baron's aid.

All at once, it seemed the battle had come to Marcus, though he still could hear fighting in the distance, so he knew it was not so. Five more men appeared and began to fight with him and the others while Tearloch finally shoved Wynfield into the loch, turned, and attacked Marcus.

Wearing heavy chainmail, the baron struggled to keep afloat, sputtering and flailing his arms, unable to make it to shore and would surely drown.

"Let me go!" Isobel said to Finbar. "Lord Wynfield will drown."

"Stay," Finbar ordered, and then he ran out of the enclosure to reach the baron.

Marcus prayed Isobel would stay put as Tearloch attempted to injure Marcus's horse. Marcus jumped down from his saddle and engaged Tearloch face to face. The Highlander had a strong swing and he was fast. But Marcus struck just as hard and quickly as his opponent, one gaining ground and then the other.

Finbar was still struggling to pull Wynfield out of the water when Gunnolf slayed his opponent and sprinted to help him, knowing one man would never be able to save the baron from drowning in the lake, wearing the heavy mail.

Isobel screamed, and Marcus turned his attention for a slip of a moment toward the enclosure. Tearloch slashed at Marcus's belly and he only just managed to block the blow that could have killed him.

Still, he had to reach Isobel and protect her.

Two of Chattan's men were still in the enclosure with Isobel, he thought. Then the sound of swords clanking inside the walls made Marcus's blood run cold. He slashed again at Tearloch, but he dodged the slice of Marcus's sword.

Then she screamed again, and Marcus thrust his sword at Tearloch, then fell back, trying to get closer to the enclosure. Tearloch lunged forward and Marcus jumped back, stumbling over a dead body and went down.

***

To Isobel's horror, dripping wet and armed for a fight, four MacLauchlan clansmen climbed over the barrier from the back side. The two guards left behind to protect her rushed to fight them. Three of the MacLauchlan men quickly engaged them.

The fourth MacLauchlan clansman forced her into a corner so that she would not get in the way of the fighting or help the guards. His blond-bearded face stern, his blue eyes narrowed, he held her at bay with his sword. Angered and frustrated, she could do nothing to help the other men. Should they kill the other men, she couldn't fight four men with just a *sgian dubh* when they were armed with much longer swords. With her heart thundering and her skin chilled, she watched the man keeping her pinned against the wall, hoping for an opening where she could attack him and get away. To her alarm, she saw both of her guards collapse in bloody heaps before the remaining MacLauchlan men turned to face her, their chests heaving and their bearded faces flushed with exertion.

At least her back was pressed against the wall, and they couldn't reach her without her slicing at them. Everything happened so fast after that, it was almost a blur.

The blond-bearded man risked getting close to her and grabbed her left arm and yanked her away from the wall, exposing her back. She slashed at his arm, slicing it. He cursed, released her, and fell back. The other men moved in so quickly, that though she swung around to cut another, one maneuvered behind and seized her by the waist. Another captured her right wrist, twisted hard, forcing her to loosen her grip on her weapon, making her cry out in pain. Before she dropped her weapon, he yanked it out of her hand and tossed it to the earth. Two of the men fought with her to shove her over the rock wall, away from the entrance, and away from the battling men. Isobel screamed to alert Marcus or anyone she was in trouble.

They intended to steal her away while everyone else was fighting. Neither she nor the men protecting her had heard them coming.

No matter how much she struggled against the brigands, she could not break free to grab the blade. Nor could she stop them from hoisting her over the wall. She landed hard on her knees, smacking the rocks strewn there. Her pursuers heaved themselves over the wall and onto the other side, landing beside her, just as she gained her footing and ran to the other end of the peninsula. She nearly reached the loch and intended to jump into the water and swim away.

She was a good swimmer, though wearing a brat, *léine*, chemise, and shoes would weigh her down in the frigid water. Not to mention the cold could quickly affect her, but she couldn't let these men spirit her away.

She ran into the loch, but her gowns dragged at the water. She dove in and shivered as the cold water closed around her.

"Grab the woman," one of the men said.

Splashes behind her assured her that she was not swimming as fast as she needed to. Not with the way her garments were weighing her down the wetter they got. Then someone grabbed the edge of her brat, and it tightened around her throat, forcing her to stop swimming. Her fingers stiff from the cold, she fumbled with the brooch to unfasten it, but she couldn't manage it and stay afloat, too.

The four men suddenly surrounded her, grabbing at her arms, forcing her to go with them to reach a closer shore. She then saw their horses tied up to trees near there.

If they managed to get her to shore and onto one of their horses, they could ride off with her and rendezvous with the others, leaving Marcus, his cousins, and kin behind before they even realized she was gone.

She cried out, "Marcus!"

She hoped that he would realize she was in the loch and no longer in the enclosure. That she needed his help or his men's if anyone could even hear her voice.

She scuffled with them, trying to hit them with her fists, attempting to kick them. But she was having a time keeping her face above water, choking on it, gasping for breath. They kicked and swam and attempted to get her to the shore as quickly as they could. Every stroke brought her closer to their horses, and every stroke made her panic more. Kicking and trying to yank her arms free did nothing but make them angrier as they tightened their grips on her arms and dunked her to half drown her and make her behave.

"Once we reach the shore, knock her out," one of the men said.

If they knocked her out, she'd never be able to escape, she feared, as she coughed, and tried to catch her breath, but she didn't stop fighting them, praying she'd still manage to get free.

***

Sweat pouring off his face red with exertion, Tearloch nearly smiled with dark intent as he thrust his sword at Marcus, who was scrambling to get off the body of one of MacLauchlan's men and ready his sword.

Tearloch stabbed at Marcus's chest, but he managed to roll to the left and gain his feet. He was about to thrust at Tearloch, when they both heard Isobel cry out from the direction of the loch. The whoreson broke off the engagement with Marcus and ran off.

Marcus's heart beat even harder at hearing Isobel's cry of distress from the location of the loch. He sprinted to where his horse had taken refuge in the enclosure, remounted him, and raced him back to the mainland. Four MacLauchlan men were in the lake, trying to swim to shore with his wife, who was fighting them as much as she was able.

He galloped around the loch to reach them. The men were still a long ways from the shore, attempting to swim with a reluctant hostage. He cursed again under his breath, seeing red he was so angered.

Before Marcus reached the men and Isobel, someone rode after him. Hoping it was one of his own kin, he turned, only to see Tearloch on horseback, getting ready to swing his sword. God's knees! Marcus needed to rescue his wife!

Turning his horse, Marcus swung his sword with

such force, Tearloch nearly lost his weapon. Marcus thrust for the kill, but Tearloch jerked his horse to the side to avoid the impact.

The blade sliced across Tearloch's side and stained his brown tunic red. He cursed bloody murder and turned his horse again to strike at Marcus.

For the tromping footfalls of their horses, the clashing of swords, the sound of fighting in the distance, of men yelling and crying out, of swords clanking and horses neighing, Marcus couldn't hear what was going on behind him.

Isobel was too quiet and he feared someone had knocked her out to make her compliant. He was ready to kill the bloody bastard. But he was trying to concentrate fully on the menace before him and hoped he could run him through before the men reached the shore with Isobel.

Where were Marcus's men?

When he heard the sound of men splashing on the rocky shore, grunting, trying to make it to their horses, Marcus wanted to swing around and kill them all now. But he couldn't turn his back on Tearloch.

"Angus! Finbar!" Marcus called out. If any one of his men or his kin could hear his voice he would know Marcus was in dire need of help or he would not ask them to come to his aid when he knew they had to be in the thick of battle themselves.

Instead of any of his men, three of Pembroke's knights came into view, surprising Marcus. He hoped that if they slew Laren's men, that Pembroke's knights didn't try to take off with Isobel next.

"We have got her," Sir Travon said, galloping past him.

Marcus recognized the two other knights who had forced him to leave the dance held in Isobel's honor before he was bushwhacked. That realization didn't make him feel any less uneasy as he slashed again at Tearloch.

No matter how hard he swung or thrust at the villain, Marcus couldn't break free from his battle with Tearloch, both of them wearying.

"You ken I killed your da, eh?" Tearloch taunted, his face a mask of fury, as he readied to take another swing.

His blood burning with anger, Marcus blocked Tearloch's swing with a mighty clang. He hadn't known. No one had. Not only would he kill the whoreson for attempting to take Isobel, Marcus was glad to avenge his da's murder!

"And that sweet lassie will be beneath me before long. Mark my—"

Marcus thrust his sword into Tearloch's chest, saw the look of wide-eyed surprise, right before the man sputtered and tilted on his horse.

Marcus yanked out his sword and watched the bloody bastard fall to the ground, not stirring, his eyes wide in death, leaving his men to their fates.

Marcus turned his horse to join the knights and

fight the MacLauchlan clansmen who had stolen Isobel from the crannog. But Laren's men were done in by the swim in the cold loch and the fighting before this. One of the men held a sodden Isobel over his shoulder like a sack of wet grain. She wasn't stirring. And Marcus was furious with the bastard as he leapt from his horse and stalked toward the man.

Three of the soaking wet Highlanders dropped their weapons and sank to their knees. Isobel's captor waited for someone to take her from him, wisely not releasing her like they had their weapons.

One of Pembroke's knights gathered the men's weapons while another directed them to sit on the ground.

Sick with worry over Isobel, Marcus took her from the man, cradling her in his arms, holding her tight to warm her chilled, wet body. "Isobel, lass, can you hear me?"

She didn't respond, but her skin was pale pink, not blue and she was breathing, her breath warm against his chest, which were all good signs. Marcus had to get her into the enclosure right away where a fire was burning at the hearth, the smoke curling above the boulders. "Can you hold these men here, Sir Travon?"

"Aye, what of Lord Wynfield?" Sir Travon asked.

"Injured. We will take him to Lochaven as soon as my reinforcements get here." Marcus glowered at the MacLauchlan men. "What did you do to her?"

"Naught," a black-haired man growled. "She just

got quiet all of a sudden."

Marcus would ask Isobel as soon as he could revive her. "If I hear it wasna true, I will be asking you again how she came to be this way."

Then he strode off for his horse. Sir Travon ran after him. "Let me help you with the lady."

"Is it true that Lord Pembroke lives?"

"Aye." Sir Travon took Isobel from him so that Marcus could mount his horse, and then Travon lifted her up to him. "We only just learned a farmer had found Lord Pembroke and the two knights badly injured. One died. The other and Lord Pembroke lived. His lordship did not want anyone to learn of what had happened to him until he was well enough to travel."

Marcus frowned at the knight. "Lord Pembroke feared someone in his own ranks had attacked him?"

"I should not speak of it. Lord Wynfield will if he can."

"Aye. See to these men and we will have to learn what has happened to the rest of our men and theirs."

"Aye, you have but to tell us what you need us to do." Sir Travon bowed his head to Marcus.

Marcus was surprised to see the knight pledge his loyalty to him.

"Aye, thank you."

"Just…just take care of the lass."

"Aye, that I will do." Holding Isobel as close to his body as he could, Marcus rode back to the crannog and found Finbar caring for Lord Wynfield, the baron's chainmail and some of his clothes removed.

Finbar had stoked the fire and was trying to warm the man with dry wool brats and offering him ale.

"Lady Isobel." Finbar's face was a mask of alarm as he quickly rose from his crouched position, and took Isobel from Marcus.

Once Marcus dismounted, Finbar handed her over to him. Anxious about her well-being, Marcus rested her on the ground and began removing her wet clothes.

"She is…?"

"Alive." Marcus fumbled with her damnable brooch, his hands shaking from worry.

"I will get more wool blankets." Finbar rummaged around the leather bags and other spare blankets left behind.

Marcus thought he saw her stir. "Isobel."

She groaned a little, her eyes fluttering open, then widening as she saw Marcus on his knees beside her, rubbing her hands with his, trying to warm them. "Marcus."

"Aye, lass."

She closed her eyes.

"Nay, stay with me until I can get you warmed up. What happened?"

She seemed too tired to speak, and instead he began removing her shoes and hosen. Finbar handed him several dry blankets.

To Finbar, Marcus said, "We need to know the status of our men and Lord Pembroke's."

"Aye. Do you wish me to look into it?"

"Nay. When the men return here who are injured, you will be responsible for them. Just have someone else take care of it."

"Aye."

"What happened to the Chattan men who were guarding her?"

"Dead. I removed their bodies."

Marcus nodded, hating to learn of it. One of the hardest things a clan chief had to do was give the fallen clansman's family the news of his death. No matter the number of years a chief led his clan, the solemn task never got any easier.

"I will return." Finbar left the enclosure.

"Isobel." Marcus finally managed to unfasten her brooch and let her brat fall away from her shoulders. Then he pulled off her soaking wet *léine*.

"Nay." Isobel pushed his hands away.

Taking a deep breath, he was gladdened to see her react to his efforts and not lie there still as death.

"Aye, lass. Your clothes are sodden." He pulled her clinging wet chemise off, and then dried her and wrapped her in a blanket, sat down, and held her in his lap, close to his body to share his heat. She was shivering so hard, he worried she had grown too chilled this time. "How are you faring, baron?" he asked Wynfield.

"I will live." The baron's voice weary, his eyes half-lidded.

"Isobel, Lord Wynfield has brought us news. Your da is alive."

Isobel looked up at Marcus, her eyes widening. She was so pale still from the cold, he didn't think her face could lose any more color. He held her tighter. She parted her lips, but the words would not come out, and her beautiful blue eyes filled with tears.

"Aye, lass, 'tis true. He lives."

"Oh, God, Marcus..." She buried her face against his chest and soaked his tunic with her tears.

"'Tis good news, is it no'?"

She nodded, brushing her wet cheek against his chest. "'Tis really true?"

"Aye, lass." Marcus kissed the top of her wet head.

She was quiet for a long time, most likely processing the information, like he was.

"Oh, Marcus, we have agreed to wed and--"

"We are wed," Marcus corrected her.

His face as pale as Isobel's, Lord Wynfield shook his head as if he couldn't believe what he was hearing.

"He is truly alive?" Isobel asked Wynfield, freeing an arm from the cocoon of a blanket and brushing away the tears. She quickly tucked her arm back inside the blanket.

"Aye. We thought he was dead. No one knew the truth but the farmer and his wife caring for him and the knight who survived."

"Oh, thanks be to God that he is alive." But then she looked up at Marcus. "Oh, Marcus, what will he do? About you and me?"

Marcus wanted to reassure her that her da would be reasonable. At least he was hopeful he would be. Marcus wasn't giving her up, no matter what.

"Did you tell Lord Pembroke what happened to Lady Isobel and her escort, Lord Wynfield?"

"What little we knew to tell," Wynfield said. "That your man brought one of our knights back to the keep to have our physician see to him. That you and the rest of your men went in search of Isobel because she was not with her doomed escort. We fed your man and took care of his horse. He left after that. I sent men to discreetly follow him, knowing he would lead me to you and Isobel. Your man quickly lost Lord Pembroke's men and they returned to the castle. The next morn, we had word that Lord Pembroke and Sir Edward lived."

***

Isobel couldn't believe the news. She was so glad her father was alive, but she couldn't absorb the information no matter how much she tried as if her body was so numb with cold, her thoughts were also. She fought crying with joy for the welcome word all over again, but she feared what her father might still do once he learned she and Marcus had pledged themselves to each other.

"At first, he was angry that Marcus did not return you to the castle. I was sent in search of you, to locate you," Wynfield said, his voice strained, filled with pain.

She wished she could ease his discomfort, and

prayed he would get through this all right.

"We thought my father was dead, and that one of my suitors was responsible for everything that has befallen us. The attempt on Marcus's life. The murder of my father and his escort. The killing of my escort." Isobel hated that her words were so shaky because she could not stop shivering, despite the heat of Marcus's body as he tried to warm her. She loved how he did so, leading by sending other men to take care of matters, while he stayed with her, protective and endearing.

"I pray forgiveness, my lady, that I put you in such danger." Wynfield's eyes shimmered with tears.

She hated seeing him on the verge of tears when she couldn't recall a time when he'd ever revealed such an emotion to her before and it made her uncomfortable. "I forgive you, Lord Wynfield, but only because Marcus came to my rescue in time. Had he not…" She didn't bother to finish the statement. She was certain she would have been in the hands of a murderous knave. "Also, John intended to take Father's place. So there was no need for me to stay there any longer."

"His nephew John is the one who attacked Lord Pembroke and nearly killed him," Lord Wynfield said coldly.

Isobel's jaw dropped. "No," she whispered, thinking of her sullen cousin and the way he had always ignored her, until he thought to use her as a marriage pawn. How could he turn on her father like that when her father might very well have handed the earldom to John when it was time?

"It was said that my father knew his attacker, a Norman," she finally managed to choke out.

"Aye, his very own kin. John thought your father and his knights were both dead. John did not arrive until two days after I had sent you away from Torrent. Once we learned your father was alive, we realized John had been in the area the whole time, but was keeping out of sight so it would appear he had naught to do with your father's murder. When John finally arrived at Torrent, before we knew your father was alive, I told him that your escort had been murdered. John was furious that I had sent you away. He went after you, vowing to bring you home at once. He knew that Laird McEwan had to have found you and since Marcus did not return you home, we all assumed you were on your way to Lochaven with him."

Marcus cursed under his breath. "We must send word to Rondover Castle at once to let the chief know that John and his men need to be incarcerated until your men can return him to Lord Pembroke. Then he can handle the matter."

"He is at Rondover Castle?" Wynfield's eyes narrowed with hatred.

"Aye. My uncle is keeping him and his men there to allow us time to reach Lochaven. John wasna happy about me taking Isobel for my wife."

"What if John was the one who had my escort

attacked?" Isobel asked. "If he wanted to be the one who married me off for his own personal gain?"

"'Tis possible," Wynfield said.

"Would he have sent men after me to have me killed so much earlier?" Marcus asked, sounding skeptical.

"Nay, I do not think so." Isobel hated that they couldn't clear the whole matter up right away.

Gunnolf stalked into the enclosure. "One of your men, by the name of Dow, has been wounded. Two of Lord Pembroke's men are dead. Ten of MacLauchlan's are dead or wounded. Four more have been taken prisoner. The rest escaped."

"And Tearloch is dead. He said he killed my da," Marcus sounded so angry about it, and her heart went out to him.

Glad that Marcus had learned the truth of who had killed his father, she was shocked to hear that Laren's people had anything to do with it. Knowing that her real father had to have given the word to kill Marcus's father, she worried how he would feel that he had agreed to marry her when she was from the clan that had murdered his own father. She snuggled tighter against Marcus, remembering how he'd talked so fondly of him as the two would fish together in the loch and hunt in the woods. How he'd shared humorous stories of his youth, like the time he had gone off to hunt a rabbit and a wild boar had treed him, or how he met his beloved wife, Marcus's mother, at a feast that Isobel's own mother's clan had given.

His expression dark, Gunnolf nodded to Marcus. "Then 'tis good you avenged your da's death, *ja*? But I understand. Did you want MacLauchlan's wounded men brought here also?"

"Aye. Have the dead men buried. Lady Isobel's father lives. Let the others know that."

Gunnolf's eyes widened, then he looked at Isobel.

"My father will approve of our marriage and I hope that he will be well enough to travel here to attend our wedding," Isobel said, determinedly. She would have it no other way.

Wynfield shook his head. "He said if you and Laird McEwan had decided this because you believed him dead, then he would not stand in your way."

Still trembling with the cold, Isobel sagged against Marcus with profound relief. He tightened his arms around her and kissed the top of her head again. "'Tis what we always wanted, aye, lass? Your da's approval?"

She sniffled, fighting the tears again. She had always adored her father. She always would. She nodded against Marcus's chest. "But what about a successor?" Isobel asked Wynfield, saddened that John could not fill the position.

"Your father has sent word to John's younger brother."

Isobel knew even less about him, but she hoped that her people would keep a close eye on him and watch her father's back in case this cousin decided he wanted the earldom sooner.

"The only problem I now see is with MacLauchlan, should he pursue this business with saying you are his daughter," Marcus said.

"Who told MacLauchlan that?" Wynfield asked, sounding outraged.

"He somehow had word that Lord Pembroke had died and that is why he sent Tearloch and his men to seize the lady and take her with them. MacLauchlan had intended to marry her off to someone of his choosing. Though, Tearloch had been under the impression he would have wed her, if I hadna killed him."

"Laren is not her father," Wynfield said. "Who told him he was?"

Isobel stared at the baron in mute shock. Wynfield could not be trying to protect her from the truth still, could he be?

"Isobel's mother," Marcus said. "And if you must know, I dinna like that you are still trying to keep the secret from the lass when MacLauchlan is attempting to take her hostage. The lass had to know the truth!"

CHAPTER 17

Marcus didn't feel any remorse for telling Isobel the truth about her parentage. She had every right to know when MacLauchlan was trying to claim her as his own daughter. Wynfield had no cause to be angry with Marcus over it.

"My mother told me," Marcus said, "because Isobel's mother told her."

Wynfield shook his head and closed his eyes. "Lady Ciarda lost the bairn within a fortnight of reaching Torrent Castle. Three months later, she was with child again. This time with Isobel. Mary knows the truth. And several on the staff at that time still serve the earl and were witness to the events that occurred. Lord Pembroke was distraught when Lady Ciarda lost her first bairn, but he could not have been more pleased to have had a daughter from their union."

Isobel clung tighter to Marcus, still trembling from

the cold. "He *is* my father."

"Aye," Wynfield said. "No other."

"I am sorry, lass." Marcus felt sick knowing that he had told the lass wrong and upset her so. And yet, would he have gotten her to agree to marry him if he had not? Still, if he had known the truth, he would have attempted to convince her to marry him anyway, assuming John would have taken over her father's estates, and she would be free to wed whom she pleased.

He still couldn't believe the bastard had attempted to kill her da for the power it would have given him. If Marcus had only known sooner when they were still at Rondover Castle…

"What did Lord Pembroke say about me bringing Lady Isobel here instead of returning her home?" Marcus asked.

"He said had he been in your place and he was rescuing his beloved Ciarda, he would have done the same as you. I will admit he was furious with me for sending the lady away from Torrent Castle. To rectify my standing with his lordship, I came myself to give you the news and make amends. I did not expect to be in a battle with your people."

"They were no' my clansmen," Marcus said, irritated that anyone would think that.

"Aye, I know that now. But not when they first attacked. You do not know how confused I was to see you fighting them when I thought they were your own men. I had told them who I was, and that I was bringing word of Lord Pembroke's state of health. That made them attack all the more ferociously."

"Because they didna want you to aid us, nor for us to learn Lord Pembroke lived." Marcus rubbed Isobel's blanket-covered arm, trying to warm her.

"I cannot believe he is alive," Isobel murmured against Marcus's chest, her breath warm.

"Dinna fall asleep, lass," Marcus warned, wrapping her more tightly in his arms.

"I cannot get warm."

Finbar quickly scrounged for another blanket and covered her with it.

"Thank you. Bring the men here who tried to steal Isobel away," Marcus said.

"Aye, Marcus." Finbar hurried out to fetch them.

"Is my father very worried about me?" Isobel asked, her voice shaking with the cold.

"Aye," Wynfield said. "I was to make all haste to locate you and ensure you were safely with Laird McEwan."

"I am safe." She sighed deeply against Marcus's chest.

"Safer when we reach my castle." Marcus hated that she had to remain out here in the cold until more of his men arrived to escort them home.

Finbar returned with the men and two of Wynfield's knights who continued to guard them.

Laren's men quickly dropped to their knees, wet,

bedraggled, shivering, and anxious as they awaited Marcus's judgment.

"Did any of these men knock you out when they brought you to the shore of the loch?" Marcus asked Isobel.

"Nay. I think I succumbed to the cold."

"Then I will release the four of you men to return to your clan. Know this, Lady Isobel is the daughter of Lord William Pembroke and Lady Ciarda. The bairn Lady Ciarda had carried before, didna live. MacLauchlan has no claim to the lass. Lord Pembroke has agreed to my marriage to Isobel. If we see any of MacLauchlan's men on our lands again, it willna go well for them. Do you understand?"

"Lord Pembroke lives?" one of the men asked, his eyes wide.

"Aye. He, and no other mon, is Lady Isobel's father."

"Aye, my laird." All four men nodded, eager to leave with their hides intact.

"You willna have your weapons or horses. You have given them up as spoils of war."

"Our *sgian dubhs*?" the one man asked.

"Aye. But naught more."

"Aye, thank ye, laird."

"Go then and give your laird my message."

"Aye." The men quickly got to their feet and hurried past the knights.

"See that they dinna find swords or horses upon

their departure," Marcus said to Pembroke's knights.

They looked to Lord Wynfield, and he nodded. "Do as his lordship bids."

"Aye." They both bowed their heads a little to Wynfield, then hurried after Laren's men.

Isobel soaked up the heat from Marcus's body, trying to get warm, hating that she was wearing only a blanket wrapped around her and the others on top of her, yet she was still not wearing any clothes in front of the men who were coming and going and she felt...naked.

They'd brought the wounded men in and Finbar was taking care of them. She wished she could help him and them, but she felt frozen to the bone, her wet hair making her colder.

She still couldn't believe the turn of events once again. She was glad she was Lord Pembroke's true daughter as she could not see herself as any other man's child. She was sorry her mother had lost her first child, but glad MacLauchlan had no claim to her.

And she was gladder still that her father lived. Then she wondered if Marcus would have felt differently about her all those years if he'd known she wasn't all Highland lass. "Do you mind that I am Lord Pembroke's real daughter?"

Marcus smiled down at her with such tenderness, it brought tears to her eyes. She knew before he even spoke what his answer would be as he stroked her hair. "Ah, lass. You are my joy and always have been. 'Tis you that I am wedding, no' your da."

Relieved, she settled against him again. "I want my father to be here for the wedding."

Marcus looked at Wynfield. "Is he well enough to travel?"

"In a few more days, mayhap."

"Will he come?" Marcus asked.

"You will have to ask him yourself," Wynfield said.

"Nay. You cannot return to Torrent castle, Marcus. What if my father changes his mind about you and imprisons you in the dungeon instead?" Isobel dearly loved her father, but she still didn't trust him where marrying Marcus was concerned.

"He can ask him in a missive." Wynfield sounded tired, in pain, and exasperated.

The sound of horses coming from the north made Marcus set Isobel gently aside, and then he quickly rose to his feet, seizing his sword at once.

Rob shouted, "I have returned with reinforcements."

"'Tis good. Lord Wynfield has paid us a visit. We have wounded."

"The wagon is coming for the wounded." Rob dismounted and stalked into the enclosure. He looked at Isobel wrapped in the blankets on the floor. "Is Lady Isobel—"

"I am fine," she said, annoyed. "Only cold and my clothes are soaking wet."

Rob looked at Marcus for an explanation as if she were daft!

"She took a swim."

"Not by choice," she said.

Rob smiled at her. Then he looked Lord Wynfield over. "We will get you in the wagon, my lord, as soon as it arrives."

"I prefer riding," Lord Wynfield grumbled.

No one worth their salt wanted to ride in the wagons meant for hauling goods, the elderly, or the injured. But the baron would have to sacrifice his pride as Marcus knew he would suffer less, particularly if he passed out from his injury while trying to ride his horse.

"When we return, I need you to send five men to Rondover Castle with word about John attempting to murder his uncle, Lord Pembroke," Marcus said to Rob.

"The bloody fool."

"Aye. Let us get the men organized and be on our way," Marcus said.

"I cannot wear just a blanket," Isobel objected.

"Your clothes are soaked, lass. You will ride with me."

"Och, Marcus."

He smiled and mounted his horse. Finbar handed Isobel up to him as Wynfield, despite his protests, was loaded into a wagon with the other injured men who could no longer ride.

"Be gentle with Lord Wynfield," Marcus said. "He will be our honored guest."

When everyone was ready to ride, Marcus took off as Angus and his kin joined him for the rest of the journey to Lochaven.

"I cannot believe you are taking me to your home like this—naked as the day I was born."

Marcus smiled at her, and his look was more heated than sweet as if he was thinking about her being naked underneath the blanket and she suddenly felt very hot.

"You are perfectly covered or I would have come up with some other plan."

She could just imagine the first impression she would make when she arrived at Marcus's castle as his wife, her hair wet and in tangles, and all she was wearing was a blanket.

"They will love you as I do," Marcus said, and she thought she was as transparent to him as she was with Mary.

She must have fallen asleep then, because before she knew it, she was at the castle, looking at an expansive blue-green loch nearby, surrounded by trees, the castle with four round stone towers at each corner of the curtain wall stretching up to the cloudy sky, the portcullis raised and gates open in welcome.

Cheers went up from the wall walk as several men gathered up above to see them arrive.

Marcus raised his arm in greeting. More hails followed. And she smiled at him. She loved that he was so well thought of by his people, but she wanted to melt into the saddle and disappear. Never had she been wrapped in a blanket, bare naked, for all to see.

When they reached the inner bailey, Rob hurried to take her from Marcus and that made her body heat all over again. She prayed the blanket would not unwrap and reveal any part of her, other than her bare feet, which was scandalous enough.

After Marcus dismounted, he reclaimed her from Rob and stalked toward the keep, while men and women alike were eager to greet him. They seemed somewhat reserved about Isobel, probably trying to figure out who she was until Marcus said, "I bring home my bonny bride, Lady Isobel, my wife."

He smiled down at her, looking so pleased, his kin applauded and shouted well-wishes.

"We will celebrate," he said. "We have honored guests." He mentioned Lord Wynfield, Lord Pembroke's knights, Angus, Niall, Gunnolf, and Marcus's cousins. "We need a hot bath—"

"Already arranged, my laird," Siusan said, her plump cheeks full of color, her smile contagious. "We had a runner watching for you. Young Taldon. He did well, did he no'?"

Angus saw the tow-headed lad standing on a barrel, trying to see Marcus over all his kin gathered around.

"Taldon, you have done well."

He beamed.

"And a feast for you." Cook's brown eyes shifted to take a look again at Isobel, her brows raised a little.

"We will find garments for the lass," Siusan said.

"Aye good," Marcus said.

Siusan did a little curtsey, then hurried into the keep.

"Aye, our healer has made arrangements to aid the injured men. Is the lady injured as well?" Cook asked, her brow furrowing.

"She is fine," Marcus said, "but her gowns were drenched and she is still cold. Thank you," he said to the collected men and women. "I will have a word with everyone in...a bit." Then he carried Isobel through the castle and soon was climbing a set of winding stairs.

"Truth be told," he said to Isobel, "I dinna believe you need any clothes for a while."

She chuckled. "'Tis why I agreed to marry you."

He laughed.

"But what will your people think of us if you do not feast with them?"

"That I am enjoying time well-spent with my lovely wife, as it should be. They would be more than surprised if we should show up at the feast right away." He sighed. "Lass, I canna tell you enough how sorry I am to have told you wrong about your da."

"You revealed to me what you believed with all your heart, Marcus. You would not have told me if it had not been for me saying King Henry might not allow us to wed. I am glad to learn that my father truly had a daughter with my mother, and that MacLauchlan is truly not my father. That is all that matters."

Marcus stepped into his chamber and she glanced around at it. Big, the bed massive, the curtains around it gray, the wood dark, two arrow slit windows, rushes, pegs on the wall, a chest, a table, and a chair.

Her curtains were blue and she wondered if she could bring them here to soften the dark look a bit. Her curtains looked to be a richer wool and heavier. Though she did not want to offend Marcus should he feel she was not happy with the accommodations.

"If you wish anything changed, you have but to ask." Marcus set her on her feet.

She did not want to ask for anything for her personal use when she felt the moneys spent on such extravagance should be used for the benefit of all his people.

The revelry below stairs had already begun in the great hall, and she did feel a little guilty and embarrassed that she and Marcus were up here, and that everyone in his clan would miss him and know just what they were up here doing.

He unwrapped her from the blanket and helped her into the warm water. Then he crouched next to the tub, took the cloth, and began to wash her as before, only he tried to do so more slowly. But he had the same difficulty and as soon as she was wrapped in a towel, and sitting by the fire, he vigorously scrubbed himself down while she watched him, amused.

She dropped her towel, and his eyes widened. She returned to the tub, but his gaze quickly shifted from her smiling face to the rest of her, taking all of her in, making her feel desirable like when he used to look at her, interested, intrigued when they met at the loch. And she loved him for it.

She crouched next to the tub, took the cloth from him, and began to slowly clean him like he had done for her.

"You are washing so quickly, you are missing half the splatters of mud," she teased, and she loved that she could do this for him, like he had done for her.

"Ahh, lass, you will have to hurry." Marcus's voice was already rusty with lust as he focused on Isobel's touch, or attempted to, but seeing her naked as she washed his face, and neck, then his chest and waist, and lower still, was making him even harder than before.

He loved the way she ran the cloth over him with tenderness and care, not scrubbing roughly and in a rush to get it over with so he could take her to bed. He was grateful she wasn't in the least bit shy when it came to being with him. When she slipped the cloth even lower, beneath the water, he knew he had no mud splatters left there. She washed his legs, but only briefly, then began to stroke his staff with the wet cloth. Despite being tough on the battlefield, when it came to his naked wife leaning her delectable breasts over the tub and her hand so deftly stroking his staff with the cloth, he couldn't hold back the craving he had for her.

He rose from the tub, dripping wet. She dropped the wet cloth in the water, but before she could do anything else, he climbed out of the tub, grabbed a towel, and hastily dried himself off—while the brazen lass watched! Then he swept her up in his arms and carried her to the bed.

"Some things a man canna last at."

She smiled up at him. "But it felt good, aye?"

He smiled as he deposited her on the mattress and joined her. "Verra."

He loved the way she was not inhibited with him, how she touched him all over, making his blood hot for her, his heart race. He kissed her, rubbing his rigid staff against her soft body, glad she had warmed up and was not ill from all she'd had to endure.

He suddenly realized he should have asked how she was feeling now. The way she was kissing him back, her tongue teasing his lips and tongue, the way her fingers stroked his sides and back, he suspected she was perfectly fine.

He didn't want to stop kissing her or molding his body to hers, feeling her soft skin and curves, smelling her sweetness, wanting to dive deep and claim her again and again. He swept his hand upward to cup one of her heavenly breasts before he moved his mouth lower to feast on one and then the other, tonguing her taut nipples, caressing her.

She moaned and moved against him, urging him on. He wasn't sure she would be healed up enough, but he wanted to make love to her as long as she did also.

He dipped a finger and then a second deep inside

her wet sheath. She was ready for him. Then he began to stroke her swollen nub and poked his tongue into her mouth, enjoying the honeyed mead they had shared on the journey here. He was so ready for her, barely able to contain himself, the way she had aroused him, starting with him bathing her, and then her dropping her towel and washing him.

She arched against him and barely breathed, and he believed she was just about there.

He stroked her harder and she gripped his hips tightly, her eyes closed, her lips parted, but before she cried out, he kissed her, muffling her cry of pleasure. She kissed him back, wrapping her arms tightly around him.

It was time. He couldn't hold back a moment longer and spread her legs further. "Tell me if you are sore and I will stop." Even though it would nearly kill him.

"I am fine."

He centered himself between her legs and plunged his staff in deep, felt her shifting a little underneath him, and he worried that she was uncomfortable. "Are—"

She pulled him down for a kiss, silencing his question, and then he began to pump into her, needing this joining, sharing the closeness—the love that their coupling meant. He still couldn't believe that Isobel was truly his and he thanked God that it was so.

He continued to drive home, kissing her, loving

her, enjoying this intimacy that he'd wanted to share with her for so long.

Until he could not hold back any further, no matter how hard he tried, the torturous pleasure filling him with a need so great, he had to release, filling her with his seed. Her face flushed with heat, she fairly glowed as she smiled up at him.

He chuckled. "Did you finally warm up enough, lass?"

"Aye. If you had done this earlier, I would have been completely warm."

"In the crannog?" He laughed. As shy as she was around other men about wearing only a blanket in the enclosure, he could not imagine her being willing to make love with him there. "How are you feeling?"

"Wonderful." She snuggled against Marcus's chest, and he caressed her back as he listened to all the happy bantering in the great hall.

The noise in the great hall grew louder, and Marcus swore his people wanted him to know just how wondrous a time they were having, despite his not being there. But he was just where he wanted to be— with his ladylove, like this.

"So tell me, what was it that you thought of me after I left you at Torrent Castle?" He'd been curious about it ever since she had brought it up. Of course, *he'd* thought of what it would be like to see her naked, to kiss her, and bed her. But he'd never suspected her thoughts would have turned in that direction. And he was more than interested in knowing.

She began running her tantalizing, soft fingertips over his chest. "Kissing, first and foremost. I had seen men stealing kisses from maids near the stables and once in the gardens. I saw the way a man wished to touch a woman's breasts, and how after he rubbed the maid's breast with his eager hand, they both worked to pull her *léine* down so he could press his hand against her soft flesh. I had never seen a man kiss a woman's breast, or take her into his mouth."

Marcus chuckled. "You saw way too much as it was, lassie."

She smiled so wickedly at him, he wished he could have shown her all that he had much earlier. "I wished to know what it would be like with you. I could imagine all sorts of things, but never what it would truly be like. I would hug my goose-down pillow to my body, imagining you…tupping me," she finally said. "Only not from behind, like a ram and a ewe."

Marcus couldn't help the way her words made his staff rise.

"What about you, Marcus? You had already been with a woman, aye? So you knew what it would be like. Did you ever think how it would be with me?"

"You dinna know the half of it, lass. I always imagined what it would be like to kiss you and… more. I could barely ride after we kissed at the loch."

"I loved the way you kissed me there, and I will cherish those moments always. I loved how you felt against me when we were sharing that special time."

He chuckled. "I was ready to take you into the woods and have my wicked way with you, claim you for my wife right then and there, and dispense with waiting for your da to agree."

"I would have gone with you willingly." She sighed. "Even if you could have managed when you were wounded. Anything to encourage my father to capitulate." Then she frowned at Marcus. "Did the same thing happen to you while we were dancing?"

"Lass, all you have to do is breathe in the same space as me."

She smiled and kissed him soundly. "I love you, Highlander."

"My bonny lass, you are my greatest treasure." He kissed her again, then closed his eyes, wanting to cherish this time with his lovely wife, resting together in his bed, holding her sweet body against his, safe from any danger.

"And you mine." Isobel was glad she had felt nothing but pleasure with their joining this time as she luxuriated in the feel of her braw warrior. She listened to his heart thumping and the noise down below, amused at just how raucous his people were getting. "I think they are getting louder, if that is at all possible."

He smiled and tightened his hold on her. "I think they are getting closer."

She laughed. "You mean they are bringing the celebration to us?"

"In case we might have fallen asleep."

She shook her head at the notion. "Let us join them then."

He groaned and kissed her forehead. "And retire early."

"Aye." She was all for that and climbed off him, but then realized she had nothing to wear.

"I will send up a maid with some clothes." Marcus hurried to get dressed while Isobel covered herself in his furs.

When he opened the door, he found garments for Isobel to wear.

"My staff has brought you clothes." He shut the door and carried the items to the bed.

She thought that he would leave her to her dressing, but he didn't.

He seemed to take great pleasure in helping her to dress in the dark blue wool gown. She smiled when she noticed he was becoming aroused again immediately after pulling her chemise over her breasts. She loved how he said just breathing in the same space with her could do that to him.

"Aye, lass, I told you. I canna see you naked, help you to dress or undress, or hold you close without my body reacting to yours."

She loved him because of it for it made her feel adored, just as much as she appreciated his beautiful form. When she was ready, he opened the door, and they heard the sound of footfalls hurrying down the stairs.

"Was someone spying on us, do you think?" she asked, surprised.

"Aye, warning the others that we are coming down."

That gave her chill bumps. She knew as soon as they walked into the great hall, the whole place would grow quiet, in part, out of respect for their laird, and in part, because they would be curious about her. Would they be pleased that she was the lady of the manor now? Or resentful that she was a Norman earl's daughter and not all Highlander after all?

CHAPTER 18

Before Isobel and Marcus even reached the great hall, the place turned deathly quiet. Except for a few chuckles, a few clinks of tankards against the wooden trestle tables, the scurry of claws against the stone floor, there was no conversation whatsoever and Isobel knew then that someone had indeed warned everyone that she and Marcus were coming down to join them.

Suddenly, two deerhounds raced out of the great hall to greet them. Her father's deerhounds were grayer in color, whereas these wore beautiful red fawn coats. Their ears were semi-erect with excitement and the bristly-haired dogs nearly smiled as they saw Marcus and her and headed their way. Normally gentle dogs, they were also extremely friendly, and she loved them already.

Isobel braced for the impact while Marcus tried to intercept them. "Down," he ordered, but they were unruly young dogs and were jumping and licking them all over.

Laughing and greeting them back, Isobel hugged each of them before they settled down.

"They are adorable." She considered the two of them. "Male and female. When will they have pups?"

Marcus laughed and shook his head. "You will want to be mothering them."

"Aye. I am ready. I helped raise pups at my father's keep. He even gave one to King Henry. Though the man who was to raise them for hunting was supposed to keep me from playing with them and ruining them for the hunt."

"Did he?"

"Nay. I always have my way. Well, almost always. And the dogs were still great hunters. See, all you need is a bright smile and a cheerful disposition and it will make all the difference in the world in getting your way."

"I will have to remember that," he said, smiling down at her.

"You always get your own way. You are a laird in your own right."

"No' where it mattered the most. No' with you until the end."

She sighed. "Aye, 'tis true."

"But it all turned out well. That is all that matters." He escorted her into the great hall where she felt warm all over again as everyone rose from their benches and watched her walk with Marcus to the dais. The dogs hurried alongside them as if they were to sit at the high table as well.

It looked as though it was killing everyone to hold their tongues as they smiled broadly at them until Marcus took his seat alongside Isobel and gave the word to allow the festivities to continue.

He raised his tankard that a servant hastily had filled. "To my bonny wife."

"May you have dozens of bairns," Angus called out.

Everyone laughed and cheered.

Isobel felt she had been slaving over the fire all day long, her skin was so hot. Marcus leaned down and kissed her cheek, then whispered in her ear, "We will have to retire early and make it come true."

She laughed. "I am already burning up from embarrassment, husband."

"May we always have peace with the…English," Niall shouted out, raising his tankard in the direction of Lord Wynfield.

Everyone was getting loud again, whistling and whooping it up, having the time of their lives.

"Are your celebrations always this cheerful?" At least this Highland clan gathering seemed so much more boisterous and earthier.

"Aye."

They had begun to eat, though many had finished their meals by the time she and Marcus had arrived, but she noted their food was already set out on the table in anticipation of their arrival. The hounds were waiting for scraps from their plates, which made her think that was why they were sitting by them, and not entirely because they were devoted to Marcus.

"What are their names?"

"Crevan, for fox for his red coloring and his tendency to steal food if he can manage, and Oona, the female, meaning one. She is the first female deerhound the clan has owned."

"They are beautiful and I will enjoy playing with their pups when they get here." She ate some of the wild boar from her plate, but was curious about a discussion from their travels here. "Earlier you mentioned something I have wondered about—the woman who was your ward and you were trying to convince one of your cousins to wed her."

"Aye, her da had been gravely ill and he asked me to find her a husband. Someone I knew who would be good for her. Immediately, I thought of my cousins and wanted them to meet and get to know her. But her uncle stole her away when she was visiting one of her cousins. So I havena had any success in getting her back since he is her relation and I am no'."

"Why did you no' marry her?"

Marcus looked down at Isobel, his brows elevated. "I canna believe you would ask me such a question. She is like a sister to me. And you are the only one I have ever wanted to wed." He glanced at the Chattan brothers. "Among all the brothers, surely one will be the right man for her. I had hoped that while she stayed with me, they would visit and one of them would appeal. Then they were incarcerated in a dungeon, and well, by the time they were set free and arrived at Lochaven, she was gone."

"And you wanted me to meet her."

"Aye. She could use a friend, someone who would be like a sister to her."

"I can be that. I will pray she is returned to us and I will do anything to help." Isobel glanced at the Chattan brothers, seeing them anew. They were protective and good fighters, but coming to stay with Marcus as suitors for the lass when they didn't know her, well, that was more than chivalrous. "Which one would be best suited to her?"

Marcus laughed. "That is something that will have to be decided between one of them and the lass. Though it doesna mean that any of them would suit. Only that they are some of my favorite cousins, and I would love to see her wed to one of them. They are good men. And I believe any of them would make suitable husbands. Though...Drummond, the youngest, might take a little longer before he is ready for a wife."

"What about your friend Gunnolf?"

Marcus considered him as he tossed a scrap of boar to one of the dogs. "Aye, he would be an acceptable husband for the lass, though he has declared he willna marry any time soon."

She nodded, but then considered another matter that had been troubling her. "Marcus, we still have not discovered who the man was who orchestrated the killing of the men escorting me, nor who ordered the men to murder you. I had thought the one in charge was the same man who had nearly murdered my father. But that was John, and well, you do not think he was responsible for both of the other ambushes."

"Nay. I still believe, as I did then, that it is more personal. Likely one of your seven suitors. Tell me about them."

"I only know that Lord Neville, Erickson, and Hammersfield, who had been discussing my mother and me in an infuriatingly irritating way, had been given permission to court me."

"Also Lord Fenton was no longer allowed to because you broke his nose, and you finally told your da you feared Fenton would retaliate if you were to wed him."

"Aye."

"And Lord Wynfield."

"He is way too old."

"Aye, but he was given permission to court you." Marcus finished his boar and began to eat a wedge of cheese.

"Aye." She sipped some of her mead.

"That is four. Who else is left?"

"Three unnamed suitors. I do not know."

"Your da wouldna tell you?"

He seemed surprised and irritated, but she smiled. "Nay, I did not wish to know. I told my father I would marry only you."

Marcus smiled, then he frowned. "So three others. Can you guess as to who they were?"

"Mayhap the two knights who had earned manors for their service to the king. But I do not know that for certain. Sir Edward is one, and Sir Thornton, the other."

"Then we must discover from your da who the other three suitors are for certain."

"What if it *was* John? Only instead, he had you ambushed rather than showing up to fight you." She finished off her bread and looked up at Marcus and frowned.

"He had not been to Torrent Castle recently, had he?"

"Nay." She hated that they still didn't know anything more about it.

"Lord Wynfield would know, would he not? He is your da's advisor. He probably even recommended who should court you as far as the benefit it would be to your da and his name."

"Aye. After we celebrate, we must speak with him."

"I had other plans in mind. As long as you are feeling all right," Marcus quickly added.

"I so appreciate how considerate you are of how I feel, Highlander. But I am half Highland lass," she reminded him, tickled by his concern.

He chuckled and leaned over to kiss her, but when she took hold of his arm and responded in a manner highly improper for an earl's daughter, he deepened it, plunging his tongue in her mouth, and pulled her closer. She adored him for being all that he was. She didn't even realize how quiet the great hall had become until they broke off the kiss and everyone started cheering.

Marcus raised his tankard and grinned.

Amused at his very male response, she felt the heat rise all over her skin again. She would have to remember that despite how noisy the great hall was and as much fun as everyone was having, many were watching their laird and his new bride to see how they behaved during the proceedings. It might not be as formal as with the English, but the Highlanders were very much like her courtiers at home. Everyone would talk for months about this eve, she suspected.

She loved it here and loved the people so far, but she was already missing her own staff, Mary, Jane, and her father. She now knew what it must have been like for her mother when she had moved so far away from home and left her people behind to live with Isobel's father and his people. It wasn't the same as going for a visit. This was her new way of life.

Isobel could see how important it had been for Mary to stay with her mother through the years. At least her mother had Marcus to visit with, and keep her informed of what was happening back home. Isobel wouldn't have that luxury. Though she could write to her father. But it wasn't the same.

"Can we go home to see my father from time to time?" she asked Marcus.

He looked down at her so tenderly, she blinked back tears.

"Lass, are you already homesick?"

"Nay, well, once I get to know the people and Mary is here, and I learn what I need to do, I am sure I will be busy enough and feel more settled."

"I will talk your da into coming here for the wedding and bringing Mary with him. Is there anyone else you would like to have join you here?"

"Nay. I love Jane dearly, but she is a knight's daughter and has her heart set on marrying a knight. I think if she came here she would be homesick and wish to return to Torrent Castle."

"You will make friends here, of that I have no doubt."

"Aye." She sighed.

"I canna allow you to travel anywhere until we have this matter cleared up concerning who killed your escort and tried to murder me."

"Aye."

He took her hand and kissed it. "But I will do everything in my power to make you feel at home."

She nodded.

"Even encourage Oona and Crevan to have pups."

She laughed and leaned her head against his shoulder, prizing him for everything he was to her.

"Are you tired?" He wrapped his arm around her shoulder.

"A little, but I am enjoying the revelry. If we go to bed now, all the noise would keep us awake."

He smiled down at her. "That is not all."

"Are you ready again?"

He laughed out loud. "Aye. With you? Always."

If it hadn't been for wanting more than anything to take his wife to bed to ravish her again, and then sleep with her, until they wished to make love again, Marcus would take Lord Wynfield aside and ask him just who else had been given Lord Pembroke's permission to court Isobel. Marcus wouldn't discount Lord Fenton either, whose name had been stricken from the list because of the childhood incident.

Lord Wynfield looked done in, most likely from the injury to his leg. And Isobel, despite her saying she wished to stay up later, was leaning so heavily against his shoulder, he knew she was about to fall asleep. He couldn't have that.

He was certain that once she was with child, and was settled in with her new family, she would be happy.

Marcus motioned to Rob and when he joined him, Isobel didn't even straighten, and he knew then she was asleep. "Rob, see that Lord Wynfield is taken to a room and that a maid cares for his injury. I dinna want the man dying on us."

"Aye." Rob looked down at the lass. "You have worn her out."

"I hadna intended to this early. Ask Duff to see if he can...well, encourage Oona and Crevan to have some pups." As if anyone needed to encourage them when she was ready to mate.

Smiling, Rob raised his brows, then glanced from Isobel back to Marcus and whispered, "She isna already homesick, is she?"

"Some, I am afraid. We will have to keep her busy so that she feels she is important to the clan and is enjoying her home here."

"Aye. I will spread the word." Then Rob grinned. "But I dinna have to tell you how you can ensure she doesna wish to leave here."

Before Marcus could say a word to his cousin, Rob stalked off to give the order to move Lord Wynfield to a chamber. Marcus carefully rose from his chair, keeping hold of Isobel's shoulders without waking her. As soon as he stood, he lifted her in his arms and said, "As you can see, 'tis time for my bride and me to be abed. Feel free to continue to celebrate without me." Then he glanced at Finbar. "Cousin, you are in charge."

Finbar grinned and saluted him with his tankard.

Marcus carried Isobel off to bed. This time, instead of cheers, everyone was respectful and quiet, as if they feared waking the lass. He couldn't have appreciated his clansmen more.

When he reached his chamber, he found a servant had lighted the tallow candles inside, then he shut the door behind him and deposited Isobel gently on the bed.

He stripped off his clothes first before he removed hers, wishing they could have made love before they fell asleep. But after the long day they'd had, the riding, fighting, and her swimming in the loch in her gowns, she was worn out. She needn't worry about the half of her that was English. They were just as hardy as the Highlanders, and Isobel proved that time and again.

Marcus removed Isobel's clothes, admired her beauty, wishing again that she had not fallen asleep, then doused the candles, and climbed into bed. Isobel immediately curled up against him. He loved the intimacy between them, her soft, warm, naked body pressed against his. In the short time they'd been together, he couldn't imagine them ever being apart again.

Was she awake enough to want him to make love to her? He was ready.

"Lass…"

"I have been thinking," she said sleepily against his chest.

He sighed and caressed her hair. She was not thinking of what he was thinking of, he was certain.

"Aye, lass." He knew what it was about, too. Once he had safely escorted her here, he had been going over in his mind all that had happened before—who could have ambushed them. The same man? Or were two different ones involved?

"The night of the dance, my father gave the order to Lord Wynfield to have him send you away." She caressed his chest with her fingertips, which was not conducive to his thinking about them being waylaid.

"Aye. What if Lord Wynfield had it in mind that, since he was one of your suitors, he would have me eliminated because he knew you wished to wed me and no other man? Even if your da had made you marry him, you would have resented Lord Wynfield and still loved me. Unless I was dead."

"I still would have loved you with all my heart until the end of my days."

"Aye, lass, and I you."

"There is a problem with that notion. He was not one of my suitors when you left that night. I spoke with my father after you were gone and it was not until he told me that Lord Fenton had asked to court me and I explained to him about the past, that my father took him off the list. Then he said he would add Lord Wynfield. But the baron would not have known that right away."

"True. And Lord Fenton could not have known your da had decided against him courting you either, not for some time."

"Aye."

"Why did Lord Wynfield wait ten days before he sent you from Torrent Castle to stay with King Henry's court?" Marcus asked. "Why that day? Not earlier? Or later? What was the delay? Your da said he would never have sent you there. So why did Lord Wynfield believe you would be safer there?"

"Who would have known I was leaving?"

"Your staff."

"Aye."

"They could have talked to someone in the village and the word was spread to someone else. Someone who made arrangements to kill your escort."

"But if one of my suitors had thought to do that then how could he have convinced me to marry him?"

"He wouldna have been with his men. Just like he wasna with those who attempted to murder me. What if he was trying to stop you from going to King Henry's court?"

"Because he would suspect King Henry would choose a husband for me and my suitor would not have a chance."

"Aye. If your escort was murdered, you would be forced to return to the castle. You were only an hour's ride from there. He most likely would have believed you would have done so, not run off in a different direction. His men would have left you alone then, but secretly ensured your safety as you traveled back to the keep."

"Except that you arrived instead and killed off his men. Too bad he had not been with them."

"Aye. Which is why I believe it was the same man who had his men, or paid for mercenaries, to kill me. He hasna the courage to fight me. Maybe he even had a bargain with—"

"John. Oh my God, aye. What if one of my suitors tried to have you killed? But it did not work out the way he had intended. Then he speaks with John, saying if he takes me off his hands, he would make it worth his while. But, wait, then my suitor would not obtain the title and property."

"Maybe he didna want the title and property as much as he wanted you. John said that you have a substantial dowry also. Once everyone believed your da was dead, your suitor knew John was his last chance at obtaining your hand in marriage. Your suitor would have no likelihood at that point to actually take over the earldom. Unless, of course, you had a son, and John happened to die without issue."

"Aye. My suitor probably did not know that John murdered my father, only that the deed was done. Unless he was in on my father's killing. I suspect he was not, because before that happened, he still had a chance to wed me and receive the title, property, me, and my dowry."

"Which means we still need to learn who your other suitors were. John was incensed that Lord Wynfield had sent you away. At first, I thought it was because he had worried about your safety."

"What if John already had someone in mind to marry me off to?"

"What if it wasna even one of your suitors."

She took a deep breath. "I had not considered that."

"You said you had trouble with some of your suitors. That they had made disparaging remarks about you and your mother. What was that about?"

"Aye, the next morn after the dance, I was with Mary and Sir Travon and I wished to ride. My father had tasked him to follow me everywhere. Or another knight that Lord Wynfield would choose."

"Sir Travon has always had a fondness for you. I can see it in the way he looks at you, not as a dutiful and loyal knight to your da, but something more...personal."

"Aye, I am certain he would have wished to have been numbered among my suitors, but my father would not have permitted him to. But I do not think he would have had anything to do with having his fellow knights murdered. He is good friends with many."

"He did pledge his loyalty on the battlefield to me when we were through fighting Laren's men."

"He did?"

"Aye. He handed you up to me when you were unconscious after your swim in the loch. It was as if at that point, he had conceded I had won the battle with the English and had earned the prize."

She poked him in the chest. "I am not a prize to be had."

He laughed and wrapped his arms around her. "You are the greatest treasure, lass. So you said that your suitors had said something disagreeable—"

"Aye. Lord Hammersfield said that I had been wanton when I danced with you and said that I was like my mother. Or some such thing. He thought that they should use a firmer hand with me, and not be so polite.

He had fisted his hands and was filled with rage that I would defend my mother and he was dying to say something to me, but watched his tongue while the other men stood as witnesses. Lord Neville said that you had forced yourself on me. He is a sneaky one. When the other men began to talk about trouble with the Scots at the border, which is what they believed when Cantrell, one of my father's servants, gave Lord Wynfield the news that you had been injured—though we did not know it at the time—Lord Neville tried to convince me to dance with him. Lord Erickson remarked that the way I had thrown myself at you, he believed I was no longer a virgin. He is easily provoked and has a fiery temper."

"I will kill the bastards should I ever see them again," Marcus growled. "What of Fenton?"

"Lord Fenton would likely wish to see you dead also. But he was not with the other barons in the room that morn, discussing my being so wanton. I do not know what they thought when I told them I was still untried and that if I had to wed Lord Neville, he would have to force himself on me as I would never be his willing wife."

Marcus was so angry, he could have killed every last one of them.

"But you see, dear husband, it matters not what they believe. All that matters is that you are my husband and none of them will ever have the chance again."

"I canna believe you spoke thus to them." Before she could say anything, he added, "Then again, I can. But you shouldna have had to."

He kissed her tenderly on the mouth, to show her how much he treasured her, and how much he was glad she was his and no other man's.

A knock on the door had him jumping free of his wife and out of the bed, grabbing up his sword, ready for battle—stark naked.

CHAPTER 19

No one in their right mind would disturb Marcus and his bride unless trouble was brewing. "Aye," Marcus called out.

"Lord Wynfield wishes to see you," Gunnolf said. "He is adamant that he see you at once."

"Is his condition worsening?" Marcus asked, setting his sword aside and grabbing his trewes.

"Mayhap he feels such."

"Aye. I will be right there."

"Rob is seeing to him. We were still drinking when the maid came with word. Your cousin asked that I inform you of the matter. I will wait for you."

Isobel was out of bed in a hurry and slipping her chemise and then *her léine* over her head.

"You dinna need to come with me." Marcus tugged on the rest of his clothes as she pulled on her shoes.

"Aye, I do. If he doesna make it, I would feel

terrible if I had not seen him this eve."

She slipped her brat over her shoulders and Marcus quickly joined her to fasten her brooch, and then they left the chamber. Marcus escorted her to the one where Lord Wynfield was staying as Gunnolf walked beside them.

"He is feverish and is moaning in pain," Gunnolf warned.

That did not sound well. "Are you and your family leaving on the morrow?" Even though Gunnolf was not a blood relation, he was very much part of the family as they had raised him from the time he was a lad.

Marcus remembered the first time he'd met him, blue eyes wild, his hair long and unkempt, his expression grim and fierce, even though he was still suffering from a sword wound that would have killed a lesser man. In the beginning, Gunnolf had slept with the dogs. His choice because he was a Viking and not a Highlander and he had felt he did not belong with them. Until Angus's mother coaxed him into sleeping in the keep with her sons in their chamber. At two and ten, Gunnolf had still been healing from wounds he'd received in battling the English. Some of his family had been killed and those that had survived had believed him dead and left without him. Marcus sometimes wondered if the Viking was even mortal because he seemed to survive every battle no matter how badly injured he was.

"*Ja,* we are leaving after we break our fast, with all

haste, before you reclaim your ward and try to match up one of us with the lass. The Chattan brothers are willing, but me?" Gunnolf furrowed his brow at the disagreeable notion. Then he considered Isobel and smiled. "Unless I could find a lass as bonny as your lady, who would turn my world over in a heartbeat."

Grinning, Marcus shook his head. "You will fall in love, my friend, and then you will wonder why you ever delayed the matter."

They grew quiet as they reached the chamber housing the baron. Rob was standing outside, waiting for them. "He has been asking for Isobel as well."

Marcus prayed the man would survive, but feared if he did not, how Isobel would fare. She might not have wished to marry the baron, but he could see she had a deep fondness for him, and Marcus loved her loyalty.

Isobel rushed inside as Rob shook his head at Marcus. Even if it did not look good, men who appeared to be dying could sometimes recover to everyone's surprise. So Marcus was hopeful that it would be so.

Rob moved a chair close to the bed. Isobel took a seat while Marcus stood behind her and rested his hand on her shoulder, which she so appreciated. Her heart was breaking that the baron would come to give word about her father, to right a wrong with her, and then die from wounds he'd suffered from Laren MacLauchlan's men.

"I am sorry, Lady Isobel." Lord Wynfield offered his hand to her.

Isobel took his hot hand in hers and held tight, fighting the tears filling her eyes. She had seen many men die and no matter how little she knew them, she could not banish the sorrow she always felt—for them, their families, and friends. But she had known the baron since she was a wee bairn.

"I forgive you," she quickly said, afraid if she didn't, he would die and she'd never have the chance to tell him one last time that she had forgiven him with all her heart.

"I should never have sent you away."

"Why did you?"

"I…I knew we had a traitor in our midst."

Her heart nearly quit beating. "What do you mean? Who?"

He shook his head. "I sent men with you who were completely trustworthy, completely loyal to both your da and to you."

"And they died." But then she wondered who he had not trusted. "Who were my other suitors?"

"Lords Neville, Erickson, Hammersfield, me, Sir Halloran—"

"The captain of the guard."

"Aye. Sir Edward—"

"One of the knights who owns his own manor."

"Aye. And Sir Travon."

"Travon," Isobel said. "Why Sir Travon?"

"Your da knew the knight would love you dearly even though he did not have the social standing that the other men did. He is loyal to his lordship and to you. And he has always been good with dealing with the Scots at the border, so Lord Pembroke thought he might do well in his place."

"Yet you did not send him with me as part of my escort."

"I would have had he not become too ill that morning."

Thinking how convenient that was for the knight, she narrowed her eyes.

"He protested most fiercely, my lady, when I would not permit him to go. He could not hold his food down. He was in the stable saddling his own horse, when he was forced to his knees again, losing everything he had eaten to break his fast. Sir Edward fought with him to make him stay behind. Sir Edward was the only man who survived the onslaught."

"He was lucky," Marcus quickly reassured her. "He had been grievously wounded, still fighting, but was the last of the men still left alive when we killed your attackers."

Isobel agreed and was thankful that at least Sir Edward had been spared. "Did anyone know the men who killed ours?"

"Nay. Mercenaries, we suspect. I asked everyone on our staff if any of them recognized the dead men. But no one did," the baron said.

"How did my suitors react when I had disappeared?"

"All of them were furious. I could not tell if any of them had anything to do with the despicable act. Sir Travon wanted to find you when Sir Edward was returned half dead. But Sir Travon was still too sick to travel. Sir Edward was clinging to life, though even in his wounded state, he wanted to go after you, fearing for your safety. We knew Laird McEwan would find you and bring you home." Lord Wynfield cast Marcus an annoyed look.

"You canna blame me for taking Lady Isobel home with me where I knew she would be safe."

"And you would claim her for your wife." Lord Wynfield let out a ragged breath. "Nay, I cannot blame you."

"Why did you have our men escort me to King Henry's castle?" Isobel asked.

"I did not intend to. Ever. A friend of mine has a castle south of us, only a day's ride. I planned for you to stay there until I could ferret out the traitor. Only Sir Edward knew where you were truly going. And I told no one to prepare for the journey until that morn. Not even him. Everyone else was told that you would be staying with the king's court at Westminster. Even everyone who was escorting you, except for Sir Edward."

"Someone must have known the route I would take."

"It was the fastest way for you to go in the beginning. If they had not caught up to you so quickly, they would have had a more difficult time locating you. So we believe they had watched the castle until you left. Someone had to have sent word to whoever attacked your escort before you had traveled very far. Which means we still have a traitor in our midst."

"Why did you not tell me the reason and where I was going? Surely, you did not believe I would tell anyone and the word would reach those who attacked my escort."

Lord Wynfield looked steadily at her and she thought, though his face was flushed and he must be feeling badly, it did not appear that he would die. Not the way he was responding to her questions. She prayed with all her heart that his condition would not worsen and that he would still live.

When he would not say, she frowned at him. "You thought I would tell someone? Who? If you had sworn me to secrecy for my own safety and that of my escort, why would you think I would tell anyone?"

When he still didn't say, she gaped at him. "Lord Wynfield, you cannot believe if I had told Mary where I was going, that she could be at the root of all this. Nay, she would never have been."

Though Isobel was quickly thinking about how Mary had been so tearful when she had left. But that had all to do with her leaving her behind. Naught more.

"She told me the direction to go to rescue Isobel,"

Marcus said. "She wanted me to rescue her."

Lord Wynfield narrowed his eyes. "How did she know?"

"I dinna know. Maybe it was as you said. They would have gone in the one direction at the beginning. But it was her telling me that ensured I arrived in time to rescue Isobel and save Sir Edward. Mary told me that as soon as I brought Isobel safely home, she wished me to bring her to Lochaven to join Isobel. She is like a mother to her," Marcus said.

"Aye, she is." Isobel shook her head. "She would never have betrayed our men." Then she frowned. "She is who you are thinking of, aye?" When Lord Wynfield still didn't say, Isobel couldn't believe the baron would think Jane would have been behind any of this. "Jane? You do not believe she would have had anything to do with it."

"You know she has wished to wed one of your father's knights, aye?" Lord Wynfield asked.

Isobel's eyes filled with tears. Jane had been like a sister to her. A friend. Not just a companion. "Aye, she has oft mentioned it."

"Do you know which she prefers among them?"

Isobel's heart was nearly bursting with upset. "Nay," she said softly, not wishing to hear it was one of her suitors. "Sir Edward? Nay, Sir Travon, who had suddenly become ill and could not travel with us?"

"She could have been hidden, listening in when I spoke privately to Sir Edward. Everyone knew several knights were getting ready to leave before we broke our fast. Just not where they were going or for what purpose."

"A maid had to pack some of my things, and so Jane would have realized I was leaving."

"Aye."

"But she cared about the knights. Her father is one."

"He was not tasked to go with you. If he had been, would things have turned out differently? I do not know. But she is the one who tended to Sir Travon when he was so ill, making much more of a fuss over him than Sir Edward, who was in a bad way for several days."

Feeling sick to her stomach, Isobel couldn't believe it. "When Jane learned my father was alive, how did she react?"

"She was not happy about it like everyone else was. I had been watching her for her reaction, already suspecting her complicity."

"But there is more to what you suspect, is there not?"

"Aye. I was concerned that Sir Travon could not go with you. At first, I suspected he had poisoned himself so it looked as though he had accidentally eaten something that had disagreed with him. But he was so adamant about going after you, that we had to keep a guard posted at all times. Then I questioned Cook and her staff about the food that morning. No one had gotten sick. Sir Travon said he had not eaten anything other than what everyone else had to break their fast. He was talking to Sir Edward concerning where they were going that morn in the great hall, and Sir Edward could not tell him. But Jane was seated on the other side of Sir Travon."

"She knows very well what can aid a man's digestion and what can make him sick." Isobel still could not believe the woman could have been so calculating and aid in the killing of their knights. "When…when you came here and Sir Travon accompanied you—"

"She was not happy. But this time, he did not sit beside her when we broke our fast."

"And he did not get sick."

"Nay." Lord Wynfield squeezed her hand.

"You have questioned her?"

"Aye, but she swears she had naught to do with it. That she knows naught."

"What does Sir Travon believe?"

"That she poisoned him, but he does not believe she did so for any other reason than ensuring he did not go with your escort. She would not say so, but I believe she thought with you leaving, she would have a better chance to encourage a relationship with Sir Travon. But she needed him to remain behind. She seemed as distraught as anyone did when we learned your escort had been massacred. It is the only thing that has saved her from a hanging."

Isobel bit her lip. "Then who is the traitor?"

"I believe he had something to do with both Laird McEwan's attack and the slaughter of your escort," Lord Wynfield said.

"Aye. We both think so, too. Most likely my suitor had already planned to have his men in place no matter how late it was before Marcus left. But he departed much earlier than they had planned because Father only decided to send him away right before you were given word, aye?"

"True." Lord Wynfield shifted his attention to Marcus. "Did you notice anyone following you when you left?"

"Aye, half a dozen servants and a couple more of the guards, curious as to what was going on," Marcus said.

"You said that Cantrell brought the news to you that night at the celebration. What was he doing that he would have learned of it?" she asked Lord Wynfield, trying to get a clearer picture in her mind.

Lord Wynfield's lips parted, but he didn't say anything.

"You did not ask him?"

"Nay. As soon as I learned Laird McEwan had been attacked, I organized a search party. Cantrell said he was not armed, well, with a dirk, but the man he saw had a sword and was on horseback. Cantrell could not have fought him. He made haste to reach the castle and give me the news, though he said he feared the laird had died. By the time we reached the location, we found one dead man, and Laird McEwan was nowhere in sight. Our men continued to search the dark for him. I returned to the keep to inform Lord Pembroke."

"What would Cantrell have been doing out in the dark of night in the very same area as—wait! If he said only one man had attacked Marcus, he lied! Three men had attacked him. And if he saw one, he had to have seen all three. The two that Marcus managed to kill before the third man cut him across the back."

"Why would he help your suitor to kill me, then report the battle to Lord Wynfield?" Marcus asked, sounding puzzled.

Isobel chewed on her lip and pondered that. "What if he did not want to report the trouble to Lord Wynfield, as much as he had to let whoever my suitor was know the deed was done? Only he thought you had died. He left after the man cut you on the back. He had to have watched you leave and you probably were having a time of it, aye?"

"Aye. I wasna sure I would make it across the border to the tavern. I could verra well have died before I ever made it there. Why would he side with your suitor in this matter?" Marcus asked, rubbing her back.

"He will do anything for money, even get word to your people to come for me so I could travel across the border to see you when you were wounded. It appears that he has no loyalty to anyone—only greed."

"When I return, I will make sure he is detained and

questioned—thoroughly," Lord Wynfield said, and she knew he didn't mean to treat the matter lightly.

Footfalls stalked toward the chamber and Finbar appeared. "Marcus, a word with you, please."

"Aye, cousin." Marcus squeezed Isobel's shoulder with reassurance. "What is the trouble now?"

"Lady Isobel's cousin, John, is here with his men. I know I should have spoken to you first before I took action, but I assumed you would want them inside where we could take them prisoner as soon as you gave word."

Isobel's jaw dropped. Yet she should have realized her cousin would still want some satisfaction concerning her since he would not know her father lived. John would still think he was the earl and was in charge of her father's property and come here straight away once the Clan Chattan released him.

"You have done well." Marcus rubbed her shoulder in a manner meant to soothe her. She wanted to kill John herself for attempting to murder her father, and nearly succeeding.

"We allowed them into the great hall. He wishes to negotiate with you over Isobel and her dowry, since you have unlawfully absconded with her. He will seek King Henry's help in the matter, he says, if you do not come to terms," Finbar said very seriously, then smiled a little evilly.

"He does, does he?" Marcus said, darkly, his whole body stiffening beside her. "Have you disarmed his men?"

"Aye."

"Lady wife, do you wish to stay with Lord Wynfield?" Marcus asked and she appreciated that he would.

"Aye." She still held the baron's hand, not wanting to leave his side should his condition worsen.

"Do not kill him," Lord Wynfield said. "Lord Pembroke will want to decide his fate."

"Aye, I wouldna think of it." Marcus turned to Finbar. "What about the men I had sent to speak with Tibold about John's complicity in trying to murder Lord Pembroke?"

"They met John and his men on their way here. They didna tell him his uncle lived nor that they knew John had attempted to kill him. They could do naught else but escort them here as though John and his men were their honored guests as they numbered twenty and our men only five."

"Tibold must have realized we would reach Lochaven well before this, which is why he released them. We would have arrived sooner if we hadna had the trouble with Laren's men."

"Aye."

Marcus looked down again at Isobel. "I will return soon."

"I will be here."

He leaned down and kissed her cheek, and then said to Rob, "Will you stay with Lady Isobel and Lord

Wynfield?"

"As you wish."

Marcus headed out of the chamber with Finbar and Gunnolf. "Who is with John and his men?"

"Ten armed guards, in addition to Angus, Niall, and our Chattan cousins. They will see to it that neither John nor his men get out of hand. Good news, aye?" Finbar asked.

"The best. I worried that when our men reached Rondover Castle, John and his men would have left already. I really hadna believed he would come here after he had to know we would have our forces behind us."

"He is an arrogant bastard, certain his threatening you with King Henry's involvement would make you capitulate in any manner he wishes. Mayhap to say he will now allow you to wed the lass with his blessing if you would make some concession," Gunnolf said.

"Like agree to give up the dowry," Marcus said.

"*Ja.*"

Marcus and the others stalked into the great hall where his servants had hastily set up trestle tables and were offering food and drink to John and his men, which made it look like they were honored guests, despite the lateness of the hour.

His blue eyes narrowed, John smiled darkly when he saw Marcus, not bothering to rise in his presence, notwithstanding that this was Marcus's keep and John was not an earl.

"To what do we owe this pleasure?" Marcus asked.

John motioned to the chair beside him, but Marcus remained standing. John took a swig of ale, the cheese and bread at his table half eaten already. "You know I have King Henry's ear and—"

"Which of Lady Isobel's suitors killed the knights serving as her escort?"

John stared at him for a moment as if he was stunned at the direction this was going. "I know naught of what happened with regard to the men who killed her escort."

"One survived."

John was still holding the tankard of ale in his hand, but he set it down on the table. "Then you should question him."

"We did. He said you killed Lord Pembroke." Marcus knew that wasn't so, but he wasn't about to reveal that Lord Pembroke himself had identified John as his attacker.

John's face drained of all color. If he'd been angry at a wrongful accusation, he would have grown red-faced, but instead, the man suddenly looked as though he knew he'd been caught.

John's dark brow furrowed. "The man lied."

"What do you think will happen to you if King Henry learns you murdered one of his most loyal lords? Who on countless occasions has brought peace to the region?"

"I had naught to do with my uncle's death."

"Witnesses say otherwise. Who is the man behind the killing of the lady's escort?"

"I had naught to do with it. And certainly not anything to do with my uncle's murder. But I have heard rumors that Lord Fenton was behind it all." John didn't look so arrogant now. More like he was squirming to find someone else to offer up to save his own neck.

The best way to do that? Give enough of the truth that could be verified, while digging his own way out of the grave.

"Lord Fenton." Marcus had certainly considered the man as suspect, but then thought he couldn't be the one as he was no longer a suitor. But if he agreed to some terms with John, maybe the game had changed.

"Aye. I heard he hired some men to get rid of you, in truth. He was angry when not only had you survived, Lord Pembroke denied him the chance to court my cousin," John said. "So he must have murdered him in outrage. He…he must have murdered my uncle," John repeated, then rubbed his chin as if giving the matter some thought. "Then figuring he would be found out, he did not pursue marrying Isobel. He must…he must have assumed I would become the next earl and because the way had been cleared for me, he should be able to wed Isobel if I agreed. Aye, that has to be it. Not that he has asked this of me. When I return, he will probably do so. But then that fool, Lord Wynfield, sent her south to stay with King Henry's court and Lord

Fenton must have feared he would lose Isobel in that way so he had her escort murdered. Except that did not go as planned either because then there you were."

"So you told him you would, what? Give Isobel to him for some concession if Lord Pembroke suddenly— died? Would he have wanted her for her dowry? What would he do for *you*? You had to have wanted something out of the deal."

John rose from his chair and growled, "I told you I had nothing to do with any of it. I will send a missive to King Henry at once to tell him what I suspect."

"And that is?"

"That Lord Fenton hired the three men to kill you."

Soft footfalls caught Marcus's attention and he turned to see his lovely wife entering the great hall. John's men finally stood. Marcus's men and his cousins all stood ready to fight John's men if they thought to cause any trouble.

"The word was that only one man tried to kill Marcus," Isobel said, joining him.

He took her hand in his and her fingers were ice cold. He held them tight, loving his dear lass.

"When I asked Lord Wynfield why he had told me only one man had attacked Marcus, he said that was all they had found. One dead man. How did you know there were three? Only Marcus and the man who paid those men to attack him knew," Isobel said.

"And my cousin, who had located them and discovered they had been paid handsomely for the task," Marcus said. "Which means whosoever paid them must have gone back for the money when he learned I had not died. And moved most of the men, but was unable to hide the last one before Lord Pembroke's people discovered the dead man."

John clamped his lips tight.

"Why could you not have waited for my father to give you the title? Were you afraid he would learn you could not be trusted? And that you would never earn the title?"

"See? That is exactly why I had naught to do with your father's murder. I would have earned the title in due time," John said.

"Aye, but you could not risk that he would not give it to you. And you did not want to wait, either. You say Lord Fenton had my escort murdered because he did not want me to leave the area. Because he wanted you to offer me in marriage to him?"

"You allow a woman to speak on your behalf?" John asked Marcus.

Marcus bowed his head to him. "She is doing a fine job of questioning you."

"Why did you come after me at Rondover Castle? Had you promised me to Lord Fenton, and if you did not return me, then what? He would reveal the truth that you had murdered my father?"

"I will not repeat again that I had naught to do with any of it. You were brought here against my consent. That is why I followed you here. If you so choose to live with this...man, then so be it. I see there is no talking you out of this misfortune. We will be on our way."

"Your horses and your men need to rest," Marcus said. "We have the perfect place for you and your men." To his guards, he said, "Take them below."

John pulled a dirk from his boot. "You have no right—"

"For the attempted murder of Lord Pembroke, your uncle, Laird McEwan has every right," Isobel said. "Lord Wynfield is with us now as he brought us the news that my father lives. And that you are the one who tried to murder him, unsuccessfully. He and the other knight who lived are witnesses to the attempted murder."

Her hand tightened around Marcus's, and he unsheathed his sword and pointed it at John. "You will drop your dirk. Now."

CHAPTER 20

Two months had passed and yet it seemed like only days since Marcus had escorted Isobel to her new home at Lochaven Castle. Now, she sat in their new bath built for two, savoring the hot water and her even hotter Highland husband. "We make the servants work twice as hard," she told Marcus as he ran a wet cloth over her back and she adored him for it.

"They talk twice as much about their lovely mistress and how delighted she makes their laird, and that makes them happy." He smiled, lifted her suddenly out of the tub, and carried her to the fire where he set her on her feet, then began to dry her off.

She cherished how he was always eager to make love to her. All she had to do was smile at him and he'd take a break from sword practice with his men, overseeing repairs to the curtain walls, or other non-urgent issues. He always had a moment for her.

Not that she didn't reciprocate. If he came into the kitchen when she was talking to Cook about the next meal, or showing the ladies a new sewing technique, she would stop what she was doing and go away with him. Which was why all the betting was going on concerning an announcement of when their first bairn was due.

It was still dark out, the candles and the fire providing a soft light as she turned to dry him next. She'd been amused at how everyone seemed to know just when she and Marcus disappeared into their chamber for some more intimate time. She couldn't believe her father was finally coming to see her and bringing Mary. Then they'd have the wedding and a feast. Lord Wynfield was staying on at Lochaven until that happened, stating that it was his duty to still watch over Isobel until her father actually gave her away.

She assumed some of his reluctance to leave was because he was walking with a cane and riding was still giving him some difficulty, though he was getting better. Still, he probably only wanted to make one trip home, and not have to return again so soon, vowing to stay to see her married no matter what. She loved him for it.

"Marcus," she said, running the cloth over him. "I do not want you to change the way you are with me."

He lifted her face and frowned at her. "What ails you, lass? Your da's arrival? Mary's? Why would I treat you any differently?"

She smiled and moved the cloth lower to stroke his staff. "I would not want us to stop this."

He laughed, lifted her in his arms, and carried her to the bed. She tossed the damp cloth to the floor and wrapped her arms around his neck.

"Why would I ever want to stop making love to my bonny lass? There isna any chance of that."

She just smiled as he set her on the bed, then he lowered his body next to hers. He ran his hand over her breast, and she tried hard not to let on how sore they were. She knew she was carrying a bairn, but she was afraid if she told him, he'd stop making love to her. Her belly was still flat, though even she could see it was starting to grow just a wee bit. She loved the changes in her body to accommodate the bairn growing inside her. She'd been careful not to let on to any of the maids who served her. She knew when Mary was here, she'd suspect right away.

Isobel lowered his hand between her legs so that he would pleasure her there, and then began to kiss his mouth. She loved his mouth and the way he slid his tongue into hers, the way he nibbled on her lips, and kissed her all over. She still remembered that day at the loch when he had first kissed her and she had wanted the rest of what he could give her.

With his touches, she was burning for him, craving the intimacy and she was so afraid he'd want to stop.

He stroked her between her legs and made her feel deliciously wicked and loved and all his. God, how she cherished the way he touched her, eager to please her. She caressed his whiskery cheek and teased his tongue with hers. His hand went again to her breasts, and she loved that he wished to feel them, just as she craved the sensation of his touch. *Until now.* Because of the tenderness in them, she sought to distract him by touching his shaft. Her diverting his attention in such a manner had worked the last two days when he had wanted to feel her breasts, to kiss them, and lick her nipples. It worked this time, too. Besides, she loved wrapping her hand around his rigid staff and stroking him. She relished seeing the way his blue eyes clouded with lust, and hearing him moan at her touch.

He started to stroke her in that sensitive spot between her legs again, touching her, lifting her to the heavens above, ecstatic to feel that all-consuming pleasure driving her higher. She was grateful that part of her was not tender and sore, but eager for his ministrations.

She rose so high until she hit the peak and felt as if she was flying off the goose down mattress right before he plunged his staff into her. She loved feeling him inside of her, the connectedness, the closeness, the intimacy.

She rode a new wave of high, wanting them to be like this always, even after they were old and gray.

Marcus loved making love to his wife, but he knew things had changed between them. She no longer wanted him to touch her breasts, but they seemed plumper and he loved touching them. Not wanting to ask her in the middle of their lovemaking, he would question her later when they were resting afterward. He wanted only to please his wife in every way as much as she pleased him.

For now, he plunged his staff deep into his lady wife's welcoming, warm, wet sheath, felt her near the verge of coming again as her fingers dug into his hips, and he continued to drive forth. He loved these early morning wake-ups, though they usually didn't start out with a bath. Today was special because today he was marrying his bonny lass in the kirk.

Her long, dark tresses spilled across her pillow, her blue eyes filled with awe, her face flushed with pleasure, she couldn't look any more beautiful than she did this moment.

This time, he really tried to hold back, tried to make this last longer. He slowed down to savor the moment, valuing this intimate time spent with her, then gave up the battle as his seed spilled inside her. She tensed, gripped his hips with her fingers, and he rubbed against her until she cried out with pleasure.

His thirst for her slaked—for the moment—he sank down on top of her, then moved off her, pulling her into his arms. In the past, she nestled against him without any trouble, but now she seemed to have to be…well, careful, the way she rested on top of him. He caressed her arm as she resituated herself again, appearing to attempt to get comfortable.

"Are you feeling all right, lass?" He couldn't help his concern that he had done something wrong, or she'd labored at something recently and injured herself.

"Oh, aye. 'Tis a wondrous day." She was so cheerful, he wondered if he imagined her discomfort.

"You seem to be... sore. Have I hurt you in some way? Or made you feel uncomfortable?" He hated to think she didn't like him touching her breasts any longer. They were remarkable and he loved kissing them and more.

"Oh, Marcus, do not treat me any differently, I beg of you."

"What is the matter?" He began to sit up, but she pushed him back down and cuddled with him.

He sighed and caressed her back, her long hair cascading over his chest.

"We are going to have a bairn."

In disbelief, he stared at her. Then he grinned, so thrilled to hear the good news, he bolted upright again, taking her with him. "When? Why didna you tell me?"

"To begin with, I was uncertain. I was going to ask Mary. But I am certain of it now."

He kissed Isobel and held her tight, then let loose of her. "You are hurting."

She cupped her breasts lightly. "They are growing and I am a little tender. I do not want you to treat me any differently. Some husbands no longer bed their wives when they are carrying a wee one. I do not want you to—"

"I would never neglect you. Near the end, we will have to stop, but you are a Highland lass, and in the Highlands, we dinna stop. By the heavens, I couldna be more thrilled at the news. Ah, lass, you dinna know how much this means to me."

She smiled and he kissed his loving wife, thanking God that was all that had concerned her. He couldn't wait to tell all of his kin. "When can we tell the clan?"

She raised her brows. "Mayhap after we are married in the kirk? At the celebration?"

"It will kill me to keep the secret." It would. He was certain they'd guess it when they saw him fussing over his wife and grinning like a fool. "Aye, you have my word. Do you no' think the maids who attend to you know already?" If they knew, everyone else already knew. Then he wouldn't have to wait to tell the clan.

"Mayhap. If they helped me to dress and saw me wince, they might have realized it."

He nodded and looked down at his sweet wife. "I can love you no more than I do now." Then he kissed her again and hugged her gently.

"I love you, Highlander. Now, and for always."

A knock on the door startled Isobel and she jumped a little in his arms.

"Aye?" Marcus called out.

"Guests have begun to arrive. Our Chattan cousins, Gunnolf, Angus, our uncle. And, just so the lass knows," Rob said beyond the door, "Oona had her pups."

"Oh." Isobel quickly scrambled out of the bed to get dressed.

Marcus laughed. "We will be down shortly."

"Aye, I will let everyone know."

Marcus helped Isobel to dress. "She likely willna want you seeing her pups for a couple of days, lass."

"Nay. I have been with her several times a day. It was the same with my father's deerhounds, and the mother let me see her and her pups, though she hid her pups afterward. Oona will trust me. I will not touch them until they are older and she is agreeable."

They were soon dressed, much quicker than he had ever seen Isobel dress. Once they left the chamber, she practically raced down the stairs. She was about to head to the kennel when Ulicia's children, Druce and Fiona, came out of the kitchen and tackled her with hugs. Marcus was both surprised and glad to see the lass and lad.

"Druce, Fiona," Isobel said, smiling. "Are your mother and other brothers here? And is she well now?"

"Aye, she is well. And Da is with us." Druce beamed with the news.

"Da?" Marcus said, and the children looked up at him until he motioned to them to give him hugs also. They quickly obliged. Their exuberance pleased him and he thought how someday he and Isobel would cherish their own bairns just like this.

"Leith took our mother to wife." Fiona sounded as proud as could be.

Marcus laughed, glad that Leith had found a family to care for. Then he saw Leith and Ulicia with the two younger boys headed their way. "You are here for the wedding?"

"Aye, and to stay, if it is all right with you." Leith was holding each of the younger lads' hands in his. He looked like a proud da.

Ulicia looked just as cheered.

"Aye, we are happy to have you home again."

Edana and the rest of the Chattan kin headed their way, but this time Edana went to hug Isobel first. "I am so happy to see you again." She threw her arms around her and gave her a light hug. "Come, we must talk before the wedding."

As soon as they were alone in the misty, cool gardens, Edana walked hand in hand with Isobel as if they had always been sisters, which Isobel dearly loved.

Edana cleared her throat. "I have to tell you the news. I am carrying our first bairn. I knew way before I...really knew, but anyway, I have this, well, gift, and I learned that our bairns will be playing together when they are wee young'uns and that means..."

Isobel stared at her, not quite understanding Edana's meaning. "How did you know? About me? I have not told anyone. Yet."

"I have this gift, you see..."

* * *

Before her father and Mary arrived with their escort, Isobel was so excited to see Oona with her pups, she could barely contain her enthusiasm as she made her escape from everyone and slipped into the kennel. Oona allowed her to see all five before tucking them underneath her legs in a protective way.

Isobel was so engrossed with seeing Oona and her pups, she didn't realize that her father and Mary had arrived until she heard all the commotion in the inner bailey. She hurried out of the kennel to greet them.

She gave her father a hug first, tears filling her eyes. "Father," was all she was able to choke out. To think if John had his way, her father would not be here now.

"There, there, daughter. It is a happy occasion— your marriage to the man you love, just as it was when I married your mother. I am glad to be here and to see..." Her father glanced around at the castle. "Your accommodations."

"I was just checking on the deerhound's new pups," she said, smiling.

He shook his head. "You will spoil the hunting hounds here now instead of mine."

She laughed and turned to hug Mary who was just as teary-eyed. But Mary's jaw dropped when Isobel hugged her so lightly and not exuberantly like she would normally do after being separated for so long.

"Are you...?"

Isobel grinned and nodded.

Mary quickly looked at Isobel's father.

"For heaven's sake, what now?" He frowned, then

his brows shot up. He seized Isobel's arm and headed toward the kirk. "Let us get this wedding over with now."

The celebration was an extravagant affair as Marcus had made sure that everyone would have the opportunity to feast and make merry for several days. The announcement at the first of the feasts that they had a bairn on the way was met with enthusiastic cheers.

He had enjoyed dancing with his wife, and even slipped into the kennels with her to quietly check on Oona and her pups. What he witnessed was nothing less than a miracle. Oona, the pups, Isobel here with him, adoring them, and him adoring her. Even more wondrous—his own bairn on the way.

When they returned to the great hall, Lord Pembroke took Marcus and Isobel aside while pipers played in the background. Many of his people danced, drank, and talked as Lord Pembroke said, "I had planned to allow you to marry my daughter before I was left for dead, I wished you to know."

Marcus stared at him slack-jawed.

"Aye. You see, in the last missive you sent, you said something that really resonated with me. You said how much my wife had cherished me and how she gave up her close family, her home, and the rest of her kin to be with me. That she loved me for who I was, for how I handled the Scots at the border, for how I made her feel special, just as she made me feel. There was not a day that went by that I did not think of her when we were separated, or when I had seen her at the first, and wished to see her again. 'Twas not the same as the way she had felt about MacLauchlan."

"Her being with him had been a mistake," Marcus said.

"Aye. So I intended to send you a missive that said you were welcome to court my daughter and if she chose you, I would be agreeable."

"I have saved you the trouble." Marcus grinned.

"Aye. I wish I had seen that my nephew was not the man to take my place. Had Isobel been a son..."

Isobel smiled and reached across Marcus to pat her father's arm. "You would have had a worse time of it."

He chuckled. "Think you I do not know all that you were up to? Swordplay with Marcus and his cousins? Bow hunting? Fishing? And all manner of other unladylike behaviors."

"Mary told on me?"

"Nay. I had men watching out for you. They reported all that you had done."

"You... you never objected to it."

"I loved your mother. She had grown up just the way you had. How could I not love seeing you turn out as beautiful as her? So, nay, I could not keep you from doing that which made you the person you have become today. Marcus and his cousins were always careful with you and protective. Though my own men were there watching out for your welfare, they said they trusted in Marcus to keep you safe."

Lord Pembroke cleared his throat. "I…I apologize for sending Marcus away the day he was injured. I had learned that, for the first time, he had kissed you at the loch and I feared, especially after the way you danced with him, that you would end up like your mother had—with MacLauchlan."

"MacLauchlan was married! And Marcus was not. He wished to marry me."

"Aye, and I was not ready to listen to reason." Lord Pembroke took a heavy breath. "John's younger brother, Rian, has handled things nicely. He has my gift of persuasion. He has already helped me to quell two skirmishes with just a couple of talks."

"What of John?"

"He is dead. By his own hand. He knew for trying to murder me, he would not live long. He took the coward's way out."

She didn't feel any pity for the man. If he'd been decent, he could have had everything, but her. Then she wondered about the dowry. Would her father give it to Marcus? Mayhap not, because he had taken her to wife without getting her father's approval.

"Yet, if he had waited, he could have taken your place in a legitimate way," Marcus said.

Lord Pembroke shook his head. "He was a hothead. He could not wait to take my place, once he learned I was entertaining the notion of allowing Isobel to wed you and allow him to have the earldom and properties at some future date."

"What about Lord Fenton?" Marcus asked.

"I turned the matter over to King Henry. One of the knights that Lord Fenton murdered, King Henry himself had knighted. I received word that Lord Fenton and the men who helped him are in a small, filthy cell."

He deserved worse, after what he had done to both Marcus and to the good men who served as her escort. "Good. What about Jane?" Isobel asked.

"After what she did to Sir Travon? No one trusted her any longer, and she had to find a position with another household."

"I still do not understand what John would have gotten from Lord Fenton should he have handed me over to him." Isobel thought how bad it would have been for her if she had become his wife.

"Lord Fenton knew John had killed…or thought he had killed me. He threatened him with reporting it to the king if John did not give up both you and your dowry to him. He knew he had lost the earldom, but at least he would have had you. Should John have ever died unexpectedly? And you gave birth to a son in the meantime?"

"Lord Fenton would have taken over the earldom in our son's name. We had considered such," Isobel said.

"When men like that have no scruples, no telling how the game would end up playing out."

"And Cantrell? What part did he have in all this?" Isobel asked.

"He would do anything for money. Sell his soul if he had one. As soon as he overheard I had given Lord Wynfield the order to have a couple of men send Laird McEwan on his way, Cantrell sneaked out o warn Fenton's mercenaries. He was to witness the deed, then let Fenton know that Laird McEwan was dead. Fenton would have had his men get rid of the laird's body, and no one would have been the wiser." Her father took a swig of his ale.

"But Marcus did not die." Isobel squeezed Marcus's hand, thankful to God that he had managed to fight off the three men and survive his injury.

"Nay. But Cantrell could not tell Fenton right away that Laird McEwan killed his mercenaries. And he thought for certain as wounded as the laird was, he would not make it very far and die from his injury. The mercenaries were to take care of the body, only now they were dead. Fenton had to take care of all of them, finish the laird off, also. So he sent one of his men to see what happened, and he discovered the slaughter. He moved two of the mercenaries' bodies before Lord Wynfield arrived with men, searching for Laird McEwan. At that point, Fenton could do no more to cover up his foul deed."

"What has become of Cantrell?" Marcus asked.

"Hanged for the traitor he was."

Lord Pembroke sighed. "I sent a missive to Laird Laren MacLauchlan, explaining about my dear wife losing her first bairn, that was his, but I do not know if anyone can even read in his clan. Even if someone can, it will not guarantee he will believe me. As to a more important matter, I do not want you traveling all that way to see me, daughter. When the time comes, I will visit with you and the wee one."

Isobel smiled and gave him a hug.

"You have not asked me about Isobel's dowry." Her father eyed Marcus with genuine compassion.

"Under the circumstances…"

"Under the circumstances, the lady's dowry is yours, and I would hope that when you have a daughter, you will save it for her."

"We thank you." Marcus clapped his hand on Lord Pembroke's shoulder, and the older man smiled. "And welcome you into the clan."

Her father looked pleased to hear it, and nodded, smiling a little. "Now about the hunt scheduled for the morn," her father said to Marcus as though he was talking to his new son about more important business, and he walked off with him as Marcus gave her a wink over his shoulder.

Edana and Mary quickly joined her.

"So tell us, Mary," Edana said. "You took care of Isobel when she was a wee bairn, aye? But you also cared for her mother when she was carrying a bairn in her belly. What can we expect?"

Mary smiled with such joy, Isobel knew then if she had any reservations about starting over in a new household, she didn't now.

***

"I believe the wedding and the first day of the celebration was a success." Marcus wrapped his arms around Isobel in bed late that eve. He couldn't have been more pleased about how well everyone had gotten along and how much his kinsmen had jested with him about dancing with Isobel that was not like any form of dancing they'd ever seen. But he hadn't wanted to give her up for anything, after what had happened the last time he had been with her at a celebration like this.

"My father has always been the one to win men over in his quest for peace," Isobel said, "and yet you won him over so completely this day, I am in awe."

"He is a good man. He could see how happy we are together and how my people love you as one of their own."

"Aye. I am home."

"Do you miss Torrent Castle?"

"A little."

"Then I will have to work harder at keeping you perfectly happy so that you dinna think on it any longer."

She laughed, then placed his hands on her breasts. "No one can make me happier."

"Ah, lass. You are the joy of my life." He began to kiss her neck, careful to touch her breasts with the utmost tenderness.

"Hmm, I wonder who won the bet, concerning when I would be with child."

"We did."

That was all that needed to be said and she thought of nothing more but of soaring into the heavens with her heroic Highlander.

ABOUT THE AUTHOR

Bestselling and award-winning author **Terry Spear** has written over fifty paranormal romance novels and four medieval Highland historical romances. Her first werewolf romance, *Heart of the Wolf,* was named a 2008 *Publishers Weekly*'s Best Book of the Year, and her subsequent titles have garnered high praise and hit the *USA Today* bestseller list. A retired officer of the U.S. Army Reserves, Terry lives in Crawford, Texas, where she is working on her next werewolf romance, continuing her new series about shapeshifting jaguars, loving to share her hot Highlanders, and having fun with her young adult novels. For more information, please visit www.terryspear.com, or follow her on Twitter, @TerrySpear. She is also on Facebook at https://www.facebook.com/TerrySpearParanormalRom antics. And on Wordpress at:

Terry Spear's Shifters
http://terryspear.wordpress.com/

CPSIA information can be obtained at www.ICGtesting.com
Printed in the USA
LVOW11s1307060914

402789LV00001B/88/P